"I know you have good reason to suspect me. But I swear to you, I'm not that kind of person."

He studied her face, searching its depths for... something. Sincerity, perhaps, but between them, something else ignited, the spark of something far too dangerous to contemplate.

Or so she told herself, but with temptation arcing through her body, her eyes refused to obey. One glance at his lips and it was too late to step back. Too late to do anything but tilt back her head when he whispered, "I believe you."

To do anything but part her lips when his mouth fell upon hers.

His taste was bittersweet: the mint of toothpaste mingled with the darker notes of coffee. But this sensation submerged completely beneath the unexpected pleasure, her every nerve ending flaring, awakening to his touch.

Some slim margin of her brain warned this kiss, this passion, was too sudden and too needful, flung at her like a net....

Dear Reader,

As I write this morning, I'm remembering some advice my sister, a traveling hospice nurse, has shared. In the end, she tells me, people never regret not having worked more hours, acquired more things or been more successful. Instead, they worry over missed opportunities to mend relationships and spend more of their precious time with loved ones.

Lone Star Redemption is the story of two people doing their best to fix their broken families. For career-minded reporter Jessie Layton, it's all about finding her lost, chronically troubled twin sister—and honoring her vow to bring Haley home before their terminally ill mother dies. Stung by Haley's behavior once too often in the past, Jessie is leery of getting caught up in another of her sister's dramas, but she begins to rethink her position after seeing the sacrifices former marine corps fighter pilot Zach Rayford has made to return to his widowed mother and the sprawling Texas ranch she's been left alone to run.

As I wrote Jessie and Zach's story, I ached for these two wounded people, both struggling to find their way through a complex moral quagmire. And I held my breath at times, terrified they wouldn't survive a killer bent on keeping the truth hidden...no matter who must die.

I hope you'll enjoy *Lone Star Redemption* and keep your eyes open for a new tale from the Rayford Ranch at Rusted Spur, coming very soon.

Happy reading!

Colleen Thompson

LONE STAR REDEMPTION

—

Colleen Thompson

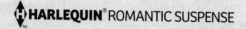

HARLEQUIN® ROMANTIC SUSPENSE

Recycling programs
for this product may
not exist in your area.

ISBN-13: 978-0-373-27876-3

LONE STAR REDEMPTION

Copyright © 2014 by Colleen Thompson

This is a work of fiction. Names, characters, places and incidents are either the product of the author's imagination or are used fictitiously, and any resemblance to actual persons, living or dead, business establishments, events or locales is entirely coincidental.

This edition published by arrangement with Harlequin Books S.A.

For questions and comments about the quality of this book, please contact us at CustomerService@Harlequin.com.

® and TM are trademarks of Harlequin Enterprises Limited or its corporate affiliates. Trademarks indicated with ® are registered in the United States Patent and Trademark Office, the Canadian Trade Marks Office and in other countries.

Printed in U.S.A.

Books by Colleen Thompson

Harlequin Romantic Suspense

Passion to Protect #1729
The Colton Heir #1776
Lone Star Redemption #1806

Silhouette Romantic Suspense

Deadlier Than the Male #1631
  "Lethal Lessons"

Harlequin Intrigue

Capturing the Commando #1286
Phantom of the French Quarter #1302
Relentless Protector #1376

COLLEEN THOMPSON

After beginning her career writing historical romance novels, in 2004 Colleen Thompson turned to writing the contemporary romantic suspense she loves. Since then, her work has been honored with a Texas Gold Award, along with nominations for a RITA® Award, a Daphne du Maurier Award and multiple reviewers' choice honors. She has also received starred reviews from *RT Book Reviews* and *Publishers Weekly*. A former teacher living with her family in the Houston area, Colleen has a passion for reading, hiking and dog rescue. Visit her online at www.colleen-thompson.com.

To strong and loving families: those we're born to, those we give birth to, and those we cobble together from the broken pieces of our hearts.

Prologue

If she couldn't have her son back, was peace too much to ask?

The question reverberated through sixty-eight-year-old Nancy Rayford's throbbing skull with an intensity untouched by the powerful prescriptions she had taken. Still, the knocking went on, a pounding at her front door. What time was it, anyway? How long since she'd drifted off?

Tossing aside the light throw she'd used as a blanket, she pushed herself up off the soft cushions of a leather sofa before blinking at the television. There, the muted figure of some late-night comedian clowned before his silent audience. All of them laughing up a storm, as though her sweetest boy had not been reduced to ashes in a small urn just two weeks before.

Not a boy; a man, she reminded herself, *Ian and his brother both.* But she'd never known either one as a grown adult, as a soldier, thanks to her husband's scorched-earth approach to fatherhood. Now *he* was gone, as well, leaving her alone here, or as alone as an aging widow could get surrounded by thousands of acres of drought-plagued range and thirsty cattle.

The pounding started again, adding a desperate edge to the insistent rhythm. It sliced through her drugged reality, reaching a part of her that understood there must be something very wrong. Shaking overtook her at the suspicion that she would find another pair of uniformed officers at her front door, somber military personnel assigned to tell her that her surviving firstborn son, her Zach, was gone, too.

With a cry of pain, she lurched through the empty house, her shaking hand reaching for the door before she could wonder if it might be unsafe to do so. Because he was all she had left; if he'd been taken from her now, too—

With her heart pounding in her throat and the world careening wildly around her, she unlocked the door and flung it open so hard that it banged against the entry wall. Staring into the dark August night, she begged the same God who'd failed at every turn to heed her prayers that it not be the news she most feared. *Please don't take him, too.*

But tonight's visitor wore faded jeans and a black T-shirt rather than the dreaded uniform. She was a gaunt and pale young woman, with eyes shadowed by exhaustion and arms that trembled with the weight of the small child she carried. The sleeping girl of three—or was it four?—years, wrapped in a blanket, her tawny hair a matted mess.

"I can't do this anymore," the young woman told her, her eyes shimmering with tears. "I just can't. I need your help, please, Nancy. C-can you take her?"

Drained from days of headaches and weak from dehydration, Nancy felt a jolt of pure energy restore her. Her long trance shattered, and a new sense of purpose moved her forward. She raised thin arms to lift the burden from the taller woman's arms, to cuddle the child close to her breast.

Rather than weighing her down, the little girl's weight made Nancy feel lighter than she had since her husband's death, six months earlier, lighter and younger than she had in decades. And when she looked down into the precious face, so smooth and unblemished and impossibly perfect, the knowledge coursed through her, a swift river of current telling her that this was no accident at all.

This was, instead, a miracle, a reason to go on.

Chapter 1

Three months later...

Stiff and tired from hours of driving across the desolate northern Texas prairie, Jessie Layton climbed from her blue hatchback and stepped into the howling wind.

Bent low against the gusts, she slung her purse over her shoulder and raced for the steps leading up to the wide white veranda without waiting for her cameraman to follow. By the time she made it to the mansion's front door, she was choking on the brick-red dust, her eyes and nose streaming and long ribbons of her reddish-blond hair whipping across her face. Shivering with a cold that her leather jacket barely cut, she felt scoured and sandblasted—and angrier than ever.

Leave it to my sister to drag me halfway to Hell.

No. That wasn't right. As she pushed the hair from her face, she reminded herself she hadn't driven all the way up to the Panhandle ranch, where her twin's trail had gone cold, for Haley's sake, no more than she was here for the "very personal human-interest story" she'd pitched to her news director as a pretext to get out of Dallas for a few days. Though the request must have come as quite a shock considering that she'd been on the verge of breaking a story bound to make national headlines, She had really come because she'd made a promise. A promise to the mother she was about to lose.

The thought brought with it a stab of fear, the same swirling sense of panic that threatened to pull Jessie under several times a day. She was still working to get past her father's sudden death two years before, and *he* had barely acknowledged her existence, except to criticize her. Now, her mother, too, was dying, the one parent she could always count on for support, for love—Jessie couldn't bear the thought.

She closed her eyes for a moment, steadying her breathing, reminding herself that they still had weeks or months left. Or maybe even longer. Aggressive as the cancer was, her mom was holding her own at the moment, and the oncologist had allowed that spontaneous remissions *had* happened in a few rare cases.

If she could find Haley and bring her home to make peace, they might get the miracle they needed. *Or maybe Mom just wants to see her one more time before she dies...* The reason didn't matter. Finding Haley, and getting her home fast, was more important to Jessie than anything else right now. Important enough that she scarcely gave a thought to the risk to her career and the story she'd been so focused on selling to her news director.

Henry Kucharski stumbled up the steps behind her, the bushy gray wreath that ringed his bald head swirling in the gale. A wiry little man with a woolly caterpillar of a mustache, he was struggling with the mini-cam, pulling off the lens cap as she pounded on the front door.

"Three in the afternoon, and it might as well be full dark," he said anxiously. "Without decent lighting, this footage won't be worth the—"

"Don't you get it, Henry? I couldn't care less about the lighting," she said, "or the footage, either."

Pried loose by the wind, a nearby shutter started banging. Concerned her own knock wouldn't be heard, Jessie tried ringing the bell but didn't hear it. As she'd suspected when she'd first spotted the darkened windows, the storm must have caused a power outage.

"That's not what you told Vivian." Behind his gold-rimmed glasses, Henry squinted against the wind. "And I'll remind you, she's my boss, too. You and I both know how she holds on to grudges. And how many ways she has of making our lives miserable."

Jessie, who towered over him in the high-heeled boots she wore with a tunic and leggings, spared him an apologetic look, remembering how allergic the poor guy was to confrontation. And how sweet he'd been to postpone his wedding anniversary dinner with his wife of twenty-six years to make the six-hour drive out here with her when it was clear that no one else would. "I'll take full responsibility. Don't worry."

She rapped at the oversize mahogany door again, more insistently this time. *Please let someone be home.* She'd spotted a big pickup parked out back, but for all she knew, the owners were off somewhere in another vehicle from the attached four-car garage.

"Oh, I'm not worried about *me,* so much. It's you, especially after you jammed that story on the mayor down her throat. Vivian has friends, I hear, including one *very close* friend supporting—" As the doorknob rattled, Henry went silent, tensing as he readied his camera.

The moment the door cracked open, a gust sent a swirl of sand spinning into Jessie's face. She cried out, covering her stinging eyes with her hands.

"Come inside, out of the wind," insisted a female voice, thin and scratchy. "Quickly, please. You're letting in the dust."

"Thank you, ma'am," said Henry as he ushered Jessie inside and pressed a handkerchief into her hands.

Blotting her streaming eyes, Jessie blinked in the dim light of a surprisingly formal entryway for this part of the world. Half a dozen tiny flames flickered, where someone had set out candles atop a fussy table with carved, curved ivory legs. The soft glow was reflected by a tall, ornately framed mirror, its illumination warming the cool marble floor beneath a vaulted ceiling. Like the huge old house, miles from its nearest neighbor, this entryway had been built to impress, even overwhelm, potential rivals.

Having grown up in Dallas's upscale Highland Park neighborhood, Jessie had long since gotten past the notion that privilege necessarily deserved protection. It was part of what made her fearless when confronting those who considered themselves untouchable, from a beloved sports legend who was systematically cheating customers at the car dealership he'd purchased, to the mayor of Dallas, who would very soon be facing his own reckoning over his crooked reelection campaign.

The lady of the house would find herself no more immune, especially if the woman kept doing everything in her power to frustrate Jessie's search.

"Mrs. Rayford? Nancy Rayford?" She blinked at an attractive older woman with a silvered pixie cut and blue eyes a shade darker than her soft cabled sweater.

It was hard to imagine this was the same woman who had answered her questions on the phone so brusquely before repeatedly hanging up on her. She was a tiny, mousy-looking thing, so frail and insubstantial that Jessie quickly closed the door behind her, half-afraid that a stray gust could waft her up into the shadow of the elegant curved staircase just behind her.

"Yes, why—" Voice faltering, Mrs. Rayford took a step back before reaching for a candle with one trembling hand. Lifting its light toward Jessie, she gasped and spread her hand over her chest. "*Haley?* Oh, my— I thought you weren't—"

Jessie shook her head. "My sister. Remember? I tried to tell you on the phone." Her heart fell with a realization. "Then, Haley really isn't here?"

She'd been banking on finding her sister hiding out here, after having talked her way into some menial job with some sob story about being pursued by an abusive stalker. It was Haley's time-honored method for avoiding creditors, former lovers and, Jessie suspected, her family, as well.

Mrs. Rayford's blue eyes widened before she flicked a fearful glance behind her, toward the stairwell. "You're— Then you're really not her? Truly?"

"We're identical twins," Jessie explained, offering a smile in an attempt to reassure the frightened woman. And more important, to gain her trust. "Our own father couldn't tell us apart."

Not that he'd ever made much effort. But Nancy Rayford didn't need to know that.

From outside came a low hum, and a moment later, the chandelier above them flickered on. The sudden illumination revealed the older woman's pallor, painting gaunt shadows in her hollowed cheeks.

Reminded of her own mother's illness, Jessie said, "I'm sorry I've upset you. Do you need to sit down?"

Taking the woman by the arm, Jessie led her to a bench seat and squatted before her when Mrs. Rayford sank down to it.

"Are you all right?" Jessie asked, thinking of heart attacks and aneurysms, and the sudden, fatal stroke that had taken her father over one of her family's mandatory Sunday dinners. "Is there something I can get you? Someone I can call?"

No sooner had she asked the questions than she heard the sounds of approaching boot heels on the marble. As Henry faded back, turning to hide the mini-cam still perched on his shoulder, a deep voice boomed, "Generator's back online, Mama. Should keep us up and running for a while, anyway—"

A tall man holding a broad-brimmed gray hat came striding through the archway and stopped short, looking in confusion from Henry to Jessie before finding Mrs. Rayford. She had leaned forward, holding her bowed head in her shaking hands.

"What's going on here? *Mama?* Is something wrong?" He rushed toward her so quickly that Jessie rose and stepped out of his way. "These people—are they bothering you?"

Blinking back tears, his mother waved off his concern. "No, no, Zach. They're just—" She looked to Jessie. "They took a wrong turn in the storm, but they saw our gate and stopped to ask directions to town."

Jessie stared in surprise. *Why on earth would you lie to your own son?*

"I was just helping them when all of a sudden, one of my headaches came on," Mrs. Rayford continued. "They've been very kind, but I'll need my prescription.

You remember where I keep it, don't you? And some water, too, please."

Clearly uneasy, he looked from Jessie to Henry.

"I'll be fine," his mother said, tenting her fingers over one side of her forehead. "Maybe it's the wind, but this migraine's getting worse. If you could get my pill right away..."

"Sure, Mama. I'll be right back," he said, his concerned eyes as vibrant a blue as his mother's. But that was where their resemblance ended.

Where Mrs. Rayford was petite and frail, her rancher son was broad-shouldered and long-limbed—a trim six-three, at least, and only a few years older than Jessie's twenty-nine. The wind, or maybe the hat, had mussed his short jet-black hair, but it was his strong jaw that caught her attention—that and the high cheekbones, deep tan and dark brows that hinted he had Native blood, despite the color of his eyes. To her surprise, there was no ring on his finger, she noticed, sneaking a glance at his strong, work-roughened hands as he rushed back in the direction he had come.

He might be wearing a barn jacket, boots and worn jeans—well fitted to the contours of his body—rather than Armani, but she knew instinctively that if a gorgeous specimen like him showed up in Highland Park, he'd have half the women in that ZIP code lined up, hoping for a ride. And if they had any idea how much land and livestock his family owned—and how much oil had been found here, according to her research—a good number would be out to permanently corral him. She couldn't imagine herself among them, though, for if she'd learned anything from her last boyfriend, it was that guys who looked that good and had the money to back it up tended to have a lot more ego than she cared to deal with.

"You'll need to leave now," Mrs. Rayford told them. "Before my son gets back. Please."

Jessie squeezed Mrs. Rayford's ice-cold hand and said, "I'm very sorry you're not feeling well, but I'm not going anywhere until I find my sister. My own mother— My mother's seriously ill and needs to see her. And every lead I've uncovered stops right here at this ranch."

Mrs. Rayford straightened to look her in the eye, her otherwise pale face marked by two splashes of bright color. "I told you on the phone, Haley Layton moved on six months back," she said, her voice going cold and brittle. "She and that good-for-nothing boyfriend of hers sneaked out of the old bunkhouse they were renting without a single word—or a penny of the three months' rent they owed me."

The part about the money didn't surprise Jessie. Haley had a long history of abusing the trust of everyone with whom she came in contact. Jessie herself had fallen for a couple of Haley's hard-luck stories—the last time to the tune of nearly five thousand dollars—all the savings she'd had at the time.

The *very* last time, she'd sworn, cutting off all contact once her sister had skipped out of a battered women's shelter and disappeared almost four years before. It had hurt Jessie, too, turning her back on someone so close. She felt almost like a part of Jessie's own body, but she knew, too, that if she kept enabling her twin, Haley would never learn to stand alone—and would never stop resenting Jessie for the accomplishments that set them apart.

"I'll write you a check right now for the back rent," she offered, now more intent on offering her mother peace than in fixing her sister's life, "if you can only tell me where she went or even this boyfriend's name. Then I'll be on my way."

The woman moaned. "I don't care about the money. As I *told* you before, I have no idea where your sister's gone."

"Then why act so evasive on the phone, and why hang up on me every time I tried to call back?" Jessie demanded. "When you saw my face, too, I saw how you—"

From behind her, Zach Rayford returned to interrupt them. "What's really going on here? Who the hell are you people, and what do you think you're doing upsetting my mother?"

"I—I'm looking for my sister, that's all," Jessie stammered, forced to step aside once more as the rancher gave his stricken mother the pill and glass of water he had brought.

Gently, he touched her rail-thin shoulder. "Don't you worry, Mama. Take this, and I'll send these people on their way."

She tensed visibly and then, a moment later, nodded.

"I—I'll do that," Nancy Rayford said, her voice small as a child's as she pressed the pill to her lips and swallowed with a sip of water. "And then, I might— I think I may go up and lie down for a bit. I'm not— I'm feeling a little—"

"Go on ahead, Mama. I'll be up in a minute to check on both of you. And I'll look after Eden, so there's no need to worry."

Bending his powerful frame, he helped the fragile woman to her feet. As soon as she was standing, she murmured to Jessie, "Forgive me," with a plea in her eyes before she started up the stairs.

"Just her boyfriend's name," Jessie called after her, caring far less about this stranger's inexplicable desire for secrecy than her promise to her mother. "Please, if you can tell me that much, I'll be on my way."

Zach Rayford narrowed his eyes. "It's time for you people to leave. Now."

Still looking at Jessie, Mrs. Rayford shook her head. "I—I'm not sure I can—"

"You don't have to answer her." Laserlike in its intensity, Zach's glare flew from Jessie's face to Henry's, where he quickly did a double take. "What the hell? Is that a camera you're hiding? You people are *filming* us? Right here in our home?"

He stalked toward Henry, saying, "Give me that right now, you little—"

Scrambling backward, Henry twisted in an attempt to keep the mini-cam out of reach, but the rancher wrested it from his hands before the older man could do anything about it.

"Wait!" Jessie said, fearing the expensive camera would be damaged. And fearing even more that her foolish attempt to appease her boss had cost her her only real chance at finding Haley.

Rayford stopped, a mirthless grin spreading across his handsome face as his gaze swung from her to Henry. "Now that I have your attention," he said, "maybe I can get some answers. First of all, you're going to tell me right this minute, who are you?"

He nodded toward the red-faced cameraman, who was rubbing his neck and darting glances toward the door. It didn't take a mind reader to see that he was thinking about bolting before the rancher's big hands found him, too.

"Henry Kucharski," he finally murmured, shoving his own hands into the pockets of his jacket. "And I'll need that camera back, or I'm a dead man when I get back to Dallas."

Ignoring him, Zach looked to Jessie. "And now you," he ordered, "the woman with the questions."

"As I've told your mother," she said, her voice tight with anger, "my name is Jessie Layton, and I'm looking for a former tenant of yours—"

"A tenant? You think we're running some sort of a boardinghouse here?" He glanced toward his mother, who lingered on the staircase, gaping at them as she clutched the railing for dear life.

She nodded, desperately, or so it seemed to Jessie. "Back before your brother..." Mrs. Rayford explained to her son. "While you were still away, I let Frankie McFarland and his girlfriend—you remember Frankie, don't you?—he grew up right here in Rusted Spur—talk me into renting them the old bunkhouse on the East Two Hundred."

Jessie threw up her hands in exasperation. "If you'd only given me that name when I asked you on the phone, I wouldn't have had to come all the way here in the first place!"

Paying no heed to her outburst, Zach stared at his mother. "That old place?" He shook his head. "But no one's lived there in years. It was falling apart."

"At the time, they seemed like such a nice young couple. Down on their luck, that's all."

"From what I remember about Frank McFarland," Zach said grimly, "there was never one nice thing about him."

"I thought he'd changed," his mother said, "but I was wrong. They disappeared six months back, without doing any of the repairs they promised in exchange for cheaper rent—or paying, either, for that matter."

Turning to look at Jessie, Zach said, "So you're looking for this woman, right? This deadbeat with the loser boyfriend really is your sister?"

"She's my *twin,* and she's missing," Jessie shot back, her face heating to hear this glorified cowboy running down the sister with whom she'd shared a womb—a sister who had shared her every day and every thought for the first sixteen years of their lives. No matter how embarrassed she felt to be judged by Haley's bad behavior, it came as second nature to defend her. "And for the record, I offered to pay your mother whatever Haley owed."

Narrowing his eyes, he glared at Henry once more. "If you're just here to find your sister, why'd you bring a cameraman? *Tell me* you're not some damned reporter—"

She pulled a card out of her purse and admitted, "Jessica Layton, Dallas Metro Update, Channel 37. But I'm really here to find my sister, for my mother's sake."

"I don't buy that for a second. You're here for some sleazy story. Here to make my mother look bad somehow," he accused as he fumbled with the camera's buttons. "How do I— Where's the release on this thing, before I have to tear it apart? There's a memory card in here, right?"

"Don't you touch that," Henry managed, but, thoroughly intimidated, he sounded more apologetic than outraged.

Finding the right lever, Rayford ejected the memory card and slipped it into the pocket of his jacket.

"No, please. I don't—" Jessie shook her head. "Forget that. You can keep it. Just— I need to ask your mother a few more questions. Please."

"What *I* need," he said as he jammed the mini-cam back at Henry, "is for the two of you to get the hell out of my house and off my property before I call the sheriff—or go get my gun."

Chapter 2

Zach was gratified to see the little cameraman scuttling out the door without a moment's hesitation.

But the slim, green-eyed woman didn't move a muscle as she stared him down. "For the record," she challenged, the wind from the open door whipping her long, red-gold hair around her, "you're threatening to shoot us?"

Though he'd like nothing more than to answer, *Hell, yes,* he hesitated for a heartbeat, remembering reporters and their underhanded ways. Innocent as this Jessica Layton appeared, with her tangled waves and a smattering of girl-next-door freckles, there was a stubborn set to her delicate jaw that promised trouble if he wasn't careful. For all he knew, she had a digital recorder hidden on her and would take his bluff to the law if he were stupid enough to threaten her. Not that Sheriff Canter would likely do anything but escort this troublemaking outsider to the county line, but Zach didn't need the aggravation.

And he didn't need her raising more questions about his mother's strange behavior. Why *hadn't* she simply told the reporter what little she knew about Layton's sister and her boyfriend instead of acting as if there was something to hide? And why had she lied to *him* about the reporter and her cameraman being lost in the storm and looking for directions?

"I'm not going to shoot you," he admitted with a shake of his head. "But I promise you, I'll pick you up like a bawling calf and carry you straight back to your car if you don't leave."

To her credit—and his irritation—Jessica Layton didn't bat an eye at the threat.

"So you're sending me back out into this storm?" she asked.

"And straight down the road to Dallas, if I have anything to say about it," he said, thinking of the tears he'd spotted in his mother's eyes. He wouldn't have her getting sick again, an illness that had alarmed him into accepting the discharge he'd been offered, as his family's sole surviving son, and into finally accepting his father's unwelcome legacy.

The reporter waited without speaking, clearly hoping to make him squirm. But as an officer of the marine corps, he was familiar with the tactic. Had used it himself upon occasion, while staring down the younger pilots he'd trained.

He waited her out, thinking how pretty he might've found this clearly smart and stubborn woman if she weren't some damned reporter, especially one who'd invaded his turf and upset his mother. Did this Jessica Layton have any idea that the woman she'd come here to grill had lost her son—his only brother, Ian—in combat a few months ago? Or that she'd still been reeling from her husband's death at the time, which had left her responsible for running an enormous spread with no one but hired hands to help her?

"I'll leave your property," the reporter finally conceded, "but I'm warning you. I'm not making the drive home until I find my sister—or at least get some straight answers about where she might've gone. Because my mother isn't dying without seeing her again."

"You—*Your* mother?" he asked. "She's—she's what? You're saying that she's sick?"

Her jaw tightening, Jessica Layton nodded. Pain cracked through the mask of fierceness, the pain of a despair barely held at bay. A reminder that death hadn't made its last stop at Zach's family's doorstep.

"I'm sorry for your family," he said, really seeing the woman behind the reporter for the first time. A gorgeous woman, not just pretty, and one that his instincts assured him wasn't lying in the hope of getting either an edge or a story. "But you just heard my mother. She has no idea where your sister's gone."

"You heard her as well as I did. It's obvious your mother's hiding something." Jessica stared in challenge at his mother on the staircase.

A challenge he cut off by stepping between them, his heart pounding out a warning that this reporter, this intruder in his home, was too dangerous to sympathize with. "You crossed a line today, barging in here with a camera, and you're crossing another, standing here and calling my mother a liar." He squared his shoulders and drew himself to his full height. "Now get out before I put you out."

"I'll be back," she assured him, turning on her heel.

And leaving him to wonder, could his mother's strange

behavior have anything to do with another woman who had shown up unexpectedly to knock at their front door?

Reminded of the miracle she'd brought, Zach glanced up toward the landing and glimpsed a tendril of soft golden-brown hair and a pair of eyes peeking through the bars of the metalwork railing.

The green eyes of his four-year-old niece, Eden, who had been dropped off by her mother—an old girlfriend of Ian's who none of them had ever heard of—in the weeks following his brother's death. Still in San Diego, packing up the contents of his room in the Bachelor Officer's Quarters, Zach had never met the woman, but Jessica Layton's green eyes nudged a suspicion…a suspicion planted by his mother's too-neat story to the night her "miracle grandchild" had appeared.

The moment the reporter closed the door behind her, the tiny girl—the child Zach swore had restored his mother's will to live—trotted down the staircase and threw herself into his mother's arms.

And in a small, sweet voice that drove a shaft of ice through his heart, Eden asked tearfully, "Grandma, is my mama coming back this time? Is she taking me away?"

"Thanks loads for the backup in there," Jessie told Henry once she'd climbed behind the wheel.

His bald scalp reddened. "Did you see the size of that guy? And the muscles? Besides, I've got at least thirty years on him, or else I would've— I could've decked him…."

When Jessie raised her brows, Henry laughed at her skepticism.

"You know me all too well," he conceded with a shrug. "Maybe I wouldn't have at that, but I could tell that cowboy wouldn't hit a woman, much less shoot one. You saw how he was with his little mama."

"I figured the same," she admitted as she started the car's engine. "But he wasn't going to back down from protecting her, either."

"Protecting? You still think she's hiding Haley?"

Jessie turned the car around and started back for the gate. "Not anymore I don't, but she's holding back. Or outright lying for some reason. I'd bet money on it."

"I sure as heck noticed how she lied to him about who we were and then popped off your sister's boyfriend's name when her son looked at her funny. And right in front of you, too, after acting like she couldn't remember."

Frowning, Jessie shook her head. "She was so flustered by that point, I'm guessing she couldn't keep it together any longer. But at least I have the boyfriend's name now, so we can check him out."

He pulled his cell phone from his pocket and glanced down at its face. "Not out here, you can't. Not online, anyway. There's no service, and—big surprise—no Wi-Fi signal, either."

"How do people *live* like this?" Hours from the nearest Starbucks, she was going into withdrawal, and being cut off from the phone, email and internet was even harder.

As if on cue, a trio of cows—or bulls, or whatever the heck they were—wandered into their path. Apparently unfazed by the wind, the big red-and-white animals stopped to chew and stare at them.

"Come on, you three. Out of the way." She tapped the horn, and one mooed. Another turned around and mooned her, before lifting its tail to…

"Not on my hood, you don't!" she said, shifting into Reverse and backing the car a safe distance. Though she'd covered far more than her share of crime scenes, accidents and fatality fires on the night beat, she crinkled her nose and *oohed* at the disgusting display.

Henry grinned and said, "I'm guessing Bossy there doesn't like us any better than that cowboy does."

Jessie snorted, then tried to decide if her Prius could make it if she drove off the graded driveway and carefully skirted the cattle. The ground to either side was lumpy with rocks, and the tough grasses and thorny shrubs could easily hide holes where they might get stuck.

Fortunately, the cattle moved on, swishing their tails smugly.

"I am so having a nice, juicy steak tonight, if I can find one…" she grumbled.

The caterpillar mustache twitched. "I'm sure our host will be glad to hear that. Good for the cattle business, after all."

"Oh, right," she said, wishing she could declare for vegetarianism, instead. But she'd been raised on good Texas beef, and she'd miss it like crazy if she had to give it up. "Well, all that aside, I think I saw a diner back in Rusted Spur. And I'm betting there's a signal there, too, so I can hop on the web."

"Glad to hear it 'cause right about now, I could eat that cow whole." Henry slanted her a look, reminding her she'd been in such a big hurry to reach the ranch, they'd had nothing since first thing that morning. Not that there had been a lot of restaurants to choose from once they'd left the state highway. "You're sure the place'll be open?"

"Judging from the number of pickups parked out front earlier, I figure it's the local hangout. Thank goodness it wasn't boarded up like most of the other businesses in town."

"*Town* seems like a stretch," said Henry, who was a city boy himself, born and raised in Chicago.

Jessie had to agree with his assessment. When they'd driven through Rusted Spur forty minutes before finding the ranch, the winds had just begun to blow, making the depressing collection of weathered, mostly wood-frame buildings, older vehicles and a single, flashing red light look positively bleak. She hoped that she was wrong, that some unexplored cross-street would reveal a thriving downtown with actual human beings she could talk to. Because even if her sister had been a stranger here, Haley's boyfriend wasn't, which made it likely he had friends or family members who would know where he had gone.

"It's late for lunch and early for dinner, but let's head that way, anyhow," she suggested. "With a little luck, we'll find some chatty local who'll tell us about Frankie McFarland."

"Could be they won't like outsiders," Henry warned. "Especially not outsiders asking questions about a local boy."

"Oh, ye of little faith," she said. "I'll bet you a nice, crisp twenty there's somebody eager to rat out old Frankie. Either because he's a jerk—my sister's boyfriends always are—or for the chance to be on TV."

"Not for some Dallas station they don't even get here."

Henry's cynicism reminded her of the other type of people news crews frequently encountered: those who called them vultures—or worse—and slammed doors in their faces. Thinking of Zach Rayford's contempt, she decided to forget about the camera and the microphone and simply play up the worried-sister angle. Her reunion with her twin later would make for more compelling viewing, anyway.

By the time they rolled into town, the storm had completely blown itself out, leaving behind a faint orange haze and chilly temperatures for late October.

Before heading toward the diner, they took the time to drive around town and found a few more going concerns, including a feed cooperative, a small post office located inside a rundown grocery store and a combination car repair shop and gas station. A lone pickup crossed the intersection ahead of them and a couple of lean brown dogs trotted along a buckled sidewalk.

"I'm starting to wonder if that storm blew us back in time," said Henry as he peered at a long-since-closed theater. "This place looks like something from another century."

"Another planet," Jessie agreed, thinking of the tangled freeways and shining skyscrapers of downtown Dallas.

They easily found parking in front of a place called Tumbleweeds, which sported a peeling, hand-lettered sign proclaiming it the HOME OF THE PANHANDLE'S BIGGEST CHICKEN-FRIED STEAK!

"I notice they didn't bother to claim 'best,'" she said, making a mental note to order something healthier than the breaded, fried and gravy-laden dish.

After hiding the mini-cam in the rear hatch, they went in to scope the place out. At only a few minutes past four, the small, wood-frame structure was deserted save for a plump, dark-haired teenager cleaning tables and an older man Jessie assumed to be the cook, judging from his hairnet and apron, dozing as he leaned against the counter.

The waitress put down the rag she'd been using and smiled at them with crooked little teeth. "Welcome to Tumbleweeds. Are y'all here for dinner?"

"Sure thing," Jessie said, unsure whether to be relieved

or disappointed that the girl—Mandy, according to the name tag on her apron—didn't seem to recognize her, which probably meant she didn't know Haley. But that didn't mean the teen couldn't be of help.

An hour later, they came out, full of saturated fats, since there hadn't been so much as a single veggie on the menu that wasn't deep-fried or infused with bacon drippings, but little wiser than they had been.

Although Mandy had seemed sympathetic when Jessie told her about her search, it was clear that she knew nothing about Haley. She had, however, told them that Frankie McFarland's brother, Danny, worked at the nearby feed store. Searches on both names with her cell phone, which was working decently if slowly, didn't turn up anything of use. Apparently, the McFarland brothers didn't stay connected with their friends on social networks, either.

Jessie and Henry had nearly reached the car when the girl from the diner came trotting out after them, her dark braid bouncing behind her and her round face pink with exertion. As soon as she caught her breath, she warned, "I didn't want to say it in there with Crabby Leonard listening, but Danny's nickname around town is Hellfire. On account of his temper."

"You mean he's violent?" Henry rushed to ask.

"He's been tryin' to pass himself off as respectable since he bought out the local watering hole, but everybody knows he'n Frankie have always been quick to take offense and even quicker with their fists. I've heard Sheriff Canter joke about naming one of his jail cells the Mc-Farland Suite."

Jessie's stomach twisted with sudden apprehension as for the first time it occurred to her that her sister might not be deliberately hiding from her family, but in trouble.

The kind of trouble that came with being involved with a violently abusive man.

An approaching rumble cut like a chainsaw through the small-town quiet. Swiveling her head, Mandy gasped and whispered, "Oh, gosh. Here he comes now. That's Hellfire."

As a big chopper-style motorcycle came into view, the waitress glanced from Henry to Jessie and begged, "Please don't tell him I said anything about his temper. Or that stupid joke the sheriff made, okay?"

"It's already forgotten," Jessie promised.

But she was talking to thin air, for Mandy was already hurrying back inside as Danny McFarland roared up, his ragged, reddish beard and hair wild in the wind beneath the level of the skull-and-crossbones bandanna he was wearing. A big man with a bigger belly, he hid a portion of his bulk beneath an oversize black leather jacket. As he dismounted, she saw the name *Prairie Rose Saloon* had been emblazoned across the back. Beneath those words, a rattlesnake, all coiled menace, gaped among yellow roses with wicked, blood-tipped thorns.

As biker art went, it was impressive. But Jessie had neither the inclination nor the time to appreciate the view as Hellfire turned around to look her over. Though his eyes were hidden behind wraparound reflective glasses, Jessie's skin crawled at the contempt that seemed to roll off him in waves.

"Careful with this guy," Henry warned, shrinking back as she stepped forward.

Though Jessie had interviewed motorcycle "thugs" who'd turned out to have hearts of gold underneath their rough exteriors, her instincts screamed at her to retreat to safety. But McFarland was the only lead she had to follow, so she held her ground, even when he removed the glasses to reveal a pair of teardrops tattooed beneath his right eye. Teardrops that often signified a stint in prison—or worse.

In a moment, the mask shifted, morphing from simple toughness into fury before he burst out with, "You stupid bitch. You think anyone's gonna be fooled by a freakin' haircut and some fancy clothes? What'd I tell you about—"

"Haley is my sister," Jessie said, jolted by the knowledge that he'd mistaken her for her twin. That he clearly knew—and hated—her. "She's also your brother's girlfriend, from what I hear. Can you tell me where they went?"

"Your *sister?* What the hell're you trying to pull, girl?" He stopped abruptly to scowl at her, grooves furrowing his weathered face before blinking in surprise. "Wait a minute. You ain't kidding, are you?"

"Our mother's— Our mom's dying," Jessie admitted. "She only wants to see my sister one more time."

"Well, I can tell you, Rusted Spur's the last place you're gonna find that girl, or my brother, either. Now you get on down the road, too—if you want to stay alive."

Jessie's jaw tightened. *Does everyone in this one-horse town intend to threaten me?* Nevertheless, she stood her ground, insisting, "I can't go anywhere without Haley."

McFarland looked from her to Henry and back again, his lip curling to reveal tobacco-stained teeth. "Maybe then you won't be leaving. Alive, anyway."

Jessie didn't give an inch, demanding, "Where is she, Hellfire? Where'd your brother take her?"

As the biker's gaze turned dangerous, Henry grabbed at her arm. "Let's get out of here, Jessie. I'll drive this time if you want."

Jerking her arm free, she didn't budge and didn't take her eyes off McFarland for a second.

Without further warning, he surged toward her, faster than she would have imagined such a big man capable of moving. With a cry of alarm, she backpedaled, choking with fear and nausea as her hands came up to ward off his attack.

Chapter 3

Zach was astonished at how swiftly his mother jumped up and trotted upstairs to the landing. Showing no sign of illness, she knelt before Eden and wrapped the tiny girl in her thin arms.

"No, sweetheart. *You remember,*" she insisted. "Your mama's job has her flying overseas now. That's why she had to leave you with me."

Zach's gut tightened as his suspicion deepened. Was she reminding Eden of a truth—or coaching the child to stick to some story she'd come up with?

Looking frightened, the girl stared into his mother's face. "I want to stay with you, Grandma, and Uncle Zach, too, and my pony. Please don't make me go back there. I don't want to leave."

"I promise, baby, you don't have to. Your mama signed the papers so you can stay with us forever."

"And get my puppies, too, soon as they're ready to

leave their mommy?" Eden asked, brightening at the mention of her favorite subject.

Zach's mother shot him an aggrieved look, since he'd been the fool who'd taken her with him to see his friend Nate, a bachelor who was even more clueless than Zach was when it came to four-year-olds. Not only had he shown Eden the litter of fluffy Australian shepherd pups in the barn, he'd encouraged her to cuddle and play with them, then pick out the one that she liked best.

When Eden, who was as crazy about animals as Ian had been at her age, had been unable to choose between a merle female and a male tricolor, Nate had joked, "Then why not take both, Eden? This week only, they're free to pretty girls."

Zach was still mad at the big idiot, though the two had been fast friends since high school. It wasn't so much that Zach minded the idea of getting a dog for the ranch— especially one from Nate's Bonnie, one of the smartest, most intuitive animals he'd ever known—but puppies were a lot of work. Besides, his mother, who had always firmly believed that animals belonged outdoors, had been quick to remind him how Eden had cried herself to sleep for days when they wouldn't let the pony come up to bed with her at night.

When his mama didn't answer right away, Eden said, "I already thought of the best names for them. The girl's gonna be Sweetheart and the boy is Lionheart. Sweetheart'll kiss me when I'm lonesome and Lionheart will chase away the scary dreams at night."

"Those *are* good names." As Zach followed Eden and his mother upstairs, he was troubled by the girl's mention of the night terrors that had her waking up screaming several times a week. During the daylight hours, she seemed happy enough to ride sweet old Mr. Butters under his watchful eye or to curl up on his mama's lap and listen to the same children's books she'd once read to him and Ian. And he'd never once heard the girl ask about the mother who'd abandoned her. And she never mentioned Ian, either, or showed any interest in looking at old photos of her father.

Her *alleged* father, he reminded himself, realizing there was not a shred of proof other than a stranger's word. How could he have been so gullible as to accept it at face value? Was he as addled by grief as the mother who had raised him? Or maybe it had been her improvement, the swift change from deep depression to life and purpose, that had convinced him. A man saw what he wanted to, when his heart got in the way.

Looking deeply troubled, his mother said, "You can bring home the puppies, darling. As soon as they're big enough…"

Her voice faltered, and she suddenly dropped to her rear on the hallway's carpeted floor.

"Mama?" he asked, taking her sagging shoulders to keep her from falling onto her side. "Are you all right?"

"Oh, my," she managed, lifting a hand to her head. "It's just my medication—I'm afraid it's made me dizzy."

He helped her to bed then, but as Eden "tucked Grandma in," he thought he glimpsed a measure of shrewdness in his mother's eyes, a look that more than half convinced him she was deliberately exaggerating whatever symptoms she'd been feeling.

And even more deliberately avoiding the hard questions that she knew he must ask.

Sheriff George Canter stepped down from his Trencher County SUV, wearing a khaki-colored uniform and a look of disapproval. A tall, chiseled man whose broad-brimmed hat shaded his eyes, he made a beeline for Jessie, who'd been waiting with Henry in the car outside the diner for almost an hour.

"He looks madder than McFarland," Henry said. "Maybe we should just forget this and move on."

Wondering how the cameraman had survived decades in their line of work without a backbone, Jessie silenced him with a look. Once she'd slipped her phone back into her pocket, she climbed out to meet what passed for law enforcement in this one-horse town.

"Sheriff Canter. Good to see you." She barely restrained herself from adding, *finally.*

He studied her carefully before replying, "So you're the little lady who felt the need to drag me halfway across the county because she got herself pushed."

Jessie struggled to hold her temper in check.

"Where I come from," she said tightly, "a shove is an assault."

He snorted. "Turns out we got the memo on that all the way up here in Rusted Spur, too, Miss Layton. But at best, it's only a Class C Misdemeanor, hardly worth the effort to write the ticket, by the time all's said and done."

"He knocked me to the ground, Sheriff. I thought he was going to stomp my head in with those studded boots he was wearing." She shuddered, remembering how he'd stopped short at her scream.

"But he didn't really hurt you, did he?" The sheriff removed his hat to push back thick, dark hair with splashes of silver at the temples. A handsome man who looked to be in his early forties, he narrowed his dark eyes.

"Not really, no, but he threatened to—"

"And where the hell were you, sir, during all this?" Canter challenged Henry, who had gotten out of the car.

Flushing fiercely, the smaller man admitted, "I was

going for my phone. I'd left it in the car, you see, and—
I did tell him to back off."

The sheriff made a scoffing sound and shook his head
in disgust, clearly unimpressed with the cameraman's
conduct.

"Listen, Sheriff," Jessie said. "Danny McFarland
threatened to kick my teeth down my throat next time,
if I didn't get in the car and go back to wherever it was
I came from."

"To your TV station back in Dallas," Canter supplied,
the creases in his forehead underscoring his disdain.

Fury fading, she blinked at him in surprise. Though
she'd given the dispatcher her name, she hadn't mentioned a word about where she lived or her profession.
She'd been hoping to enlist his help in the search for her
twin, but in her experience, small-town law enforcement
often hated big-city reporters, too many of whom were
quick to paint the local cops as ignorant yokels.

"You've been talking to Zach Rayford," she guessed.
For all she knew, the rancher and his mother were his
cousins, old friends or the elected sheriff's main campaign contributors.

Canter shook his head and smirked. "Might surprise
you to know we've got the internet at my office. When
it's working, anyhow. Your name caught my attention,
so I did a quick search. Didn't take me twenty seconds
to come across your picture on your station's website."

"So I'm a reporter. That doesn't give some tattooed
thug the right to knock me down and threaten my life."

"Threaten that pretty smile, you mean," he reminded
her. "Let's get your story straight."

She glared, unable to believe this. "Seriously, Sheriff,
what exactly is your problem with me?"

He stared at her for a long moment before shaking his

head. "Well, maybe you look a little too much like your sister," he conceded. "And maybe that just makes me want to slap a pair of cuffs on you and drag you down to my jail, out of habit."

Eden looked up at Zach with big green eyes. "Please, can I come with you? I'll be good, I promise. I won't bother you a single bit."

"I'm sorry," he told her, though he didn't blame her for wanting to come out with him instead of being cooped up with their long-time cook, the no-nonsense and even less fun Miss Althea, while his mama rested. But bored as Eden might be at home, he wasn't about to take a four-year-old with him to help supervise the cowboys as they resumed the dirty, sometimes dangerous work of separating out the older calves from the herd, now that the storm was over.

For one thing, he knew the tenderhearted four-year-old would burst into tears once she figured out the mama cows were bawling for their babies. But even more, he needed time to think through this situation with his mother and their unwelcome visitor. Wishing he had never set eyes on Jessica Layton, he gently unwrapped Eden's arms from his leg and said, "I'm going to expect an excellent report from Miss Althea."

The broad-hipped, graying woman nodded her approval.

"I'll let you help me make a batch of thumbprint cookies," she told the girl, "with real raspberry jam."

"Those were your daddy's favorites," Zach added, smiling at Eden. "Mine, too, for that matter, so you be sure to save me some."

"I wanna go with you," said Eden stubbornly, her tiny hands balling into fists. "Wanna see the cows and horses."

Hoping to avert a full-fledged tantrum, Zach shrugged at Miss Althea. "Well, I *was* going to take this young lady to visit those puppies later on," he said, "but if she's not even willing to help you make your famous cookies…"

"I can help!" Eden exploded, jumping with excitement. "I'll be the best helper!"

"And you won't pester Miss Althea or your grandma by asking when I'll be home?" he prompted.

When she crossed her heart and hoped to cry, he knelt for another hug and ruffled her silky, golden-brown hair. "Be good, now," he said, grabbing his jacket and making his escape while he still could.

He cleared his throat the moment he was outdoors, trying to break up the lump of dread lodged firmly inside it. Anger, too, that he'd let himself be suckered. Allowed himself to believe that, against all odds, some part of his brother had survived.

He cranked the big pickup's engine and listened to it roar to life. *How stupid can you get?* The Ian he knew and loved never would have kept a child secret, never would've failed to see to Eden's support or named her as a beneficiary in the event of his death, either. Sure, their father would have cursed him for a fool for fathering a child out of wedlock, but like Zach, his younger brother had used the military to put distance between himself and the harshness of the old man's judgment.

To put distance between himself and the legacy of dust and duty that was all Zach had left now.

He was pulling up to the corral when a call came through on the satellite phone he'd purchased to keep in touch with his cowboys anywhere on the ranch.

"Zach, this is Sheriff Canter," said the caller as soon as he had answered.

Hearing the agitation in the man's voice, Zach guessed,

"That reporter stopped by your office to see you, did she? I figured she might, after we told her we hadn't seen her sister."

"Not exactly, she didn't. She had a little run-in with ole Hellfire over by Tumbleweeds."

"Danny McFarland?" Zach swore under his breath. Unwelcome visitor or not, he should've warned the Layton woman about tracking down and questioning Frankie's ex-con brother. Probably, that would have only made the mule-headed reporter more eager to find and question the man, but still… "He didn't hurt her, did he?"

An image of her pretty face, bruised and bloodied, flashed across his vision. He swallowed hard, jaw stiffening, though he couldn't say for certain why it was any of his business.

"Nah," said Canter, the casual contempt in his tone reminding Zach why he hadn't liked him years before and still didn't. "Hellfire looks big and bad, but he's toned down his act these days, now that he's a *man of bidness*. Just made her mad enough to call and insist on pressing charges. Waste of time was what I told her. Sooner she heads home and forgets about this nonsense, the better. From what your mama told me months ago, the sister skipped rent and skipped town with her lowlife boyfriend. Which suits me just fine, I can tell you. I was gettin' mighty tired of driving out there to make sure they weren't at each other's throats again."

Zach rubbed his forehead, feeling a headache of his own coming on. "So Frankie was violent with her?"

"Hell, when those two got to drinkin', they were violent with each other. I had to put 'em both in separate cells one night to cool off after they got into a knockdown drag-out over at the Prairie Rose."

Despite the sweetness of its name, the century-old saloon perched on the town's outskirts was as famous for its rowdy brawls as its watered-down liquor. Zach remembered a handful of fights he'd taken part in back in the day, burning off his restless energy and frustration in the weeks before he'd left home. In fact, it had been George Canter—still a deputy at that time—who'd advised him to *get your sorry ass off the ranch and out of this town before it completely ruins you.*

"Hellfire was tryin' his best to reform him, but the rest of the Prairie Rose crowd had been layin' odds on how long it would be till Frankie finally up and killed her."

What if he had, Zach wondered, then taken off for parts unknown? Could Jessica Layton, with those green eyes that looked so uncomfortably like Eden's, be looking for a living sister when she should be searching for a corpse? It would certainly explain why Frankie had suddenly skipped town, and possibly why his mother had been so quick to react—or *over*react—when Haley's twin showed up asking questions.

"What I don't understand," Zach said as another thought struck him, "is why're you calling me about this." Had the reporter said something to Canter, something that might raise the sheriff's suspicions about his mother?

His gut twisted with the thought—and with the certainty that a third loss would utterly destroy her. Especially the loss of a child as sweet and full of life as Eden.

"I'm calling to find out a little more about Jessica Layton's visit out to your place this afternoon."

"Mama told her on the phone that Haley had moved on," Zach said, struggling to sound casual, "but Jessica had to come see for herself, I guess, make sure we weren't hiding her twin under a cow pie or something."

"I guess you know as well as anyone how these reporters are, always smelling a conspiracy," Canter said, his pointed look reminding Zach of the incident that had cost him his wings. "And that young woman—I'm thinkin' that she's not finished sniffing around here yet."

"You're sure? You said that Hellfire knocked her down, and you warned her yourself to move along."

"I didn't *warn* her." Canter sounded testy at the suggestion. "I just gave her a little friendly advice. But when she and that sawed-off excuse for a man she's got with her rolled out of town, I noticed that she didn't take the road toward Dallas. Best that I can figure, she's headin' straight back to your ranch."

The hell she is, Zach decided, intent on heading her off and sending her packing before she had the chance to bother his mama again—or get a closer look at his supposed niece.

Chapter 4

The light was almost gone by the time the dusty blue Prius followed the power lines that led them to the old bunkhouse.

"You sure this is it?"

Jessie peered past Henry and nodded. "Has to be. Nancy Rayford said herself the place was on the East Two Hundred—and you saw what I brought up on the satellite map."

During their long wait for the sheriff's arrival, Jessie had taken full advantage of a nearby cell tower, using the connection to pore over the area surrounding the Rayford ranch. Sure enough, there was a large parcel to the east of the ranch house, and she'd been able to zoom in on the only rooftop, which appeared to belong to a small outbuilding. Some days, she absolutely *loved* technology.

Despite her show of confidence, however, she hadn't been entirely certain whether they would come across the bunkhouse or a half-collapsed barn—not until her head-lights skimmed the front porch of the narrow structure. Putting the car in park, Jessie took note of the boarded windows, the sagging roof and the tall brush. Piles of spindly tumbleweeds had blown up against the west side of the narrow building, mounding like a snowdrift. As sad and lonely as the place looked, she was almost certain it had served as someone's living quarters. But had her sister and her boyfriend lived here recently?

"Looks like it's been empty for a while," she said, pointing out the unbroken yellow stalks of grasses that had come up in front of the steps. "Months, at least."

"If I didn't know better," said Henry, "I'd say the place has been abandoned for years."

Jessie nodded, speechless as she took in the warped, unpainted wood and the air of desperation. Despite the presence of electricity and what she thought might be a well house, Jessie ached imagining her twin living in a shelter that barely looked fit for animals.

If their father could have seen this place, would he have relented on his own vow to never give Haley another penny? Would Jessie herself have driven here to get her?

Maybe not, though the sight of this place would have given her nightmares for months afterward. Especially if it was as infested with rats and spiders—or even snakes—as its appearance suggested.

Her stomach crawled at the thought, but she forced herself to trot out her best intrepid young reporter act. "Flashlights are in the back. You ready?"

"Ready for what?" Henry asked. "You can't mean we're going in there. This is private property. If the owner doesn't outright shoot us, that sheriff will throw us both in the hoosegow for the sheer pleasure of it."

"Hoosegow?" She grinned, wondering when the last

time was she'd heard someone refer to a jail by that name.
But then again, Rusted Spur was an outdated place, its
sweeping plains reminding her of the Spaghetti Westerns
her father had once loved.

At the thought, her imagination conjured the image
of Zach Rayford, long and lean and tough as nails as
he scowled down from the saddle aboard a coal-black
stallion. As the soundtrack whistled a cinematic warning, sheeplike townsfolk scurried out of sight. Still, she
couldn't help thinking about how handsome the guy was.
How smoking hot, despite the glower.

"You think I'm kidding?" Henry went on. "Because
I'm telling you, the sheriff wasn't. He wants us gone
from here, and I'm starting to think that's a damned good
idea."

She frowned, wishing she'd left her cameraman in
Dallas. But that would have meant bucking her news director, and Jessie had no intention of losing her job, not
when she was so close to breaking a story she had risked
so much to chase down. *So why didn't Vivian run the
piece live before I left? Could there be another reason
she'd seemed relieved when I asked to leave town right
before the date we had agreed on?*

Unfortunately, she was afraid she already knew the
reason; she simply didn't want to believe it could be true.

"Quit worrying so much," she said, hoping a display
of girl-reporter spunkiness might move him. "Seriously,
who's going to see us?" She gestured at the rolling range-
land all around them, its bleakness broken only by a
smear of rose and orange that stained the western horizon. "Maybe you could get some footage for your— You
brought an extra memory card, right?"

"Of course I did, but it's too dark now. We'd only have
to come back later, anyway. So let's wait till tomorrow."

"We can't afford to, Henry. You know as well as I do, by the time Rayford and Canter get through laying down the law around here, we won't be able to buy so much as a glass of water, let alone a tank of gas or a scrap of information. And I'll never find my sister, at least not before our mom's—before she's too sick for it to make a difference."

"If we started now," said Henry, "we could reach Marston before nine. That's where you made our reservation, isn't it?"

"Closest lodging I could find."

"We can rest up and make a new plan for the morning."

"I'm not going anywhere until we take a look inside that house," she said, "before somebody hightails it out here to clean up any evidence."

Henry frowned. "Evidence of *what?*"

"Whatever really happened to Haley." A chill crawled down her neck like some many-legged insect. "Whether it's a forwarding address or—or something worse."

"Like what? You don't seriously think a tiny little thing like Mrs. Rayford's done something to your sister?"

"Not her, but what about Hellfire's brother, Frankie?" Jessie shook her head and climbed out into the breezy chill, not wanting to think about the kind of damage a violent man could inflict on a woman. Beatings, strangulations, shootings—she'd covered nearly every brand of bad news on the night beat.

Haley couldn't be dead; it was impossible. Close as they had once been, Jessie would have felt the void.

Wouldn't she? Or had Haley's choices—and Jessie's own—forever severed the connection? The questions whistled past her on a hollow wind, eliciting a shiver.

Leaving the headlights on and the car idling, she retrieved two flashlights from the rear and then passed a rusted barbecue grill on her way to the porch. As her foot creaked on the first step, she heard Henry coming up behind her.

"Think it's safe?" he asked. "The last thing we need is for one of us to fall through."

"Just a little noisy, that's all," she said, grabbing the wooden railing as she turned to look at him.

With a loud *crack,* a section of the railing snapped off in her hand.

"Or maybe not," she said. "Be careful, Henry."

"My middle name," he joked, accepting the flashlight she offered with a shaky hand. "At least that's what my wife claims."

On the porch itself, they found a sand-filled coffee can bristling with ancient cigarette butts. Broken pieces of beer bottles lay scattered, along with a few crushed cans. Beneath a rough-hewn bench, she spotted a soiled wad of cloth. Using the broken length of railing, Jessie poked at the cloth, then jumped reflexively as a couple of scorpions disappeared into the crevices between boards.

Jessie shivered, but she forgot the nasty little things as she turned her attention to what turned out to be a worn T-shirt.

As she poked and then lifted it with the piece of railing, the torn and holey shirt's design sent a jolt of recognition through her. With its feminine scooped neck and its red-and-white Texas Rangers logo, she felt certain it had to be her sister's.

Seeing her face, Henry frowned. "You recognize it, then?"

"Haley's favorite team." A memory of a family trip to the stadium in Arlington—of a time they'd still been a real family—froze the breath in Jessie's lungs.

She shook it off and said, "You see the stains here?" With her flashlight's beam, she indicated darker splotches. Large splotches.

"Mold?" he asked.

"Or blood." She used her on-air voice, its calm confidence belying the panic that gripped her, the desire to scream or cry or pray her way out of this possibility. *It could be Haley's blood here, right here, the DNA so close to mine it would take a team of scientists to tease out the differences.*

"Should we call the sheriff?" Henry asked.

"Are you kidding?" she asked. "Like you said before, he'd just arrest us for trespassing, and nine chances out of ten, this shirt would disappear before it could get tested. We'll bag it before we leave, get an independent lab to check it out."

"But it could be—I'm sorry to say this, Jessie, this being your sister—but this might be evidence of a crime. You can't take it."

"What else would you suggest? Leave it here and run home to tell my mom some fairy story? Because I'm not going to do that. And I'm not trusting Canter with this."

"What about someone else?" He pointed at the shirt's logo. "Maybe the real rangers?"

"Great idea," she said, thinking that the legendary Texas Rangers would be perfect, "but before they'll come, we'll have to convince them the locals aren't willing or able to handle this investigation. And that there's more to this than some reporter's overactive imagination."

"Or an attempt to add a little 'sex appeal' to a routine missing person story." He sketched air quotes around the phrase, alluding to the Ranger mystique viewing audiences lapped up so eagerly.

She felt her face harden. "You really think I'm *angling* here? We're talking about my family."

Raising his palms in surrender, Henry quickly back-pedaled. "I didn't mean you, personally. Only that's what these law-enforcement types are gonna think you're up to."

She sighed before admitting, "A lot of times, I would be."

"Not you, Jessie, not that I've ever noticed. You're not like that at all."

She skewered him with a look, reminded of a recent conversation. "I'm *not* too soft for real news. Look how long I've covered the overnight crime beat."

"I didn't mean it that way."

"I have plenty of ambition. Look at that story I just did on the mayor," she insisted.

"You mean the one that Vivian wouldn't let run before we left?"

"She'll run it," Jessie insisted. "When the time is right, she'll—"

"It's locked," he interrupted, trying to hide his enthusiasm as he pointed out the padlock on the bunkhouse door. "Guess we'll have to leave, after all. Wait. What're you doing? You aren't seriously thinking of breaking and—"

Using a small folding knife she'd pulled from her pocket, Jessie pried at the latch that held the lock in place.

"Entering," Henry finished. "You surprise me, Jessie."

"Which part?" she asked, easily dragging one screw from the dry-rotted wood. "The knife or the ambition?"

"You're not letting me forget that, are you?"

"Not likely." Her pulse jumped as the latch fell away. Rusty hinges squealed in protest as the bunkhouse door swung open.

She grabbed the porch rail, which she'd leaned against

the wall, and gestured toward the black maw. "After you, sir."

"Ladies first," Henry said. "Though for the record, I still think this is the worst idea you've had all day. And considering some of the other ones, that's really saying something."

Jessie ducked beneath a cobweb that draped the upper portion of the doorway and stepped inside. But the chance that the stains on the old T-shirt might be blood had her heart pounding. Was it possible her sister had never left this glorified shack alive?

No way, she told herself, even as the fine hairs on the back of her neck rose. Surely, whoever had come to put on the padlock would have noticed something as obvious as a dead body—or its odor.

Shaking off her jitters, Jessie aimed her flashlight down the long and narrow space. Startled by her entrance, something scuttled across the floor, and she swallowed back revulsion.

There wasn't much to see: a grimy tunnel-like room with a stained mattress pushed off to one side, a threadbare, plaid sofa with a distinct sag in the middle. Feet crunching over grit, she took another two steps inside. Enough to spotlight the kitchenette, with its rusty sink and a plug-in electric burner on a plywood countertop. At the far end was a single doorway, which must lead to the bathroom.

Jessie tried a light switch, found it dead as she'd expected, and walked the length of the bunkhouse, her eyes straining for forgotten oddments: a bent fork, a piece of junk mail—anything that might convey the slightest clue.

But there was nothing, no trash or personal possessions in the kitchen drawers or the tiny pantry. Even the dented refrigerator had been left unplugged with its doors propped open. Since Jessie couldn't imagine her sister or her boyfriend taking the trouble to clean before running out on the rent, she supposed that Mrs. Rayford had had whomever she'd sent to secure the door deal with the mess.

Sighing, Jessie lowered her light. "Guess you're right. There's nothing left to see."

Henry sidled toward the door. "Let's get out, then. Before somebody catches us here."

"Might as well check the bathroom first," she said. "Then I'll be right behind you."

The beam of light preceded her, sweeping dated fixtures. A strand of hair lay in the sink, reddish-gold and longer than her own. Unease crawled on spider's legs up her neck. *Haley's hair,* she thought, raising her eyes to the mottled glass of a partially de-silvered mirror.

There, her attention zoomed in on the brownish speckles along the lower edge—speckles that made her think of dried blood.

"Henry!" she called.

But he was shouting her name even louder, screaming, "Jessie, don't come out!"

Heart contracting, Jessie reached for the bathroom door to slam it shut. But in that fractured second, she looked out through the narrowing gap to see Henry's splayed hands rising, his feet scrambling backward as he struggled to escape.

Reacting on pure reflex, she flung open the door rather than retreating. Unable to bear the thought of anyone hurting her reluctant partner, she launched herself forward, intent on dragging him out of harm's way before—

She had barely made it a step when an impossibly loud boom exploded.

With that single blast, Henry was falling, crumpling

as an arc of scarlet sprouted from his back. In the span
of that same panicked heartbeat, an invisible blow caught
her right hand, a shock that brought with it a wave of dizziness that dropped her to her knees. And pain, pain like
she had never known, turned her vision red and dragged
a cry from her lungs, sending streamers of shock cascad-
ing through her.

Abruptly biting back her scream, she looked at Henry:
her coworker, her friend. A man she'd known for every
day of the four years she had worked for Metro Update,
a family man with a devoted wife and three grown children, with his first grandchild on the way.

He lay twitching in an expanding puddle, as his choking rattle gave way to a sigh, then utter stillness. *Gone.
He's gone,* she understood, the dark certainty slamming
her like a mallet. And the bullet that had killed him must
have passed through and caught her hand, too.

Get inside that bathroom, his voice seemed to shout
inside her brain, *before the shooter comes to finish you,
too.*

Adrenaline pounding through her, she fought to get
up, to get away, but panic tangled her legs. So she moved
as best she could, crawling toward the bathroom using
knees and elbows while struggling to keep her throbbing
right hand off the filthy floor…and to keep herself from
looking back again at Henry—or checking for the gunman in the empty bunkhouse doorway.

Instead, she swore to herself she was going to get
through this. Going to survive to make the animal who
had gunned down Henry pay.

At least, she would if the shooter got in his vehicle
and drove away now.

But that hope died moments later, when she smelled
the first acrid wisp of smoke.

* * *

It was the dust that gave away the intruders, dust rising from the dirt road leading to the East Two Hundred. Thick as it was, the cloud lay heavy along the horizon, reminding Zach of smoke as he raced toward it, hell bent on throwing the reporter and her cameraman off his land before Jessie Layton found the proof that could upend all their lives.

If he was right in his suspicions, that same proof might end his mother's. Even if it didn't outright kill her, the web of lies she'd told could easily lead to lawsuits or even prison if the wrong jury got hold of the case.

The thought of his frail, grief-stricken mother in a cell turned his guts to ice water, and his skin grew clammy beneath the jacket he was wearing. But as horrible as it was imagining himself unable to protect her, the possibility that she hadn't actually lied but somehow *believed* what she'd been claiming disturbed him even more.

Could Ian's death have pushed her beyond the bounds of reason? Or was Zach himself the crazy one, imagining that his mother would spin such a tale? Back when he and Ian were kids, nothing would get them sent to their rooms (or whipped with their dad's belt, if he happened to hear them) faster than telling lies, and Zach had never—not even in these past few stressful months— seen any signs that she might be delusional. Fragile and often ill, yes, but never out of touch with the sad reality of their recent losses.

As he lowered the window, the ashen odor filtered into his truck, and his heart lurched at the realization that what he'd been seeing really *was* smoke, not dust, and that the flickering glow could only mean one thing. *Fire.* Had the Layton woman and her cameraman somehow accidentally set it? Or was she so upset about what had happened with his mother and then later in town, she'd taken out her frustrations with a lit match?

Furious at the thought that the flames might spread to the drought-plagued pasture and threaten his livestock, he mashed the pedal to the floorboard and crested a low hill.

From that vantage, he saw flames leaping from the collapsed front porch of the structure. Just as he'd suspected, he spotted a car there, too, the same blue hybrid he'd watched Jessica Layton and her cameraman climb into before leaving his house this afternoon.

A new worry goosed his heartbeat. Could the two still be inside?

He reached for his phone to call for help a split second before he started around a curve and was blinded by the high-beam headlights of a fleeing pickup. The blare of a horn followed, flooding him with adrenaline as he wrenched the wheel to the right.

The two speeding trucks came within inches of colliding head-on, but Zach didn't have a moment to celebrate his survival as his vehicle careened down the steep side of a gully. He fought to regain control, to steer or brake to halt the bone-jarring descent, but the truck slid sideways until the right front tire struck something unyielding and the wheel crumpled, the axle snapping audibly.

After that, there was a single, confused moment as the pickup leaned, then started over, and before he understood what was happening, there was a tremendous crunching and the sounds of shattering glass and screaming metal, followed by a pain shooting through his jaw as it struck the steering wheel.

It might have been five seconds or an hour later when his senses returned and his eyes opened. Though his dash lights remained on, the stars above had vanished, and blood was running the wrong way, dripping from the top of his head....

He was hanging in his seat belt, he realized, upside-down in the darkness. But as he blinked, he spotted a glow on the horizon. A glow that looked like firelight.

Had Jessie and her cameraman gotten out, or were they still inside the burning bunkhouse? Fumbling for the seat belt latch, he depressed the button and dropped down with a thump. For several minutes he struggled to extricate himself from the tangled belt before crawling out through the open window. His body aching with the effort, he rose to his feet, dizzy and wobbling but relieved that he could still stand.

A few steps later, a fresh wave of dizziness had Zach staggering to a stop. He bent forward, resting his hands above his knees before reaching up to probe his bloody chin. When his finger found the spot where the steering wheel had split the skin, bursts of color exploded in his vision and sirens wailed, so loud and so close he covered his ears with his hands.

It took him several moments to remember that he'd never called anyone for help. The sirens, maybe even the fire and smoke he had been seeing, couldn't be real. Instead, they were from *there,* he realized with a shudder. Another crash, another time.

Only that time, he had parachuted down to safety, watching his jet nosedive, watching a second explosion blossom, a lethal flower that consumed houses, cars and twenty-two lives, including that of his best friend. Lives lost while he hung helpless in the air above them, his chest split in two by a howl of pain and grief. The echo of that cry still woke him some nights, two years later, along with the sound of sirens in Kabul and the sense of utter helplessness.

But that time wasn't this one, he understood as the phantom sirens abruptly fell silent. Here, there might be something he could do, not only for himself but for anyone still trapped inside the bunkhouse....

His burning bunkhouse? He drew in a breath of air, and quickly understood that it *was* real smoke he smelled.

Remembering his phone, he pulled it out and was grateful to discover it hadn't been damaged in the accident. He punched in 9-1-1 and quickly got out his location to the dispatcher who picked up.

With a glance toward the glowing horizon, he added, "Send an ambulance along with a fire crew. Send everything you've got. I think there might be people trapped inside a burning building."

"I'll have first responders there as soon as I can," the dispatcher promised. "You need to wait for them outside, sir. Well beyond the fire's radius."

"I understand," he told her, cutting off the call before he could say more. Before he could lie to her, because there was no way in this world he was letting it happen again, allowing himself to waft downward on a gentle breeze while others burned to death.

Shaking off his swirling vision, he lurched forward through the dry grasses, desperate to get there as fast as possible, to change the outcome of his nightmares, if only he could keep focused on the here and now.

He dropped the phone into his pocket, then dragged out a wadded bandanna. Holding it to his chin, he broke into the fastest pace he could manage with his vision fraying like an old rug at its edges. Unsteady as his gait was, his long strides quickly ate up the distance, and soon he crested the hill—and saw the reporter's Prius parked there, its headlights trained on the last few flickering flames licking lazily up the side of the bunkhouse doorway. He stared for a moment, confused to see that the blaze had died down considerably from the initial glow.

Why? Had some accelerant burned off before it had had time to soak in? An accelerant meant to burn the evidence of a crime?

Angry as he'd been about the reporter trespassing, he thought of the fleeing truck and felt a rush of apprehension. For the rising moon revealed there was no sign of either the Layton woman or her cameraman. No sign of life at all, save for the distant yipping of coyotes.

Zach approached cautiously, relying on the same instincts and training that had kept him alive through three deployments. His mind was clear, his senses sharp as he pushed back both the pain of his injuries and his emotions to circle the bunkhouse at a distance, alert for any sound or movement.

Seeing nothing, he called out, "Anybody in there? Miss Layton? Henry!" He couldn't recall the cameraman's last name, but it didn't matter, he realized, as he got his first good look at the open doorway.

Gut tightening, he sucked in a sharp breath at the lump that blocked the entrance, a clearly human, and partially burned, body. Hurrying up the steps, Zach checked for signs of life, but quickly realized that the small man who'd sneaked the camera into his home was beyond help.

But what about the woman traveling with him?

Looking past the body, Zach made out the dim shapes of furniture, but the rest of the room lay in shadow.

"Miss Layton? Jessica? You in here?" He stripped off his jacket and beat down the last few flames at the base of the doorway. As he stamped out the embers, he raised his voice. "It's Rayford—Zach. I'm here to help you. It's safe to come out now."

There was a faint echo but no other answer. Pulse pounding, he stepped over the dead man and moved deeper, using the faint illumination from the headlights of the Prius as his guide.

For a moment, he wondered if the driver of the pickup could have taken her. Then he spotted the blood trail, and what looked like drag marks leading to the closed door of the bathroom. A door that gave only an inch or so when he tried to push it open.

"Jessica!" he shouted, giving it a hard pop with his shoulder. But the door stubbornly refused to yield, as if something heavy blocked its progress....

Something he very much feared would prove to be the beautiful reporter's corpse.

Chapter 5

Something bumped against Jessie's back, thumping repeatedly until it woke her. Her heart stumbled as she peered into the darkness. Where was she? What was happening?

Remembering, she gasped and tried to sit up. Making the mistake of pushing off the floor with her injured hand, she shrieked with the agony shooting up her right arm into her shoulder.

She nearly blacked out again, pale stars streaking across her inky vision. But the knocking and the noisy rattling of the knob above her head refused to allow her to escape the pain.

"Move back from the door," a muffled male voice instructed. "Let me help you."

Help...yes. She had to have help to get out before the place burned with her in it. But what if it was the shooter out there, trying to trick her into letting him inside to kill her?

Not right, she realized, for why would the man urge her to let him help when he could simply shoot her through the closed door? Or leave her here to die, as she surely would without help?

Her mind conjured an image of her mother, the mother she couldn't risk leaving to die alone. With the thought, she focused on dragging her body farther back into the bathroom, gritting her teeth as she slid through something wet and slimy. Blood, she realized, her blood, and she wondered if the pool was anywhere near the size of Henry's. Was it already too late for her, as well?

The door pushed into her again, this time opening wide enough to smell the ash and hear the speaker.

"That's good." His words were calm and reassuring, a lifeline to grasp and cling to. "A little more now. You can do this."

"I—I can do this," she echoed, moving onto her side and sliding back a little farther.

This time it was far enough.

A moment later, a big man crouched beside her, silhouetted by a dim light behind him.

"You're going to be okay," he said, finding the flashlight she'd dropped earlier.

When he switched it on, she saw red. So much red, on the floor, on her clothes. Had it all come from her? Looking up at the man who loomed above her, she recognized Zach Rayford, from the ranch.

He was bleeding, too, she saw, blood that ran from chin to neck, painting a dark bib down the front of his shirt. But there was nothing frightened or confused in his face, only grim determination. "We're going to get you to the hospital," he told her. "Don't worry. An ambulance is on the way."

"Fire," she murmured. "I—I smelled fire."

"The fire's out," he assured her. "It's okay."

"No, it's not okay!" she burst out, her mind leaping to another fear. "What if he comes back? Comes back and shoots us, too, like Henry?"

"Like *who* shot Henry? Do you know who did this?"

"I didn't see, but Henry—he's really dead, isn't he? It wasn't just a nightmare?"

"You're safe now," Zach told her, laying a big hand on her shoulder.

"Henry—he didn't want to come here. He argued after you told me, the sheriff told me, too, to go home. But I—I had to see if Haley had left something, anything to help me trace her."

"For your mother," he finished for her, with what might have been understanding in his voice.

"Yes." She nodded, half choked on her own tears. "But someone must've followed us. I was back here, and Henry shouted. There was a boom—and he was falling, and I—I was hit, too, and then I watched him—I saw him—"

She couldn't make herself say *die.*

"I know," Rayford told her, just as if she had. "But right now, I'm worried about you. Now tell me, Jessica, are you hit anywhere else? We need to see if we can stop this bleeding."

"Only—only here." She glanced down at the hand she cradled, then sucked in a sharp breath and jerked her gaze from the bloody hole and the white glints of bone in it.

"Try not to look at it, all right? Any other injuries?"

She shook her head, her stomach threatening upheaval and the pain spiraling in on her. "I don't think so. I only remember hearing one shot, anyway."

"Then I'm going to move you outside now, where

there's more light and the air is better. Can you help me get you up?"

"I—I'll try."

Taking her uninjured arm, he got her to her feet.

"Now close your eyes," he instructed.

"Why? I don't want—"

"Just close your eyes, Jessica. I need you to trust me."

Something in his voice made her obey, made her follow his lead, though her legs were so wobbly she only made it a few steps.

"That's fine," he said, lifting her in his arms and carrying her outside, to the fresher air.

Carrying her past Henry's body, she realized, when she unclenched her eyelids after he'd set her down a few steps from the bunkhouse's front porch, beside the old barbecue grill she'd spotted earlier.

"Th-thank you." Her teeth chattered, her limbs so shaky, she had to cling to him to keep on her feet.

He wrapped an arm around her, giving her a squeeze before easing her to the ground. "I need you to sit right here for a minute, Jessica. We've got to get this bleeding stopped now before you black out again."

"We have to go!" she tried to tell him, but he was stripping off his shirt already. The bright moonlight revealed the chest of a man who kept himself in peak physical condition.

Shrugging back into his jacket, he tore the shirt along a side seam.

"Now!" she begged, peering all around the darkness. "Before he comes back to finish this."

"Whoever shot you isn't coming back," Zach Rayford reassured her as he tore another strip from the shirt. "Not the way he lit out of here. Nearly crashed into me. Ran my truck right off the road."

That must have been what happened to his chin, she thought, unable to believe how calm and in control he seemed. How focused on her welfare while he, too, was bleeding and in danger. "Did you see him? Did you see who did it?"

"I'm sorry, no. Nothing but a pair of headlights. Happened way too fast." He squatted beside her, warning, "Sorry, but this is going to hurt."

"No! Don't touch it," she begged, but he was already grasping her wrist and shining the flashlight at the hand with a bloody hole drilled through its center.

Drilled through—she was sure of it—by the same bullet that had first torn through Henry's body.

Because of me, she thought, collapsing into sobs at the thought of how she'd verbally pushed at Hellfire before he'd pushed back, how she'd disobeyed Zach Rayford's order to leave his ranch and ignored the sheriff's warning to leave town.

"All my fault," she wept. "It's all my fault—poor Henry."

"Shh," he told her. "Hold still, Jessica. I need you to hold still for me right now so I can get this bandaged, so you can live. So you can live to figure out who would do this to your friend."

Both firm and kind, his voice punched through her despair. Reached through to offer her the courage to draw another breath.

"So you can make who did this pay," he said.

"So I can—make him pay." She looked up into his face, her body going still as she repeated the words. Words that gave her purpose, even as the strength drained from her.

But the respite didn't last long. As the rancher bound her injured hand, agony and anguish forged a pain so overwhelming, she cried out and fought to pull away from his grasp. Fought until the blackness rose up, offering the only real release from pain and guilt.

Chapter 6

"C'mon, Doctor. You can tell me," Zach coaxed as he sat on an exam table in the E.R. "Is she going to be all right? Has she been admitted?"

The harried older doctor gave him a look of pure exasperation. "If you don't hold still and be quiet, I swear these stitches are going to end up looking like somebody's second grade craft project. I've told you again and again, there are privacy laws. We can get in trouble."

Seeing that he was getting nowhere, Zach held his peace for the moment, but he couldn't stop thinking about the size of that bloody puddle, where he'd found Jessica Layton, or hearing the grief in her sobs as she'd broken down. He felt her, too, the warmth of her in his arms, the tight curves that had felt so right against his body. Even if he felt like a total jerk for noticing under such horrific circumstances.

She could be dead right now, he told himself, though

he suspected they would have told him that much. And even though some selfish corner of his brain realized that might solve a lot of problems, he couldn't wish it on her, couldn't do anything but pray that she'd pull through.

The doctor had just finished stitching up Zach's chin when George Canter strode into the exam room, carrying the brown Stetson he always wore with his sheriff's uniform. Except for the patches of gray at his temples and a few more creases at the corners of his brown eyes, he looked nearly the same as Zach remembered, right down to the contempt etched into his face.

It reminded him uncomfortably of those times Canter had dragged his drunken ass home, reckoning that Zach's old man would be a hell of a lot harder on him—and often as not, his brother, Ian—than a night inside a jail cell.

He'd figured right, as Zach remembered, recalling the bruises he had worn the day he'd stuffed a few clothes and what little money he'd saved working part-time for neighboring ranchers and hitched a ride to see the marine corps recruiter in Amarillo. The next time he'd come home was for his father's funeral.

Remembering his mother's tears, her gratitude, the day he'd knocked at the front door like a stranger, it still shamed him to realize how he'd punished her for his father's sins. Punished a woman who had never had the strength to stand up to John Rayford, even when she'd been young and healthy.

Still, Zach couldn't resist asking him the question foremost on his mind. "Is she gonna make it? Jessica Layton, I mean?"

As badly as he wanted to shake an answer out of Canter, Zach forced himself to sit there, while the man considered.

Finally, he nodded. "Yeah, she is. But I'm only telling

you that much to get you off the staff's backs. That her blood you're wearing?"

Zach glanced down at the dark stains on his pants and jacket. "Lot of it."

"Well, you'd better plan on changing before your mama catches sight of you, if you don't want to scare the liver out of her."

It grated on Zach the way the sheriff treated him—both here and when they'd spoken at the scene—as if he were the same know-nothing high school punk he'd dragged home years before. "One of the hands is driving over, bringing me a change of clothes."

Earlier, he'd phoned Miss Althea and asked her to bag up a fresh shirt, a pair of jeans and another jacket to be delivered. If Zach's mother were to wake up, she would be told that Zach had stopped by to visit a friend and would be home late, since he'd already caused her enough grief to last a lifetime.

"Hellfire's got an alibi," said Canter. "The way his latest girlfriend tells it, he was home with her the whole time."

"You believe it?"

"I wouldn't put it past Lisette to bend the truth for her meal ticket."

"So are you holding him?"

"At least till morning, but it's no good. He'd just climbed out of the shower when I got there, so there's no gunpowder residue to test for, and Lisette had just thrown his clothes in with the wash that she was doing."

"Pretty convenient timing," Zach said.

Canter nodded. "They don't own a pickup, either, and I'm not optimistic that any of his useless friends is about to admit a loan. Unless, maybe you could come up with some details, like what kind of truck it was that ran you off the road tonight? Or whether you happened to see his face behind the wheel?"

There was an edge to Canter's questions, a suggestion that Zach might "happen to" remember enough to convince a prosecutor that McFarland should be charged.

But convenience didn't cut it, not when accusing a man of murder. "Sorry, Sheriff. All I saw were those high beams, and just enough of the vehicle to get the impression of a pickup."

Canter's brows knit as he considered, "You know the make, at least?"

Zach shook his head, "I only got a glimpse, and then I was too busy trying to keep my truck from flipping over."

"And a fine job you made of that, too."

With a shrug, Zach said, "My jet could've handled a simple barrel roll like that, no problem."

The attempt at humor fell flat, partly because it reminded him too sharply of the last occasion he had flown and mostly because he couldn't forget that a man had been brutally killed, and Jessica Layton seriously injured, on his property this evening.

"You think he's good for it?" Zach asked the sheriff. "Danny McFarland, I mean."

"It'd be easier if he was. Then at least this might make sense. Reporter comes to town, asks questions about his missing brother. Maybe Hellfire figures Frankie's in some sort of trouble, wants to head it off."

"Seems a little drastic, following them to a remote spot, gunning them both down. Especially for a guy who's got something to lose." Though Zach hadn't set foot back in the Prairie Rose in years, Danny McFarland's buyout had been big news around Rusted Spur for months now. Nobody could believe an ex-con from one of Rusted Spur's poorest and most troubled families could pull off such a feat.

"Hellfire might've cleaned up his act long enough to fool the bankers, but you give a McFarland enough booze, and he's bound to revert to form. And now that he's got his own bar..."

"So was he drunk when you picked him up?"

Canter gave him an indecipherable look and then shook his head. "I've already said more than I should've, this being a murder investigation."

The words were innocuous enough, but the tone behind them had suspicion prickling at the back of Zach's neck. For all he knew, there might be some other reason Canter had decided to close down the information pipeline. After what Zach had told him about the reporter and her cameraman showing up with questions about her missing sister, had he made himself a suspect? Was it even possible?

Testing the theory, he said, "I figure I've got a dog in this hunt, too, what with the killing taking place on my land."

"You want to press charges against the Layton woman for trespassing?"

In his mind, he saw her looking up at him, her large green eyes dilated with terror and the darkness: a woman who his every instinct demanded he protect. "Hell, no, I'm not pressing charges. She's been through enough already."

"You sure? Might be a good idea, discourage her from coming back."

"If she wasn't discouraged by a bullet, I can't imagine some two-bit nuisance charge would do the trick."

Canter's expression soured. "Fine, then. Do what you want. Or better yet, step back from it entirely."

"What's that supposed to mean, Sheriff?"

"It means, don't go running off to investigate on your own like you did tonight. Because in case you hadn't noticed, it nearly cost your mama one more funeral."

"You seem awfully concerned about my mama this evening."

"Somebody ought to be, after everything she's been through."

"I've got it covered, Canter."

"Just like I've got this investigation covered."

"I hope so. 'Cause this murder's hit a little close to home." Zach gestured toward his stitched and bandaged chin, though the injury was a small thing compared to the real worry gnawing at him. The worry that somehow at its root, this crime might involve the only family he had left.

Canter leaned forward to look down on him, a look more grating than Zach remembered from his youth. "I'm not asking you to steer clear, I'm telling you, Rayford. And don't think for a minute that just 'cause you've come back to play lord of the manor on your daddy's spread, I won't toss your carcass in my jail if you don't keep out of my way."

Admitted for overnight observation in Marston's small hospital, Jessie drifted in the darkness on a raft of strong narcotics. So long as she lay absolutely still, the pain in her right hand was no more than a whisper, a dull reminder of the wreckage of tendon, ligament and bone— damage that the doctor had informed her would require a specialized hand surgeon to put the pieces back together, if she were to have a chance to regain even partial function.

Despite the drugs, her sleep was fitful, as time after

time, memories crowded in on her: Henry's shouted warning, the arc of blood from his back, the sweet kiss his wife had planted on his cheek when Jessie had picked him up that very morning. With each fractured shard of nightmare, she jerked awake, fresh torment connecting hand and heart.

To guard against it, she fought to stay awake, haunted by the sense of isolation, the feeling that the tether that linked her to her own life had been severed. Somehow, she had been marooned out here, six hours from anyone she'd ever known or loved. Because she was absolutely certain Haley was no longer here, not even in spirit. When Jessie had reached out, feeling for the slender thread of a connection that had been part of her as long as she remembered, she'd felt only an absence, a terrifying void.

Too long. I waited too long, she realized, cursing all the time she'd wasted agonizing over her career and the breakup with her longtime boyfriend. And then there had been the fallout from her father's death and her mother's cancer to deal with, pushing whatever concerns she had about her sister to the backburner.

Now, remembering the bloody T-shirt and the fine spray on the mirror, Jessie shivered. *Did the man you loved kill you, Haley?* Was her twin's body buried somewhere on the empty plains, the coyotes her only mourners?

Sometime after midnight, a dark silhouette filled the doorway. Too large to be the nurse on duty and too broad-shouldered to be female, her visitor hesitated, and Jessie's blood ran cold. Had the killer—perhaps Henry's and her sister's both—come to finish what he'd started?

There was a soft knock, followed by a quiet voice. "You awake in there?"

"I'm awake," she confirmed, relief flooding her. "Is that you, Mr. Rayford? I thought I heard you'd be admitted, too."

"I think we've moved past the formalities by this point," he said, his deep, rich tones somehow reassuring. "Call me Zach, why don't you?"

"Only if you call me Jessie." At his nod, she asked him, "So Zach, are you all right?"

He moved to her bedside. "Got a few stitches in my chin, maybe a little shook up in the wreck, but it'll sort itself out."

"There's no concussion or anything?" She vaguely remembered overhearing one of the EMTs questioning him at the scene, asking how many fingers he was holding up, but couldn't recall anything more. What she did remember was how strong he'd been, when she'd needed strength the way she needed oxygen to breathe, how he'd taken care of her wound, taken care of her. Made her want to lean into his strength and close her eyes.

"I'll be fine," he said, "but they wouldn't tell me much of anything about you."

"Thanks to you, I'm not in any danger. But I'll have to see a hand surgeon back in Dallas if I'm to regain any sort of function."

"You should go then, right away. You don't want it to heal wrong."

"But my sister."

"Your sister isn't here," he said. "And your friend—"

Moisture made a soft smear of her vision. "I know. I'll need to go for him. For his family."

"They've been told?" he asked quietly. "Or do you need someone to make the call?"

The genuine concern she heard in his voice moved her. "Sheriff Canter's taken care of it. I think he called someone in Dallas. But it should've been me. I should have told them...." She sucked in a deep breath, and bit her lip to keep from crying. "H-Henry begged me to leave, to drive us to the motel. If I'd only listened—"

Zach's big hand reached out to cover her uninjured left hand. "Don't do this to yourself. Don't, Jessie. It changes nothing."

His warmth spread over her like a warm blanket, along with the understanding that he spoke from hard experience. She wanted to thank him for it, and for what he had done at the bunkhouse, but before she could think of what to say, he withdrew abruptly.

"Listen," he said bluntly, "I can't stay much longer. My mother wouldn't take it well. Not since my brother was killed."

"I read about that," she said, realizing that whatever connection she'd imagined, he was cutting it off right now, reminding her—or maybe himself—that nothing had really changed between them. "I'm sorry for your family's loss."

"And yet you came to our home. Upset her, anyway."

"I had no other choice." Jessie shook her head. "I only wish I'd come alone."

"*Now* you're sorry. But you *made* a choice, to try to film your little story. To try to turn my mother's kindness to your sister against her in some shady ambush interview."

Anger heated her face, burning off the opiate haze. Filming *her little story,* as he put it, had been the only way to find her sister without losing her job. "So you came here to do what? Rub in my friend's murder? Make me feel even worse?"

"No, I didn't."

"Then why? Did you think you'd convince me nothing

strange is going on in Rusted Spur? Because the way I see it, the fact that I was first attacked in town and then—"

"Canter told me there was an incident with Hellfire, that you reported that McFarland pushed you."

"*After* mistaking me for Haley. Not that your sheriff buddy was much troubled about it—until after the shooting, that is. Even then, Canter still didn't act as if he half-believed the guy was capable."

"*I'd* believe it," Zach said, his tone sober. "Danny might have people thinking he's turned over a new leaf, but he's always had a temper. And he's never meaner than when he's covering for his little brother. He's been doing it since junior high, when their mama's liver finally gave up the ghost."

"Protecting a sibling's a hard habit to break," she said, thinking of how long and how often she had covered for her own twin before Haley had finally gone too far.

"As far back as I can remember, Danny'd take the blame for Frankie, or beat down witnesses if he thought he could keep the kid in school and out of trouble. Not that it worked. They both were long gone before graduation."

"I can believe he'd pull the trigger," she said. "The question is, how do I prove it, especially if I have to go back home to—"

"Is there anyone you'd like me to call to come and get you? A friend or a boyfriend?"

"I've already talked to a coworker," she said, not wanting to confess that, since she'd centered her life around a guy not worth the effort and a job that kept her working all hours these past few years, she no longer had close friends—or anyone besides the mother she was losing. "But thank you, Mr. Rayfo—Zach. It's kind of you to ask."

"Don't mistake me for a kind man," he warned. "It just seemed the decent thing to offer."

The words were harsh, and if she hadn't seen that earlier flash of sympathy in his eyes, felt it in his touch, she might have believed him. Why was Zach Rayford pretending to be so hard? Her reporter's instincts told her this was a facade he'd adopted. Because what she'd seen at the bunkhouse, what she'd felt when his hand touched her, told Jessie that Zach Rayford *was* a kind man. Kind and honest, good—everything her ex had not been, all wrapped up in a drop-dead gorgeous package.

Deciding to call him on it, she said, "And risking your life to go looking for me in that bunkhouse? Did that seem the decent thing, too?"

"Maybe," he said. "Just like offering to look into your sister's disappearance feels like the right thing now."

"Wait. After telling me to get lost—pretty darned emphatically, as I remember—you're offering to *help* me? Why?"

He glanced back to the open door and then nudged it closed with a boot. A moment later she heard his soft footsteps moving closer, and the fine hairs on her neck rose with sudden apprehension. What if she had been wrong, and it really hadn't been Danny McFarland who had pulled the trigger earlier? After all, Zach Rayford *had* threatened to get his gun before.

For all she knew, Zach's story about a speeding pickup running his off the road had been just that—a story. Wasn't it just as possible that *he'd* been fleeing the bunkhouse after firing on Henry, that he'd overturned his vehicle in his hurry to get away? Knowing there was no way to put distance between himself and the shooting, he could have panicked and then switched roles, covering his own involvement by playing the part of the hero.

A part he'd played so convincingly, she'd trusted him without reservation.

Had that instinct been the right one, or had she been out of her mind with pain and shock?

He flipped on the bathroom light, which offered enough illumination to ease her mind as he moved to her bedside. "I'm offering to help because I want to know that whatever happened at the bunkhouse isn't a threat to my family." His face hardened as he added, "And because I don't appreciate being warned off like some punk teenager."

"Warned off?" she echoed, her head whirling. "You're saying the sheriff told you to stay clear of his investigation?"

"Let's just say he suggested it would be in my best interest. Says he and his men will make sure this is taken care of."

"And my sister's found?"

"He didn't mention that."

"Because, for whatever reason, the man wants her to stay gone."

After considering the statement, Zach nodded, his blue eyes boring into hers. "I figure that's a fair assessment. Now, all I need to do is find out why while you're away."

Chapter 7

"This is devastating, just devastating," Jessie's news director, Vivian Monroe, said for what had to be the tenth time over the phone the following morning. "You poor thing—what you've been through."

Yet to Jessie's ears, each time the woman said it, it somehow sounded less sincere.

"So of course, you'll want some time off," Vivian added. "Several weeks, at least, to recover from the shock and have your surgery."

And track down my sister, Jessie thought, but important as that was, it wasn't her only obligation.

Had someone broken into the newsroom and stolen her boss's personality? "Are you kidding?" Jessie sat up in the hospital bed so abruptly that a jolt of pain ran from her bad hand to her spine. "You—you don't want me on the air with this right away, bringing pressure to bear on the investigation? This is one of our own, Vivian. It's Henry. We have to do everything we can to—"

"Of course we'll cover the story. And we'll do a nice little 'In Memoriam' segment, whenever there's time to fit it in."

"Wait a minute. *What? What* do you mean, *whenever there's time to fit it in?* If Paul or Brenda had been shot to death, you'd have everybody we have on it. And you'd never let up until there was an arrest. A conviction and an execution, if you had anything to say about it."

"But Paul and Brenda are our *anchors.* They're like *family.* Viewers invite them into their living rooms every day of the week."

"Henry had a family, Vivian," Jessie said, her outrage growing by the minute.

"Yes, of course he did, but let's be realistic, darling. Viewers aren't nearly as interested in hearing about some part-time freelancer behind the camera as they are—"

"You know as well as I do that part-time, freelance garbage only started because management decided to solve its budget issues by cheating people out of their benefits and pensions. He's worked for the station for decades, as long as you have. And longer than any of our on-air personalities." She *knew,* right down to her core, why Vivian wanted her off the air for the duration. The duration of the mayoral campaign, at least.

"Besides," Jessie went on, "unsolved mysteries are always of interest, especially one involving a missing young woman who just so happens to be the identical twin of one of your station's reporters."

"You're overwrought, and I can't blame you," Vivian said, her crisply polished words a testimony to the years she'd spent as an anchor in her own right. Years that ended too abruptly, as the result of a plastic surgery gone wrong. "With your mother so ill, your sister missing and now this—"

"What about my campaign story? We were going to break the news this week."

"Listen, Jessica. I know how hard you worked on that story. But after reviewing it again, I'm not so certain that your sources—"

"You know me. I'm always careful, and that story's as airtight as they get. Certainly, we've run with evidence far less conclusive. Of course, *those* stories wouldn't have caused trouble for any of your friends." *Especially a friend everyone knows that you've been sleeping with.* Because Vivian Monroe might no longer be camera flawless, with her stretched skin and oddly shaped nose, but even at sixty, she was still a polished, slim and beautifully put-together woman, a woman who fit in well with the Botoxed socialites of Dallas.

A woman who'd attracted the attention of a recently divorced, obscenely wealthy and notoriously opinionated wildcatter who had no qualms about using his fortune to influence local, state and even national elections. And next week's mayoral contest was currently high on his agenda.

"*What* did you say?" Vivian asked, an unmistakable warning in her voice.

"Perhaps I didn't phrase that quite right," Jessie answered, something shattering inside her. The part of her that cared whether or not this cost her her job. Because in the past twenty-four hours, she'd learned some hard lessons about what really mattered. And toadying up to Vivian hadn't made the cut. "I'm saying you're more worried about your chances of snagging yourself a billionaire— who happens to be the mayor's number one contributor— than you are of breaking a story that raises legitimate questions, important questions, about the mayor's fundraising tactics."

They both knew the story did more than raise questions. Jessie had obtained the proof, surveillance footage showing the mayor strong-arming contributions from bidders for a huge new airport project.

Vivian's answer was a silence so glacial that it all but froze the cell phone in Jessie's hand. As the seconds ticked past, she felt the throbbing in her right hand deepen, as if the chill had gone straight to her bones. Wishing the nurse would come soon with more morphine, she hoped she would survive saying what everyone in the newsroom had been tiptoeing around these past few weeks—the idea that Vivian's involvement with a man whose deep pockets had swayed many a campaign had seriously compromised her judgment.

Maybe Jessie already had too much of the painkiller in her system, because she couldn't resist asking, "Do we have a bad connection? Because I want to make sure you heard what—"

"Oh, I heard you," came the cold reply. "I'm only trying to find enough compassion in my heart for what you're going through not to fire you on the spot for that truly vile lie. For you to dare suggest that I would for a single moment put my personal feelings for a man I've—I've been in this business for longer than you've been on this planet, have put up with impediments women of your generation can't imagine. And you dare to accuse me—*me*—of stalling on a story we both know is thinner than a sheet of bargain-basement toilet paper, a story that has more to do with your own political agenda than—"

"My political *what?*" Jessie asked, genuinely startled by the accusation.

"Everyone knows your family's contributed to the mayor's opponents for years."

"That was my father," Jessie said, "my father, who is

dead. And I can assure you, he'd be laughing in his grave at the notion that his political views in any way impacted mine. Not that it's any of your business, but I voted for the mayor in the last election. Which is one of the reasons I'm so deeply disappointed in him right now."

"You're on leave, Jessica," Vivian said. "One month's leave, which will give you time to recover and me time to imagine how we might possibly move beyond this conversation."

"Understood," said Jessie, comprehending as well that the only reason Vivian didn't cut her loose right now was the fear that, despite the non-compete clause in her contract, she would find a way to take the story to a rival station—or use her injury and Henry's murder to garner support on social media. This way, her boss could use the possibility of salvaging her career to keep her under control.

Good luck with that, thought Jessie as she switched off the phone, *because I'm not going to be finessed and managed into keeping my mouth shut for long.*

"If you're the *best* friend I've got, I'd sure hate to see the worst," Zach told Nate Wheeler the following afternoon, outside what everyone in the area referred to as the Lone Star Barn. The sloped roof, first painted by Nate's grandfather fifty years before to resemble the Texas state flag, was a local landmark, visible from the state highway that ran through town.

Aggravated as Zach was, he kept his voice low, mindful that Eden was playing with the puppies just inside.

Raking a hand through sandy-brown hair that had grown even shaggier than usual, Nate winced, his copper-colored gaze contrite. "I'm sorry, man. How was I supposed to know you hadn't told your mama?"

Zach snatched off his own hat and whacked the big doofus on his brawny shoulder. A champion bull rider, Nate probably didn't feel a thing. "After everything she's been through lately, do you honestly think I was going to tell her how close a brush I had with a killer who shot down a man on our ranch?"

"She was bound to hear it pretty quick. I had three people call me by the time I finally decided it was a decent enough hour to check on you."

Zach should've known that any story involving a murdered cameraman, an injured—and beautiful—reporter and a Rayford would've grown legs in a hurry. But he wasn't yet ready to let go of his exasperation with his longtime friend.

"Sure, my mama would've heard it," he said, wondering how Jessie was this morning. Wondering if she had been discharged yet and headed home. Once again, he cursed himself for offering to look into her sister's disappearance—a disappearance that he feared would lead straight back to his fragile mother. "But maybe that would've been *after* I'd had the chance to break it to her gently, instead of you calling at the crack of dawn, scaring her half out of her mind with some wild tale about a shooting, a fire and her son's brush with the killer."

"How is it *some wild tale* when you've already told me it was all true?

"You didn't have to be so blunt with her, that's all."

"I just called to check on you, and honest to Pete, she acted exactly like she knew already. Otherwise, I would've—"

"*Acted* being the key word," Zach said, "because the second she hung up, she came flying into my room, half-hysterical. I think the scare brought back everything with Ian."

Nate's tanned face reddened. "Shoot, I'm really sorry. She okay?"

"She will be, I think. At least once things calm down and Canter locks up whoever did this." *If he ever does.*

"How 'bout I bring by one of my mama's homemade apple-pecan cakes and a fresh bouquet of—"

"No flowers, man," Zach warned him. "I tried that a while back and they just ended up reminding her of the funerals. And much as I love your mama's baking, I'm pretty sure we still have one of her cakes in the freezer with the others."

Following both his father's and his brother's funerals, his mother had been deluged in food offerings from family friends and church members, food she could do little more than stare at.

Nate pressed his lips together, shaking his head. "You're walkin' a real tightrope with her since you came home, aren't you?"

As the heady music of Eden's giggles floated through the open barn door, Zach blew out a breath. "You don't know the half of it."

Again, his mind returned to Jessie, to how dangerous it was, feeling for her the way he did. Maybe it was because the responsibilities she bore toward her family felt so similar to his own, and the grief and guilt so like what he'd been carrying since the crash eight months before. But as badly as he wanted to reach out, to walk her along this hard path, he told himself that this reporter—this woman who had triggered some latent need he hadn't even been aware of—wasn't his to protect and never could be.

He had a duty and a family he must put first, no matter what the cost.

"How 'bout I just stop by for a visit sometime," Nate offered. "Try to cheer her up."

Zach forced a grin. "I don't know. You might want to make yourself scarce till after we get those puppies housebroken."

Nate snorted and then quickly sobered. "Seriously, man. How are you? Really?"

"The cut on my chin'll leave a scar, but I still have a long way to go to catch up to your vast collection," he said.

Nate grimaced at the reminder of the back surgery that had sidelined him these past six months, a sign that soon, all the years and all the injuries he'd suffered would force him to step out of the limelight and return to the reality of helping his dad run the family business, whether or not he felt ready.

"And the rest?" Nate managed, pretending his brief hesitation had meant nothing.

"I'm dealing with it," Zach said. "All of it." It was a lie, for he'd been far too busy grappling with his mother's health, his niece's presence and the ranch's endless needs to begin to take stock of his own losses. Not only of his brother and the old man, but of the career he'd taken so much pride in, the wings that had failed to achieve enough altitude to keep his past from swallowing him whole. And now, on top of all that, there were the troubling questions raised by Jessie Layton—along with his inability to stop thinking about her.

"You sure?" Nate asked, but instead of answering, Zach held up a hand, disturbed by something he heard. Or more precisely, what he didn't, for the sounds of Eden and the puppies playing had turned to a silence still as stone, an absence that caught in his gut and had him stepping through the open door, peering into the box stall where he had left her a few minutes before.

There, he found no puppies and no Eden, just fluffy piles of clean straw.

"Eden?" he called, trying to drown out the drumming of his heart with the certainty that a four-year-old and eight puppies couldn't have gone far. But neither logic nor his experience in combat kept the panic from crowding into his chest when she didn't answer. "Eden!"

From a nearby stall, one of the ranch's quarter horses whinnied, and farther down the row, a set of steel-shod hooves kicked out, striking wood with a sharp *rat-tat*. Zach swallowed hard, trying not to think of what could happen if a tiny girl got on the wrong side of twelve hundred pounds of horseflesh. It would be all his fault, too, for not working hard enough to teach her to respect as well as love the beasts, for not keeping a close eye on her.

Coming in behind him, Nate called Eden's name, too, saying, "Come out, come out, wherever you are," as if the stakes were no higher than a game of hide-and-seek.

When there was no response, he whistled and called, "Bonnie! Come here, girl."

The puppies' mother, a big, tricolor ball of fur, emerged yawning from some dark corner, then trotted toward them, her thick tail wagging lazily. If she was half as worried about her little ones as Zach felt, she gave no sign of it.

"Where're your puppies? Find the puppies," Nate said, sounding eager and enthusiastic.

Bonnie came fully alive, her ears pricking, and her eyes excited as she dove into the "game" full throttle, running around the barn and searching. But no matter how many times she was redirected, she kept circling back and sitting beside the same stall where he'd last seen Eden and the litter.

"I thought this dog was supposed to be some kind of

genius," complained Zach, who had been running from stall to stall to look inside each one. Meanwhile, his brain kept circling back, too, returning to the green-eyed reporter's visit yesterday, and the violent fallout that had followed.

Could whoever had attempted to kill Jessie Layton have some connection to the child that had, like the reporter, shown up at their doorstep? What if the same violent criminal had followed him here this morning with the intention of taking Eden—or worse yet, hurting her?

Realizing that the fear eating at him was weaving the unlikeliest of scenarios, he told himself, "Ridiculous."

But it was Nate, standing by his dog, who burst out laughing as he stepped inside the stall and swept aside a pile of straw. "There you are! Wake up, sweetie."

He was laughing as he said it, as Zach ran, heart in throat, to see Eden stir where she'd been lying, her small hands ever so slowly stroking the bellies of two puppies while the others, all eight in the litter, lay curled around her like snoring whorls of fur.

As she stirred, Nate chuckled, speaking in low tones. "Look at that. They've gone and worn each other out."

"And off she goes again," Zach added as Eden's green eyes fluttered closed and her small hands once more fell still. Watching her, he felt something tightening inside his chest, the grip of a fierce possessiveness like nothing he had ever known. For at some point—he had no idea when—he'd come to think of this tiny wisp of light as not only another burden he was obligated to provide for, but as family. *His* family, almost as if she'd been his daughter and not his brother's.

A child he would do everything in his power to keep where she belonged, no matter what the facts of her biology. Or what anybody did to try to stop him, including his own unwise attraction to the one woman who might destroy them all.

Chapter 8

Zach awakened with a start, tangled in his sweat-soaked sheets and telling himself that it was over. *He* was over, when it came to flying, stripped of all his military duties for failing to report that Lieutenant Hernandez was a danger, failing to see beyond friendship and loyalty. For the past month, Zach had been restless, his sleep fractured night after night by the harrowing moments he'd spent floating helpless above Kabul, where he'd been forced to watch while his protégé's jet incinerated buildings and lives.

It was the phone calls that were responsible for the nightmares, the calls he'd made to Jessie Layton that were tearing him up inside. Though he had nothing to report, he'd first phoned her to find out how she was doing after surgery and how Henry's family was dealing with their grief. But the longer he listened, the more he'd found himself caring and—worse yet—wanting more. Not only to get to know her better, but to give her and her mother the answers that they needed. Answers he feared would destroy the people who he loved.

Realizing the situation was hopeless, he forced himself to go cold turkey. No more calls, no contact, and he deleted all her messages unread, reminding himself of his responsibility, not to his fellow marine corps pilots, his nation or the people they protected any longer, but to his ailing mother and a tiny girl. A little girl who he feared Jessie would soon return to discover, maybe even wrest away.

He'd asked, over and over, for more details about Eden's mother, Lila Germaine. He was troubled to imagine that his mother might have made up the whole story about Ian's alleged former girlfriend, who, after four years of raising the child on her own, had suddenly grown overwhelmed enough to dump the little girl—along with a signed form giving up all her parental rights.

"Oh, Zach, I don't know why you'd want to dwell on that," his mama had said dismissively, hands fluttering pale and mothlike to her bony neck. "There's been pain enough around here. Why worry a miracle half to death? Just thank God that Lila brought her here to live with us instead of to some awful foster home."

Each time he pressed her further, fatigue set in, or one of the headaches. Her face going gray, she would shake and cover her blue eyes against the pain light brought her. Tears came next, and then vomiting, if she didn't take her medication and lie in the quiet darkness fast enough.

As if that weren't enough to deal with, the holidays were soon upon them—her first Christmas without her husband, her first knowing that Ian was dead. Zach tiptoed around her grief, burying his own sadness deep, along with the endless, maddening questions still running through his brain, no matter how hard he fought to push them out of his mind.

When was Jessie coming back? Would she shatter their peace—and his mother's health—before the year ended? Or had something happened to her? Maybe the hand surgery had gone wrong. Or perhaps her mother had taken a turn for the worse, never guessing that her missing daughter might have given her a granddaughter of her own to cherish...

Just as his mother clearly cherished Eden in the weeks that followed, desperately grasping onto the little girl's wide-eyed excitement for all the joy and anticipation the season had to offer. Though he tried to resist, reminding himself it could all come crashing down at any moment, he ended up swept up in the spirit, too, especially on the day he came home with the biggest tree he could find. Once he and ranch foreman, Virgil Straughn, a grandfatherly type who'd do anything to make a child smile, finally had the thing set up, they'd grabbed a couple of ladders and spent an evening trimming it in Eden's favorite hot-pink as she directed from below.

They laughed that night, each one of them. The first laughter that had rung through the Rayford mansion in heaven only knew how many years.

But by January second, the spell had ended, the gifts and decorations packed away. As Zach fed the horses and started on his daily chore list, his brain burned with every worry he'd managed to suppress—and the necessity on getting the truth out of his mother before it blew up in their faces.

Before he could think of a way to finally pin her down, Eden came bubbling outside with her puppies, pleading for him to take her with him as he drove to drop off supplemental feed cakes for the cattle. It was a chore she often begged to "help" with, laughing whenever the cows and yearlings came running at the sight of his truck.

"How'd you figure out that's where I was going?" he asked, as if he couldn't guess.

"One of the cowboys came in to help Miss Althea test out the cinnamon rolls. To see if they were really good enough to eat."

"And were they?" Zach asked.

"Oh, yes. I got to be a taster, too, and we gave Miss Althea an A-plus with extra sparkles!" Eden nodded happily before wiping her mouth with the back of her hot-pink jacket's sleeve.

"You and those sparkles," Zach muttered, thinking that the inventors of glitter ought to be roped and dragged buck naked through a patch of prickly pear.

But when Eden remembered the crumpled bag in her hand and said, "I brought you one, too!" he smiled and took it from her, devil's fairy dust and all.

"Thanks," he said, finishing the slightly squashed but still delicious offering in three bites. "Miss Althea gets a gold star. And since you've been such a good delivery girl, we'll go ahead and take that ride, but first we have to tell your grandma where we're off to, and the puppies have to stay at home and guard the house."

With the wear and tear of daily ranch chores, the truck he'd bought might not long stay shiny, but that new-car smell would last a whole lot better if no one piddled in the cab.

As they headed out a few minutes later, Eden chattered away behind him, sitting like a princess in her booster seat. "Can I go cowboyin' with you later, Uncle Zach? I'll ride Mr. Butters and help you and the cowboys."

"Sorry, honey, no," he said, knowing the work was far too dangerous and dirty to risk having her in tow. "I'm afraid Mr. Butters couldn't keep up with Ace's long legs, and that would make your pony feel sad."

In the rearview mirror, her face screwed up in concentration before she suggested, "You could walk."

"Then we'd never catch all the yearlings, and they might get sick without their vaccinations."

He pulled to the top of a rise, knowing he'd seen a number of cows bedded down in this area just last night. But moments later, he realized his mistake as he spotted Eden staring at the bunkhouse in the distance.

"I want to go back home now," she whimpered, her tiny body trembling. "Want to crawl under the covers and take a nap with Sweetheart and Lionheart right now."

Zach hit the brakes, his heart sinking through the floorboards as his earlier foreboding came roaring back full blown. Eden hated napping, fought it tooth and nail until his mother had finally given up the battle. Which meant that the child must be sick. Either sick or terrified of the bunkhouse—or something that had happened in it.

Ask her, his conscience whispered. *Ask her right now.*

Eden shook her head emphatically, tears shining in her eyes. "Wanna go home, Uncle Zach. My tummy hurts real bad."

You're a marine, damn it. You can do this. But when the first drops spilled down her soft pink cheeks, he sighed and turned back toward the house, where he knew his mother would stroke Eden's hair as she consoled her… and whisper that she'd never have to go back to that awful place again.

Less than an hour later, he was back at the bunkhouse, thinking that if he couldn't bear to ask the questions, neither could he turn his back on any answers that might remain to be found. A toy left in the yard, a crayoned scribble inside a closet—surely some evidence would remain if his niece had once lived there.

Leaving his pickup, he carried a flashlight over a sagging and tattered line of yellow crime-scene tape and stared down at the burn marks still visible on the front porch. Looking around, he realized the area was cleaner than it had been. The empty cans and bottles that had been out here were all gone. Collected for analysis, perhaps? Or maybe only cleaned up, for inside, he found the old place surprisingly devoid of trash. No furniture at all remained, though he was certain he remembered a bed, at least, and maybe a junked sofa that had been here before. But the blood stains were still evident, not only the half-burned ones where he could still imagine seeing the ghostly afterimage of Henry Kucharski's body, but the reddish-brown trail Jessie had left as she'd dragged herself into the bathroom.

Nothing else remained, and try as he might, he couldn't find a single shred of evidence that any child had ever resided within these walls. Was that because Eden had never actually lived here? Or had whoever swept this place clean been careful to remove the proof?

It could be that Canter was doing his job like he'd said, his vague claim of trying to track some mysterious tattooed man with a shaved head who'd been seen around town more than the excuse it sounded like. But Zach couldn't make himself believe it, not considering the way the sheriff had been acting lately.

Giving up, he left the bunkhouse and started back to his truck. But only a few steps off the porch, he stopped short, his attention drawn to a tiny line of silvery ash.

A chill wind rose, lifting some of it, a hazy ribbon. Following the airborne trail, he was led to a low dip filled with weeds and bramble, with a scraped and dented barbecue grill lying on its side. A contraption made from a cut oil drum on a broken wheeled frame, the thing must have weighed a ton. Had it collapsed when a leg gave way and then proved too unwieldy to move? Or maybe whoever had been hired to clean the site had figured that no one would even notice it, rusting out here in this pasture.

With another puff, more of the spilled ash rode the breeze, prompting Zach's attempt to open the mouth of the drum. The way the grill had fallen made it awkward, but he kept at it, lifting and hauling for no better reason than gut instinct, until the barrel turned and the frozen hinges gave way with a squeal of protest.

More ash tumbled through the widened opening, a river of dust with blackened chunks of coal, some of which collapsed into powder when he poked them with a board. But not the bigger pieces, pieces whose shapes and sizes triggered a low groan as recognition dawned....

Along with the awareness that those dark remnants definitely weren't charcoal.

Stomach knotting painfully, Zach jerked his cell phone from his pocket and started snapping photos, one after another. And all the while he prayed that the burnt bones he had discovered were the vestiges of a meal of pork or beef or venison rather than the woman he had promised Jessie Layton he would help to find.

Two weeks to the day after her mother's death, Jessie finally made it back to Rusted Spur, her heart heavy and her eyes sore. Unlike that ominous November day of her first visit, the sky was clear and blue. But the sun looked small and distant, and the outside gauge of her mother's Cadillac SUV pegged the current temperature in the high thirties, a temperature she suspected would feel colder, judging from the way the frost-brown grasses were swaying in the wind.

For a while, she'd imagined she'd found an ally in Zach Rayford, someone who'd offer a warm welcome. She'd felt a connection taking root during their phone conversations, had heard what sounded like real concern. She'd even imagined she'd sensed an undercurrent of sexual awareness, one she couldn't quite ignore in spite of her mother's decline. Sometimes, the memory of his handsome face was the only thing that kept her from collapsing into tears.

But that had been before he'd cut her off, ruthlessly and permanently breaking contact with her. And before he'd given her a single, useful lead regarding either Henry's murder or her sister's disappearance. Vulnerable as she'd been, the rejection had stung at first, but by now she was just plain mad—furious he'd played her for a fool.

She thought of going straight to town, blasting into Sheriff Canter's office to demand an explanation for why he'd been ducking her calls for the past few weeks. And if he refused to answer, she'd give her silent backseat companion the cue to peel back her lips and show off those fearsome fangs of hers, along with the low rumble of a growl guaranteed to get anyone's attention.

But as satisfying as she found that fantasy, she knew it would be a bad idea. She wasn't going to find her sister from a jail cell, which was exactly where she'd end up if she pushed her luck so soon. Besides, she would never do anything to endanger Gretel, the expensive home protection dog her dad had had imported from Germany a short time before his death.

Though her dad had claimed that he was buying the muscular black-and-tan Rottweiler to make her mother—her poor mother—feel safe after a pair of frightening home invasions in their neighborhood, Jessie had always suspected he'd mostly enjoyed "complaining" about the fifteen-thousand-dollar price of the dog to his golf buddies at the club. After her dad's stroke, Gretel had quickly gone from "strictly business" to her mother's best friend. A best friend that could easily take down and put a bite hold on anyone or anything that she perceived as a threat.

But months before, Jessie had moved back home and taken over the big bear of a dog's care. Had bonded with her, especially just lately, when a string of disasters had delayed her return to Rusted Spur far too long.

She swallowed hard, her thoughts turning as they did too often to the pneumonia that had sickened her mother only a few days after her own surgery. And to the new promise she had made before that illness stole the weeks and months she had allowed herself to hope they would have together.

Before it had stolen, too, her mother's chance to make peace with her missing daughter. Jessie wiped at a tear, her heart breaking at the failure. If only she had started looking sooner!

But there was nothing to be done now, nothing except to find a way to keep her vow to the woman she still missed so sharply, she drew in pain with every breath.

"We'll bring Haley home," she told the dog, digging for the stubbornness that had made her such a good reporter. "We won't stop till we do."

Swallowing back the lump in her throat, she pushed past her fear of returning to the place where Henry had been killed and she'd been injured, and turned toward the Rayford ranch and the bunkhouse on the East Two Hundred. There, she planned to snoop around, taking photos of any evidence she might find. Only this time, she'd brought plastic bags and tweezers to collect anything she wanted, along with a laptop with a satellite card so she could upload the pictures to an online vault.

She told herself that by driving her mom's Escalade and avoiding town on the way in, she would be far safer. Still, she was shaking by the time she turned in on the ranch road, her brain crackling with fractured images that flipped through it from the day of her last visit. Pain spiked through her still-bandaged hand, a pain so sharp and fresh it had her reflexively stamping on the brakes.

The Cadillac stopped short, and she felt a solid thump behind her. Gretel whined in protest, offended by her lousy driving.

"Sorry about that, girl," Jessie said as the dog climbed, panting, back up on the seat.

The pain's not real, she reminded herself. *Those memories aren't now.*

To distract herself, she imagined how angry Haley would be, once she learned that, as soon as the estate was settled, Jessie would be managing a trust to be set up for her sister, a trust thoughtfully constructed to save her from her own disastrous choices.

Haley would rail at the restrictions, at the fact that Jessie's share would have none, but Jessie vowed she wouldn't complain, as long as her sister was still alive to give her grief. With both their parents now gone, that last link to her family was all that mattered to her.

And if she's dead already? Dead and buried somewhere out here?

Gritting her teeth, Jessie vowed, "Then I swear I'll find you, bring you home, where you belong."

Channeling weeks of grief into raw anger, she mashed down on the gas, sending pebbles spraying from the tires. But when she crested the hill that should have revealed the bunkhouse, she sucked in a startled breath and stared.

Nothing. There was nothing remaining of her sister's last known residence but a scraped-bare wound in the earth and a few last boards and shingles.

Heat threatened to consume her, a burning that had her instantly soaked in perspiration. When she swore, Gretel rose like a thunderhead in the seat behind her, suspicious as she scanned the area, her hackles rising and her deep growl vibrating in the air.

"Platz," she said, using the German command. As she'd been trained to do, the Rottweiler dropped to the down position, where she lay perfectly still but alert.

Sucking in a deep breath, Jessie ground out, "Damn them. Damn all of them," feeling a sense of deep betrayal, of the loss of something she had never even had, as she turned the SUV around and made for the mansion that served as headquarters for the ranch.

Only this time she wasn't leaving until she had solid answers, even if she had to set her dog to rearranging Zach Rayford's all-too-handsome face to get them.

Chapter 9

"That's right, Eden," Zach told his niece as he guided her hand. "Always brush in one direction, the same way his hair grows."

She brushed the pony's fuzzy winter coat just as he had shown her, though she could only reach halfway up Mr. Butters's rib cage by standing on her tiptoes.

"How 'bout a boost so you can do his back?" Zach invited.

Eden looked up and sighed. "Why can't I just ride him now? My arm's getting *really tired.*"

Zach lifted her with one arm. With the other hand, he patted the pony's golden back, raising dust. "If you don't brush him, he'll have grit under the saddle, and it'll make him all sore when you ride him. You don't want to hurt him, do you?"

She hesitated, her mouth pursing before she thrust the brush at Zach. "You do it, then. Don't want to."

She'd been trying his patience for the past hour, fussing and demanding and getting into so much mischief with those hell-spawned puppies of hers that his first impulse was to threaten to take her over his knee. But as he opened his mouth to speak, the words reverberated through his mind—his father's words, along with harsher ones, all spoken in anger before the blows rained down.

I'm not him. I won't be, Zach told himself, wrestling his frustration as he'd once wrestled men during hand-to-hand combat training.

"If you want to ride," he said, a thin veneer of calm covering his impatience, "you'll have to brush him yourself. Otherwise, you're welcome to spend the rest of the afternoon in your room. Only *this* time, your puppies will be staying in their kennel inside the barn, where you can't dress them in your grandma's Sunday best."

Eden giggled, "But they looked so *funny* wearing dresses!"

"I'm sure they did—for the three seconds before they shredded them."

Eden laughed, and he was explaining to her why her behavior wasn't appropriate when he spotted an unfamiliar SUV barreling down the drive. Apparently, the driver of the pearl-white Escalade saw them, too, standing by the hitching rail just outside the main barn, for it sped past the house. The Caddy pulled up short, causing the normally sedate pony to prance and whinny, struggling to get away.

Zach snatched Eden out of harm's way, holding her in his arms with the intent of giving the idiot behind the wheel a piece of his mind. But as the driver bailed out and marched toward him, leaving the door open behind her, he froze, barely biting back a curse as his hope collapsed.

The hope that she wouldn't prove half as gorgeous

as he remembered—and, even more important, that she would stay away forever. But those disappointments were nothing when compared to the guilt he felt—and the fear that she knew everything already, that she was coming to destroy everyone he held dear.

What the hell have I done, letting things go this far?

"What on earth do you mean, Zach Rayford," Jessie demanded, fury sparking in her green eyes, "tearing down that bunkhouse without a word to me about it?"

Ignoring the question he couldn't answer, he scraped up as much righteous anger as he could. "What do *you* mean, roaring up here and scaring my niece and her pony half to death?"

"I'm not going with her!" Eden insisted as she wriggled down from his arms, the stubborn fierceness of her gaze mirroring Jessie's. "I won't!"

Eden's voice wound down, the defiance in her expression collapsing into what looked like confusion. She blinked, then shook her head and muttered, "Go away! You're not my mama."

Panic slicing through him, Zach searched Jessie's face for some reaction. But intent as she was on ripping into him, she clearly hadn't heard the damning words.

"Eden, I need you to go inside now," Zach said, keeping his voice calm but firm in the hope she wouldn't argue. "Go inside and ask Miss Althea—nicely—if we can have some mac and cheese with dinner."

The child hesitated, looked from him to Jessie and back again and then asked, "Tater tots, too?"

"One or the other, if you'll eat your baby carrots," he said.

Eden looked at him suspiciously. "What about my pony ride?"

"We'll talk about it later—if you do as I ask right now."

He saw the bright flare of the child's temper and thought Eden might balk—or worse yet, shout what she'd said earlier loudly enough that Jessie couldn't miss it. No more than he could miss the strong resemblance between the two.

"Inside, Eden. Now," he ordered.

Huffing an exasperated sigh, she dragged out, "Okaaaayyy." After shooting Jessie one last, defiant look, she took off running for the house.

Jessie barely glanced at her before returning her attention to Zach. "So why'd you tear it down?" she demanded. "What are you trying to hide?"

He held up a finger in a wait-a-second gesture, delaying his answer until the child was safely inside the house. "I didn't, but it's for the best. It was a safety hazard to anybody who got curious enough to come snooping around. And people were. My mother told me just last week she'd spotted a truckload of teenagers checking the place out, checking out where the—the murder took place."

Though his mother rarely went out, she'd been adamant about that, insisting that was what had convinced her to have the place demolished, after clearing it with Canter and supposedly forgetting to mention it to Zach.

It was a coincidence, he tried to tell himself, that the crew had shown up only hours after Zach had snapped those damning photos, before he'd had time to do anything about what he'd found.

"My *friend's* murder might never be solved now," Jessie continued, "with any evidence destroyed. Is this why you quit calling, why you stopped returning my calls?

Because you were planning this—this *cover-up?*" Tears stood in her eyes, but she had never looked fiercer.

Or more stunning, thought Zach, even if she was a damned reporter. But with her reddish-blond hair blowing in the chill breeze and her green eyes blazing, there was no denying how gorgeous she looked, wearing jeans that hugged her tight curves and a royal-blue ski jacket. Even if she was about as cuddly as the bobcat he'd spotted tearing apart a jackrabbit last week.

"Honestly, Jessie, I didn't know about the demolition until it was a done deal. It was Canter—he arranged it after my mother complained about those teenagers getting in there."

"You should have told me," she repeated, and this time, he glimpsed the hurt and the sadness behind her hostility.

"I—um—I lost your cell phone number," he added, not explaining that by *lost* he meant *deleted,* "so I called the television station and asked to leave a message. The person I spoke to told me you don't work there anymore. Is that right?"

Jessie shook her head, her eyes glittering with anger. "Nothing's right about any of this. There was evidence inside that bunkhouse—I swear to you, I saw it when I was there before. How could Canter just pull down the scene of an unsolved— Did he even bother investigating it first?"

"He was out there several times. And the place was torn down just yesterday. I'm sorry to tell you, you just missed it."

"Fabulous," she murmured. "And did this all happen before or after he bribed or threatened you into doing a total one-eighty about finding Haley? Or did you decide it wasn't worth the bother, caring what happened to some out-of-towner?"

Guilt sliced through him, his gut twisting with the memory of what he'd witnessed yesterday. What he still had on his cell phone. He could reach for it, could show her.

Painful as it might prove, he knew, if it were Ian who was missing, he'd want to see the evidence, no matter where it led. And he'd want to kill anyone who withheld such important information from him.

But a simple vision stopped him, a memory of Eden clapping her hands in delight as he had stood high on the ladder, repositioning a hot-pink Christmas bulb more to her liking as joy lit his mother's eyes. If it turned out his suspicions were correct, there was no way any big-city reporter was going to let it go, much less allow the family who had hidden the truth from her to be involved in Eden's life.

So instead, he buried his doubts over whether he was protecting his niece, his mother or his own selfish desire to keep his family together. Instead, he hardened his heart and said goodbye to his fantasies about Jessie. Looming over her, he hid his fear and regret with anger. "What do you mean, trespassing on my land again, tossing off a bunch of crazy accusations?"

She drew back slightly, clearly startled, before turning toward the Cadillac and calling, *"Achtung, Gretel! Hier!"*

"What the—" he began, cutting himself off as a shadow leaped from the SUV's open front door, the dark bulk of a Rottweiler that rushed up and stood poised beside her elbow, its hackles raised and its dark eyes glittering with anticipation.

"I wouldn't advise you come any closer," she warned.

"Do you really think that's necessary?" he asked before

turning to Mr. Butters, who struggled nervously against his lead. As Zach unwound the rope and tried to settle the frightened pony, his temper flared. "It's okay, little fella. I won't let the bitch eat you. Or the big dog, either."

Ignoring the comment, she said, "As a matter of fact, I *do* think Gretel's necessary. You might, too, if you'd been knocked down, shot and watched your partner—your friend—die."

Seeing her point, he pulled himself together. "Well, before you call out Hansel, too, you should know I'm not about to hurt you. Pushy and annoying as I find you." That wasn't all he found her, he thought, unable to keep himself from admiring her courage.

"Glad we've got that clear," she said. "Now, maybe you can turn around and tell me what's really going on here—and why you're participating in it this time."

He frowned at her over his shoulder. "It's been pretty quiet since you left here. And come to think of it, things were running awful smoothly before you showed up, too."

"Really? Well, my sister's still missing, and Henry's murderer's still on the loose." Using her bandaged hand, she pushed a windblown strand of hair from her eyes, the fingers moving stiffly. "That's not what I'd call *running smoothly*."

Reminded of her injury, he changed the subject. "So how's the hand? You get it taken care of?"

She glared at him. "Don't try to pretend you give a damn about me."

"You mean, like I pretended the night I bandaged your wound so you wouldn't bleed to death?"

She grimaced. "Not like that night, no. Like now, because I'm a trained reporter, and I know you're lying to me, Rayford."

He tipped his hat back and blew out a breath. "It's Zach, remember? Now how 'bout you let me take care of my niece's pony, and we start this conversation over? Maybe on a civil note this time. You think we can do that?"

Part of him hoped she would say no, would stalk back to her vehicle, her storm trooper's dog at her side, and tear off to stir up trouble elsewhere. But foolish and irrational as it was, another part of him wanted her to stay here—to stay and let him get to know her better and see how she was with Eden. *Are you crazy...or just suicidal?*

She studied him through narrowed eyes before nodding. "Okay, Zach. We'll try it your way."

"Great. I'll be right back."

He took his time with sweet, old Mr. Butters, turning the gentle pony into his stall with a few soothing words and some fresh hay in his rack. He checked water buckets, too, then gave his big bay, Ace, a neck scratch, all the while taking deep breaths as he tried to figure what to do, what to say to get Jessie out of here before his mother saw that she'd come back.

But could he really do that—blow off the reporter without a word about what he'd seen? Pretend this all away while she continued to search frantically for Haley? Was that the kind of man he had become?

Jessie appeared in the doorway, the light behind her silhouetting her lithe body. "You coming back out? Or you want to talk in here?"

What he wanted to do was sling a leg over his horse and gallop off where she couldn't follow. Or maybe yank her into his arms and kiss her senseless.

But one idea was as insane as the other—and as likely to get him torn to pieces by her dog.

"I've got a little office right inside the barn here," he

said, gesturing toward the room his father had had built into the corner of the building, where he could work the business side of the ranch without interruption. There, Zach could talk to Jessie without his mother's knowledge. "Why don't you come on inside where it's warm? I'll make us some coffee."

"All right," she said, "but Gretel comes with me."

"I'll make her coffee, too, if you want."

A ghost of a smile played about Jessie's lips but didn't touch her eyes. "She's watching her caffeine intake. It makes her a little tense. Or *in*tense."

"I have to tell you," he said, working to dredge up a little long-lost charm in an attempt to disguise his rising panic, "I thought it was kind of sexy when you spoke German earlier. But I like it when you speak badass even better."

Definitely hiding something, Jessie thought, homing in on the awkwardness of his flirtation, on the way his gaze shifted away from hers so quickly. If she was reading him right, he was both nervous and conflicted by whatever it was he knew.

She almost felt sorry for him, but she pushed those feelings aside. She couldn't afford to allow empathy—and the undeniable attraction she felt every time she was in his presence—to cloud her judgment. Not when her promise to her mother to find Haley was at stake.

So for the time being, she played along, following him into a small, paneled office area: a simple affair with a big desk—a Texas lone star design carved into the front panel—a couple of well-made leather chairs, a phone and a closed laptop computer. Behind the desk, a small pair of windows allowed in light and let him see the house while on the opposite wall was a sink and countertop, along with an espresso machine with more buttons and levers than she'd ever seen in her life.

"Pretty fancy," she said as he fiddled with the settings. "I'd sort of figured you for the macho type who tosses back his coffee black and boiling, a big, bad fighter jock like you."

He went stiff for a moment, long enough for it to sink in that she'd used part of her time away to do more research on him, including the brilliant military career that had gone down on the wings of two fighter jets in an Afghan city. A career to be proud of, in the service of his country—all ending with an accident he could have prevented.

He gestured toward the machine. "Everybody has his vices. So how do you take yours?"

She grinned at the question and admitted, "Black and boiling. I was on the overnight crime beat so long, sometimes I just chew grounds."

He smiled back, a hint of wickedness in his expression. "Are you sure I can't corrupt you?"

She held his gaze a beat too long and said, "I suppose you can try."

Jessie gave him a few minutes to collect himself, watching him attend to details like a pilot going through his preflight checklist. Not that he was technically a fighter pilot any longer.

"Gretel, *platz,*" she said, and the big dog dropped into the down position. But she was still alert and watching, clearly uncertain whether the tall rancher was someone who could be trusted.

That makes two of us, Jessie thought, telling herself not to let her own renegade hormones rob her of common sense.

At his invitation, Jessie claimed one of the chairs and

forced herself to wait in silence, in spite of the impatience clamoring inside her. As she waited, she noticed the framed photos sitting by a small clock on the desktop: a portrait of a handsome soldier and another of the pretty little girl she'd glimpsed so briefly, a child with a smile full of life and mischief. The girl somehow seemed familiar, though Jessie couldn't put her finger on why that would be.

It wasn't as if she'd been around very many children, though the idea had been stirring in her subconscious lately, making her wonder what it would be like to have a family of her own. To have someone who depended on her, someone she could love.

Maybe her recent losses had started her biological clock ticking. She reminded herself that with her future so uncertain and her promise to her mother unfulfilled, she had no business thinking about starting a family. And even less, wondering what kind of a father a man like Zach would make.

Embarrassed by the thought, she felt herself flush as Zach brought her a white porcelain cup, brimming with a warm froth and smelling like heaven.

"There you go," he said, sitting with his own cup.

"Thanks," she said, nodding toward the pictures to distract him from her face. "This one has to be your younger brother. You have the same jawline, same nose."

The brother's hair was shorter and a rich brown as opposed to Zach's glossy black. Though the younger man's eyes were a darker blue, they looked just as serious, as thoughtful, as Zach's did now.

"Yeah. That's Ian," Zach said, his voice roughening. "Last good picture we have of him."

"I'm sorry," she said, a sense of profound loss washing over her, at the thought of a man who should have had decades to enjoy his life and family. Another brave man, who had sacrificed his all for home and country. "Is the little girl his? Your niece?"

He drank from his coffee, giving her time to add, "She's absolutely precious. Reminds me a little of my—"

"Having Eden means an awful lot to all of us around here," Zach interrupted, his gaze boring into hers, "especially my mama."

Jessie hesitated for a moment and then nodded, thinking how much of a comfort it must be to have something of the son she'd lost.

"You see, she lost my father, too," Zach continued, "just six months before Ian. Sometimes, I figure that tiny little handful of spunk and attitude's the only thing that's keeping my poor mama afloat."

When he looked at Jessie, there was something so raw, so painful in his blue eyes that it threatened to tear her wide-open. Which was ridiculous, she told herself. She barely knew this family and didn't trust Zach Rayford as far as she could throw him. So what if they'd both lost fathers close to the same time and he had a frail mother to watch out for, just as she'd had? She couldn't afford to feel for him, or let him get her off track.

Uncomfortable, she cleared her throat and raised her mug before admitting, "I have to tell you, this is actually one heck of a lot better than any grounds I've chewed on lately. Maybe there's something to this fancy coffee business, after all."

He smiled. "I told you I'd corrupt you. But I notice you're still favoring that right hand."

"I will be for a while longer," she said, though the truth was, her dominant hand would never be as strong or dexterous as it had been. The sooner she accepted it, her surgeon has advised her, the sooner she could do what was needed to recover whatever she had left. "But I'll be okay, thanks. At least I will be if people around here will ever quit stonewalling."

He took a thoughtful sip, the vibrant blue of his gaze—those eyes of his really were to die for—penetrating the veil of steam. "I can tell you one thing, Jessie. You come charging in, riding roughshod over people's feelings, and that's how it's gonna go around here. This is a tight community, where if folks aren't sure who you are and how you fit into the big picture, there's no way they're going to open up."

"Tell me, how am I supposed to pussyfoot around a dead friend and a missing sister? You explain that, and I'll do it. Because I'm bringing her home this time, and if that hurts some yokels' feelings, too bad."

"If you're in that big a hurry, maybe you shouldn't have let two months pass before you came back."

She glared at him. "Don't you dare judge me, after everything I've— A few days after my surgery, after you decided to quit speaking to me, my mother—"

She choked down on the words, still too raw and fresh to speak aloud.

"Your mother..." he said, his eyes softening. "You're not saying that you've lost her?"

She answered with a nod.

"I'm very sorry." The words might be simple, but they held the compassion of someone who knew grief all too well.

"Not half as sorry as I am that I didn't have my sister there beside me."

To his credit, he didn't rush to fill the awkward silence that followed with the usual platitudes. Instead, he said, "Hell, isn't it? Pure hell. One there's no way around but straight through."

"Before my mother—" She took a deep breath. "Before it got too bad, I promised her I'd come back for Haley. That this time I wouldn't take no for an answer. Not even the kind of no that comes with a bullet. And I will. I swear I will. I'll bring her home for my mom."

Her throat closed, and she looked away, not wanting him to see her get any more emotional than she was. Not wanting him to guess how hard it had been to come back or how deeply she feared the answers she might find here.

"I respect that," he said, "and if I had it in my power to help you bring your sister home today, I promise you, I'd do whatever it took to make it happen…even if it's not the happy ending you're hoping for."

She speared him with a look. "Are you telling me she's dead? Is that what you're saying?"

The room grew so quiet she heard Gretel's breathing and the ticking of the desk clock, sounds drowned out by the pounding of her heart as she waited for an answer.

Finally, he caved, his shoulders slumping. "I can't tell you for certain. But I'm afraid that's what you might find."

She nodded. "I saw blood there, in the bunkhouse."

"A lot of it," he agreed. "Between yours and your cameraman's—"

"I found it before the shooting," she said, "or at least I'm pretty sure that's what it was. There was a stained T-shirt on the front porch, some spatter on the bathroom mirror. Did Canter take samples before the place was torn down?"

"I don't know what he did there. I only know what I said before, that he went out a couple times. Took a deputy with him," Zach said, the words spilling more freely. "He never mentioned what he found, but he did tell me the investigation was still active."

"That's all he would tell me when I called him, aside from some stupid theory that it must've been a stranger, since nobody around here would ever do such a thing." She rolled her eyes at the assertion. "Wouldn't say if he had any suspects who weren't figments of his imagination, like this bald guy with the odd tats he claims people saw around that day. Wouldn't confirm that he'd cleared Danny McFarland, either."

"Hellfire's walking around a free man, tats and all," Zach told her. "I know that much for sure. I headed over to the Prairie Rose and tried to talk to him myself about it one night."

So he *had* been keeping his promise to help her, in spite of his silence. "And how'd that go down?"

He snorted. "About like you would expect with him. A couple of bruises and a scrape or two."

"He hit *you?* I figured he was just the type to bully women."

Zach's blue eyes lit up with dark amusement. "I didn't say he hit me, but he took his best shot. And I didn't say the bruises and the scrapes were mine."

"Ah," she said, wishing she'd been there to see it. "But I take it you didn't get any information."

"That, and I'm banned for life from the only watering hole in Rusted Spur."

"My condolences."

"I suppose I'll manage."

"I suggested to Canter he might want to call in outside help," she said, "maybe the Texas Rangers, if he was having so much trouble."

Zach winced. "Knowing him, I'll bet that went over like a skunk at a watermelon social."

She nodded, smiling at the image. "You've got that right. He said a few choice words about the idea of calling in the Rangers—apparently, there's some bad blood there—and assured me he had everything completely under control. Then he quit returning my calls, never mind answering his phone."

"I hate to tell you this, but he hasn't been any more forthcoming with me. Just keeps saying he's playing this one close to the vest."

"You buying it?"

"I'm not sure what to think," Zach told her. "I just thought it might be a problem with me in particular."

"You?" she asked. "How come?"

Zach grimaced. "Let's just say I wasn't exactly a choirboy before the corps made something of me."

She snorted. "You look awfully clean cut for a teenage hell-raiser."

He shrugged. "It was either that or punch out my old man, and he would've kicked my ass from one end of the county to the other. Come to think of it, he did that, more or less regularly."

"My dad was a little like that, only he kicked our tails with words. That's what drove Haley to take off—well, my father's constant harping on her about some guy. One in a series of the worst guys she could come up with. Sometimes, I think it was her way of getting back at him, embarrassing him by living down to his expectations."

"I did the same thing with my hell-raising, until I realized I was the one getting bloody," he said, his eyes misting over with the distant past.

"My sister's never learned that lesson," she said, her worry for her family overwhelming her caution, "and now I'm scared to death that it's already too late for her. If—if it turns out that Haley's really gone, how will I ever forgive myself for turning my back on my own twin— giving up and leaving her out here to die alone?"

She felt herself begin to tremble, and Gretel must have sensed it, too, for the dog lifted her head from her paws, her ears rising and her muscles gathering beneath her gleaming coat. Wanting to sink her teeth into whatever was causing her mistress distress, Jessie supposed. Which made two of them at this point; she definitely felt like biting someone.

"I was eighteen when I walked out on this ranch," Zach admitted, regret passing like a shadow over his strong features. "Left to find my future. Didn't look back, not for years. I didn't even come back for the old man's funeral. Only Ian's. It took that much—that and the mess I'd make of my career—to get me to finally step up."

Jessie stared at him, wondering what any of what he'd said had to do with her and Haley.

He shrugged and said, "What I'm saying is that no one could have stopped me. I had to make the decision for myself to finally grow up and do the right thing, just the way your sister had her choice to make."

"Speaking of doing the right thing," Jessie said, abruptly tired of talking around the real point of her visit, "don't you think it's time you try it right now? Only this time, you tell me the truth. Tell me what you're hiding from me."

Chapter 10

Zach pressed his lips together and pinned her with a hard look. A look he'd used to send the younger pilots he'd once trained scrambling for cover.

"I think we've already established that it'll take a whole lot more than a little manly scowling to get me off your case."

With a wry grin, he shook his head, thinking that he should have known better than imagining this woman, gutsy enough to return alone to face a hostile sheriff and a murderous attacker, was about to back down. "Anybody ever tell you you're as stubborn as sin?"

"In my profession, they give out awards for it," she said before adding a self-deprecating shrug, "except those days when you try it on the boss."

"So you really did get fired?" He wondered what kind of boss canned a woman who'd just lost her mother— after having been shot on the job.

"I've had all the luck, just lately. Which only means that I'm a woman with nothing but time to nail any butt to the wall that stands in my way. Including yours, cowboy."

He snorted, enjoying the sparring far more than he had any right to. "Better women than you have tried to nail my ass. A few of them ended up getting nailed themselves."

That earned him another eye-roll. "You fly-boys and your boasting. Or is it being filthy rich that makes you so obnoxious?"

"Maybe it's just you," he said, wondering what it would be like to nail *her*. And immediately quashing the most dangerous idea he'd ever had. So what if he was attracted to her, if the perfect package of face and body, courage and determination made him eager to find out if she'd give as good as she got in bed, too?

If she had her way, his family could be torn to pieces, and family was the one line he was never again crossing. Especially not now that that family included a little girl who, as secure and loved as she was, still woke screaming with night terrors several times a week.

But Jessie had a family, too, a family that had dwindled down to a single missing woman. And she would never rest until she found her missing twin. Would never back off her search. Partially because it was the only thing that she had left.

Grimacing, he said, "How about we ride back over there? There's something I want to show you."

Want to was a gross overstatement, but the truth was, he knew he had to, even if he didn't plan to tell her everything. But she deserved to know what he'd found, and only by going there could he put it all in context.

"Ride over where?" she asked. "To where the bunkhouse used to be?"

At his nod, she added, "You want me to go with you? Alone?"

"I could point out that we're alone now, or as alone as we can get with your friend there watching." He gestured toward the dog, which eyed him with obvious suspicion. "But we won't be for long if we don't head out. If my foreman or some of the hands don't show up and interrupt us, Eden'll get curious and head back out here, or, worse yet, my mama. And what I have to say, I'm only going to tell you once. Without interruption."

She considered for a moment before saying, "I'll drive."

"Paranoid much, Jessie?" he asked. "You don't seriously think I'd take you there to jump you."

"I'm sorry. You're right. It's just that even the thought of that place creeps me out a little."

When he raised his eyebrows, she sighed. "Okay. A lot."

"No surprise there," he said, "but I'm not the person you ought to be afraid of."

"The trouble is, I don't know who is. But I'm hoping that whatever you tell me will help me."

Not as much as it's going to hurt me, he worried, *if I'm not very careful.*

He rode beside her in the Escalade, the black-and-tan dog breathing down his neck from the backseat.

Turning to look the animal in the eye, he said, "If you're going to hang this close, someone should at least offer you a breath mint."

The Rottweiler peeled back her lips, revealing a set of fangs better suited to a T-rex.

"*Platz,* why don't you?" he suggested, test-driving Jessie's German.

It wasn't until she repeated the command—smugly—that the animal relaxed and lay down on the rear seat.

"Where'd you come up with a dog like that?" he asked. "They have a Rent-a-Menace center down in Dallas?"

Jessie laughed. "Sorry if she's a little hyped up today. She senses when I'm nervous, and reacts accordingly."

"In that case, I'm making you the decaf brew from now on."

"Perish the thought," she said. "And to answer your question, she was my mom's dog. My dad had his faults, and plenty of them, but he always wanted her to feel safe, and there was one home invasion too many on the evening news."

"Not much of an issue way out here," he said as the mansion shrank down to a distant dot behind them. "That's one thing to like about it. It's a damn sight safer."

"Tell that to my right hand—and especially to Henry," she said.

And maybe to your twin, he thought, dreading what was coming.

It took them fifteen minutes to get back to the old bunkhouse location, time enough for him to wonder why he was opening this can of worms. But there was no taking back his offer, and there'd be no more putting her off, either. He saw that in the fierce look on Jessie's face, the determination in her left-handed grip on the wheel.

He felt a stab of dismay, realizing it was a glimpse into the future. Eden's future, he was certain, considering the child's willful moments. But she was sweet, too, gentle with the animals and so full of life and imagination.

And every day he spent with her, every hour, every minute, it was going to get harder to do the right thing, the moral thing. Until it became impossible to straighten out the situation—and not only for his mother's sake.

"Pull up right over there," he said.

Jessie peered into the weeds ahead. "But there's nothing left."

"It'll be easier to explain it outside the car."

They left the SUV, the dog following to sniff around them. The animal's activity flushed a pheasant, and her ears pricked, but at a word from Jessie, she returned her attention to her mistress.

He opened his mouth to speak, then noticed Jessie peering at him oddly.

"What?" he asked, annoyed at the interruption.

She fought a smile with little success. "It's just—" her hand moved toward his jawline but stopped just short of touching "—someone's got a little shine this morning."

He huffed an irritated sigh and scrubbed at his unshaven jaw. "That kid and her glitter. I'd have that stuff banned from the county if I could. Ranchers *aren't* supposed to sparkle, damn it!"

Jessie looked away, biting her lip, but a bubble of laughter escaped.

Ignoring it, he gestured toward the scraped spot where the bunkhouse had stood. "A couple of weeks ago, I came to check on the place, but there was nothing inside or around it. No furniture, no junk, like somebody swept it clean."

She immediately sobered. "Nothing on the porch?"

He shook his head and then shrugged. "Maybe Canter and his people cleared it, logged things into evidence."

"Or had every last bit hauled to the dump," she said. "You do have a dump somewhere around here, don't you?"

"Not officially," Zach said, "but one of the locals has a pit dug, and for thirty bucks a pickup load, you can get junk buried. A hundred bucks if you're not from around here."

"So welcoming to visitors. Sounds exactly like the Rusted Spur I've come to know and love," she said flatly. "But I'll want to get directions from you later."

"Clem Elam won't like you snooping around his place. He's a friend of Hellfire's, for one thing, and rougher than an old cob."

"Maybe Gretel here'll charm him into it," she said, smiling as she scratched the Rottweiler's sleek black ears.

"Or maybe Canter's already warned him you mean trouble."

"The way he warned you off?"

Did the woman ever give an inch? "Tried to, don't you mean? Cause I'm here talking to you. And telling you what it was I *did* find, right over here." He took a few steps downward, into the depression, and pointed out a spot where the dried grasses lay flat. "Before somebody came back for it."

At her questioning look, he told her about the silvery trail of cinders. And about the charred chunks he suspected had been bone.

"*Human* bone?" Her face paled. "Tell me that isn't what you're saying."

"I'm not sure. I'm no expert. But I snapped some pictures with my phone."

"Let me see. You *do* still have them?"

Nodding, he pulled his phone out of the pocket of his jeans and found the photos he'd been so tempted to delete. As soon as he passed them to her, she scrolled through the short series, squinting at each image, pinching and enlarging, and turning her head as if she were imagining what she was seeing from a variety of angles. He knew because he'd repeatedly done the same thing, attempting to convince himself he was seeing the remnants of burnt wood or butchered animals.

And not a murdered woman.

"Who else have you shown these to?" she finally asked.

"I tried to talk to Canter. He scoffed about 'getting all excited over what was left of someone's dinner' but promised to come take a look. Next thing I knew, the grill was gone. Not only the grill, either. The whole bunkhouse."

She stared in disbelief. "What? You're saying he was the one who tore the place down? Without your permission? How could he possibly—"

"He showed up at the house while I was out on the range. Told my mama all about these kids he'd run off—kids my mama swore she'd seen, too—and said it was a safety hazard, practically falling down."

"It was definitely run-down," said Jessie, "but the building seemed basically sound."

"I thought the same, but our opinions aren't the ones that matter. Canter talked my mama into signing off on having Clem Elam and his helpers tear it down and haul it off that very hour. Since they just so happened to be right there, heavy equipment and all."

"That has to be illegal," she said, her voice colder than the prairie wind.

He shook his head. "My mama may have turned over the running of this ranch to me, but she still has full decision-making power when she chooses to exert it."

"Has she ever used this power before? Since you've come back, I mean."

"No." Normally, his mother referred every question, no matter how small, to him, and he was still going through bags of unsorted receipts, unopened mail—all sorts of detritus—from her brief tenure as the head of the ranch. When he'd confronted her about the bunkhouse, she'd told him she'd been having nightmares about the place and the murder that had taken place there.

Eden's scared of it, too, his mother had added, as if Henry Kucharski's death were the only reason. *She's overheard us talking about that poor man, and that reporter who stopped by—Haley's sister. It's upset her.*

"What did Canter say when you went to him about it?" Jessie demanded.

"He said he had the right to see to unsafe structures, especially when he had the landowner's permission. Unless I wanted to take a shot at having my own mama declared incompetent."

She made a rude noise. "What a piece of work this guy is. What'd he say about the grill?"

"He claims he didn't find it—and that sucker weighed a ton."

"So he didn't see the bones? Did you show him?"

Zach shook his head. "Didn't think it was such a good idea to let him know I had those pictures. Just in case..."

"So you just dropped it?" she asked, her gaze challenging him to admit the truth.

That he'd been too sickened by the thought that whatever he learned would somehow implicate his mother, who had pleaded with him to let this go, to not take any action.

"I went back to running my cattle ranch, taking care of Eden and my mama, and worrying about my business like I oughta," he said, feeling heat waves rising, cooking him in his boots. Because he couldn't help remembering the last time he'd decided to mind his own business, that time with a member of his squadron. A younger pilot who had clipped him, dooming both planes, dooming so many innocents in the sleeping city below.

"Wait, what are you doing?" he asked as he noticed her fiddling with his phone again, clicking away with her left hand.

He reached for it, panic stabbing through him. Stepping away, she turned her back, and that dog of hers slipped between them, hackles raised and teeth bared, a low growl rumbling in her chest.

"Calm down, Gretel. *Platz,*" Jessie said before looking to Zach. "It's okay, isn't it, if I forward these to my phone?"

"What do you plan to do with them?"

"Make contact with a source of mine, a forensic anthropology professor. Dr. Pollard's the director of the Body Farm run by Sam Houston State in Huntsville, north of Houston. If he says those bones are human, then they're human."

"But whether they are or not, they're gone."

"Those photographs might serve as proof, along with your testimony." When he didn't respond, she shook her head and added, "Come on, Zach. You know this is all wrong. You've known it from the start. Otherwise, why would you have kept these pictures, much less shown them to me?"

"Might not've been one of my better ideas."

"Admit it," she said. "You're a good guy. And you know as well as I do that this situation is seriously messed up."

"Yeah," he said, "I do."

Even though the implications were tearing him apart.

They looked around for only a few minutes before Jessie realized it was a complete waste of time. Canter and this Elam person he'd brought in to do the demolition had been thorough; she'd give them that. There was no way she was ever going to find a piece of evidence as flimsy as a soiled T-shirt or fragile as a mirror. She'd scarcely found more than a two-by-four and a few shards of broken glass on the scraped site.

"So what's next?" Zach asked her after they'd returned to the SUV.

"We have to find those bones," she said. "We need to secure the grill and any remains for further testing after I contact the Texas Rangers."

"The Rangers won't come out on the basis of a few pictures."

"Surely, after Henry's murder, they'll take this seriously. They'll have to."

He frowned, looking skeptical. "Maybe, maybe not. Depends on what Canter tells them."

"I'll make them listen. I swear I will," she lashed out, choked with unexpected tears. Because at that moment, it hit her: they weren't just talking about *someone's* bones, found in an old grill, or *someone's* blood soaked into a wadded T-shirt. They were talking about Haley's. *Her* Haley.

She's gone, long gone. I'll never see another member of my family again.

The world spinning dizzily around her, Jessie would swear she felt her sister's presence, felt Haley's fear, her anguish—a wave of it so strong that she jammed on the brakes and put the SUV in Park. Bailing out, she slammed the door behind her and staggered a few steps before bending to brace her hands about her knees.

Moments later, Zach was there beside her, holding her hair out of the way and rubbing her back as her stomach pitched and spasmed and she drew in deep breaths of chilly air. Inside the Escalade, Gretel barked aggressively, apparently convinced that she was being hurt.

Unable to bring anything up, Jessie finally rose, tears streaming down her hot face.

"It just hit me," she said, wiping her face with the clean bandanna he produced from somewhere. "It has to be my sister, burned like that. Like trash, like she meant nothing."

Beneath the brim of his silver hat, the tall rancher's deep, blue eyes looked into hers. And in their depths, she saw both comprehension and compassion, tempered by some worry of his own.

"She meant something, no matter what," he told her. "She had a family who loved her. She had you."

"Not enough," Jessie said as she moved toward the Escalade's hood and braced herself against it. "Never enough. She's— Haley's my twin, my mirror image. For so long, she was always there. And always in here, too, even after things went sideways." She laid her hand on her chest, feeling the heart pumping beneath it.

A heart that would beat alone, forever, with no chance of the reconciliation she had always believed would someday be possible. Someday, when her sister tired of the lifestyle she had chosen, when she tired of the resentment she'd felt toward Jessie, with her straight A's and steady job.

You act like it does any good, always playing the good twin, Haley had shouted the last time they had spoken, her tone as caustic as her words, *like he'll ever think you're good enough, no matter what you do.*

Had that been four years ago, already? Four years since Jessie had even tried to get in contact with her. But that didn't mean she didn't love her, as maddening as Haley's descent was.

"We don't even know those bones were human," Zach said, "and we for sure can't prove they were hers."

"Why else would someone go through so much trouble to take them?" she asked. "They're Haley's bones. I know it. I swear, I can feel her, feel how terrified she was, how lonely. That monster she was with, that Frankie, must've killed her. He cut her up like an animal to burn the evidence." Jessie couldn't stop herself, her fear and horror spilling over.

"Stop," he told her, surprising her by taking her wrist and then pulling her close. Pulling her against a wall of hard muscle and the scent of leather. Into an embrace so big and masculine that it was overwhelming. "Don't go there."

For one brief moment she sank into his arms, before her body stiffened, too agitated to accept the comfort. "No. Please. Let me go."

Releasing her, he shook his head. "I'm sorry, Jessie. Sorry. It's just, I've done the same thing with my brother, imagining what he felt, what was done to him in those final minutes. Short on facts, the human mind will do that, will torture itself endlessly. And it does no damned good at all, only makes you crazy. Keeps you from doing what you have to."

"So what am I supposed to do?" she asked, wishing she had even a fraction of his strength and wisdom. "Just go home? Forget my promise to my mother? Try to pretend Haley and I never dressed in matching outfits, that we never shared our toys, our crib, a womb before that? How? You tell me how, Zach, and I'll be glad to do it. And while you're at it, you can tell me how to keep on breathing, too."

He pulled off his hat to rake a hand through his hair. "I wish I had the answers for you. Wish I had them for myself."

She stumbled off, and this time really was sick, again

and again, the world around her dimming. By the time she finished, she felt emptied, and not only physically. Numbly, she allowed Zach to help her up and lead her back to the vehicle's passenger side, her knees so weak that they threatened to give way with every step.

"Let me drive the rest of the way," he said. "You're in no condition. But before I open that door for you, you better tell your dog to stand down."

She silenced Gretel with a hand signal and said, "I have a cooler in the back with water," she said. "I just need to rinse my mouth."

"Unlocked?" he asked, and at her nod, he retrieved it for her, cracking the top open with a twist.

"Thanks," she told him, and when she took the bottle from him, their hands accidentally brushed. And need opened up inside her, a yawning void that made her wish he'd pull her into those strong arms again and fill it. Fill her with presence, staving off the grief blowing through her, like the January wind.

Inside the Escalade, he said, "Convincing the Rangers to investigate those bones will be a whole lot easier if we can get our hands on the evidence. So how 'bout let's take a drive over to Clem Elam's dump. You up to that?"

Fighting hard to keep the tears from spilling, she could only nod.

They drove for about fifteen minutes, the stark winter landscape stretching out on either side. Here and there, she spotted cattle, horned heads down and backs to the light wind. Otherwise, the view was as bleak and empty as her soul.

Zach must have shared her mood, or at least sensed it, for he didn't say a word until after he'd climbed out of the SUV and unhooked a length of chain serving as a makeshift gate. The sign hanging from it read *Private Property* and gave a local number.

Once back inside the vehicle, he said, "I hate to call and warn him that we're coming, but if I don't he's likely to set loose his pack of mutts to run us off. Or if he's in an especially good mood, he'll just shoot first and ask questions later."

"I guess you'd better go ahead and call, then," she said. "My New Year's resolution involved cutting the lead out of my diet."

Zach made the call, asking the man about his luck hunting, his dogs and finally his wife before finally getting to the point of the conversation. "I'm up by your front gate right now. Mind if I drive back to the dump?"

There was a pause as Elam answered, and Zach responded a moment later. "Absolutely, buddy. I wouldn't think of using your place without paying. I'll stop by the trailer after, if you don't mind… Sure, okay. I'll head there first."

A moment later, he disconnected and drove in through the gate, explaining, "The man has his priorities. And every one of them involves cash payment."

"I got that," she said, wondering if there was any limit to the type of things that such a man might do for money.

They drove along a rutted track, turning right just past a clump of scraggly trees. Soon, a battered silver travel trailer came into view, along with a dozen coonhound mixes, each one chained to a doghouse. All of them began to bay at the Cadillac's approach. There was a ramshackle shed in back, and inside it she saw a mud-plastered yellow bulldozer. But it was the vehicles parked out front that attracted her attention. Not the old charcoal-gray pickup so much as the big chopper motorcycle, which jangled a memory.

"The Rebel flags on the gas tank," she said, nodding toward them. "I recognize that bike. It's Hellfire's."

"Great," said Zach. "Just what we needed. But at least now we know the answer to one question."

"What question's that?"

"Which one of McFarland's pals has a dark-colored pickup that he could've borrowed that night in November. The pickup that he could've used to wreck my truck after he shot you and your friend."

When Jessie opened the door to bail out, Zach caught her left wrist. He recognized that eager, almost predatory, gleam in her eye, and he meant to nip it in the bud before it cost one or both of them more trouble.

"You'll need to stay out here," he told her. "Don't get out of the vehicle for any reason."

"Why on earth not?" she asked. "It's not like they can't see me through the window. Look there—the curtain's moving."

Sure enough, when he followed her gaze, a grimy scrap of cloth twitched closed.

"Just trust me on this, all right?" Zach continued, wondering if this was the same woman he had just watched fall apart, too upset to accept the comfort he had offered. But that didn't mean he was going to let her ignore his attempts to keep her safe. "You've already had one run-in with Hellfire, and Clem's not exactly known for his way with the ladies. But he *is* known to keep a loaded shotgun just inside his door."

"I can handle myself," she said, bailing out of the car with her dog.

Cursing her under his breath, Zach followed the stubborn woman as Clem Elam climbed down a set of rickety wooden boxes used for stair steps. He wore a scraggly salt-and-pepper beard over a filthy wool plaid jacket, along with a moth-eaten brown hat with earflaps to protect him from the cold.

Expression souring, Clem hollered at his hounds, who were by now going crazy, to quit their carrying on.

A few rebellious howls and a lot more yelling followed before the noise finally subsided. Clem glared, first at Jessie and then at the silent sentinel sitting with deceptive calmness at her side.

"You didn't tell me you were bringing a coupla bitches here to stir them dogs up," he told Zach.

"*Excuse* me—" Jessie started, anger sparking in her green eyes before she glanced at Zach and cut herself off, apparently remembering that he had tried to warn her.

But that didn't mean he was about to put up with Elam's garbage, either. "You'll call her Ms. Layton," Zach said. "Or we won't be doing business." *And I might just decide to leave you lying on those steps.*

Looking down at Gretel, Elam spat on the ground. "Others might feel different on the subject, but I never did have any use for bitches. Except for breedin' dogs, that is. That's about all they're good for."

"I'll be waiting in the car," Jessie grumbled, clearly not trusting herself to deal with the man's provocation.

Once he heard the door slam, Zach told Clem, "You're a smooth old cuss, you know that?"

Elam laughed. "So I've been told," he said and then sobered in an instant. "You come to pay the dump fee?"

"Maybe," Zach said, reaching into his front pocket and then withdrawing his hand, as if he'd changed his mind. "Or maybe I was wondering what the charge would be if I was thinking on picking something up, instead."

Elam licked at dry lips. "What you lookin' for exactly? Maybe I can help you find it…for an extra twenty."

Zach shrugged, trying to make it seem as if what he wanted was no big deal. And sensing, rather than seeing, Hellfire's presence in the open doorway. Yet Zach knew he was there, trusted the knowledge as if he still had use of his crashed jet's radar.

"It really isn't worth much," he said, as casually as he could manage. "Just some old furniture I promised Reverend Jacobs from the church he could take and clean up for a family that could use it. A little down on their luck, the way he put it." Belatedly, Zach remembered finding the bunkhouse had been emptied, but Elam and Danny didn't have to know he knew that.

"A lot down on their luck," said Hellfire from the doorway, "if they're thinkin' of usin' anything outta that dump."

Zach met the biker's gaze and held it, in case his words had been intended as a challenge. When McFarland said nothing, Zach said, "You been on my property, Danny? Because I don't recall inviting any ex-cons."

Hellfire came down the steps to glare at him, and Zach noticed that he, too, had dirt smudges on his leather jacket. Even his beard had traces of the stuff.

What had the two men been up to?

Finally, McFarland mumbled, "I was helpin' Clem here with the demolition, lending one of my saloon's best customers a hand."

Just like Clem had lent Hellfire his pickup to commit a murder that night back in November, Zach figured. But as much as he wanted to lay out the accusation, he wasn't fool enough to escalate this argument here. Because, Rayford or not, he was well aware he could end up buried in the nearby landfill—and Jessie with him.

So instead, Zach walked over to McFarland and offered his hand. "We go back a long way, Danny. So no hard feelings about our little conversation at the Prairie Rose the other day?"

Hellfire blinked hard, clearly confused by the gesture. But some dormant patch of manners lurking in his gray matter won the day, and he accepted Zach's handshake with a bruising grip.

"No hard feelings," Danny mumbled, not much sounding like he meant it. "And about what I said that night— you're welcome to come by anytime. And spread around some of that Rayford money while you're at it."

"I'll be sure and do that," Zach promised, though both of them knew he never would. "So whatcha hearing from your little brother these days?"

The handshake over, Hellfire made a move, but it was only to drop the mirrored shades sitting on the top of his head down over his eyes.

"People've been asking me a lot about him lately," he said. "You, the sheriff, couple of others who don't know any better than to stick their nose in a man's family business."

With this, Hellfire glanced meaningfully at Jessie, in the Escalade's front seat. She raised her chin a little higher, her look pure defiance, and Zach felt proud of her fire, as proud as if he had some claim on her.

"Fine-looking woman you got right there," Danny remarked. "Glad to see she's finally learned her place."

"I wouldn't say that too loud if I were you," Zach told him, envisioning the Rottweiler ripping out the man's throat. "It could come back to haunt you."

Hellfire made a scoffing sound. "She oughta go back where she came from. She's not gonna find what she's looking for anywhere in these parts."

"And you know this for a fact because...?"

"Maybe that sister of hers don't want to be found,"

Hellfire told him. "Or my brother, either. She ever think of that?"

"Pretty sure it's occurred to her," Zach managed. "And I'm not sure she'd bother for her own sake, except she made a promise to her and Haley's mama, rest her soul."

He let the words hang, noticing the way Hellfire's gaze reddened before sliding toward Jessie.

"Their mama?" said the huge man.

"She just died recently," Zach told them, sensing some seismic shift inside the mountain of a biker, "without seeing her daughter. But she made Jessie promise that she'd still bring Haley home."

"Just another bitch stirring up trouble," Elam said. "Why should anybody give a rat's—"

Hellfire glared a warning his way. "C'mon, Clem. Don't be trash-talking anybody's mama up in heaven. That's sacred ground you're treading on there."

Zach stared for a moment, trying to make out whether to take those words seriously, considering the reputation the McFarland brothers' mother had had for heavy drinking. She had died young, though, maybe young enough that time had buffed away bad memories, leaving an odd residue of reverence in their place.

Before Zach could be certain, Hellfire stalked off, making for the Cadillac's passenger side. Ready for trouble, Zach followed closely enough to see Jessie's eyes widen at the huge man's approach, but she was smart enough to hide her fear and put down the window.

"So you weren't lyin' before," Hellfire asked her, "when you said you were lookin' for your sister on account of your sick mama?"

Jessie narrowed her eyes. "I *told* you it was about my mother—just before you knocked me down. And threatened to knock my teeth out, the way I remember."

He shook his head. "I just figured you were lookin' for your sister so you could get back your money."

"It was never about that, but what do you know about the money? Did Haley say something about me?"

The massive shoulders shrugged. "We were all sittin' around havin' a few beers one night last summer, and she was sayin' how she missed her family, especially her sister, but she could never go back. She'd played you all for patsies until you finally cut her off."

Anguish etched itself in Jessie's beautiful face, a yearning that made Zach ache for her. "She *said* that? That she missed us?"

The huge head nodded. "Yeah, she did. Not long before they lit out."

Recovering, Jessie speared him with a look. "For where?" she demanded before leaving the vehicle to face him directly. "Please. Hell— Please, Danny. I made a promise. A promise at my mother's deathbed."

His homely face troubled, he shook his head. "Truth is, I don't know where they went, on account of we had a falling out."

"A falling out? About what?"

"Everybody said I'd never do it, never get a bar of my own. That a fella like me, come up outta nothin', would never be a man of property. A business owner."

"You sure as hell showed them!" hooted Clem, fist-pumping the air while Danny ignored his racket.

"You gotta understand," Danny said. "I was workin' two jobs, pullin' crazy hours, sellin' nearly everything I owned. But every time I'd get a stake up, Frankie figured he had money, too. Money for food and beer and bail for him and Haley—it was like trying to swim for shore with an anchor chain still wrapped around your neck. So I told him I was finished coverin' for him, that I'd raised him up as long as I could—"

"Are you sure you're finished, Danny?" Jessie challenged, looking so small in comparison to the mountain of a man she faced that Zach came forward, fully prepared to step between them. "Or are you still covering for Frankie? Covering for the murder he committed even now?"

After Jessie's question, Hellfire turned away. "I'm not gonna stand here and listen to you trash-talking the only family I got. I gotta go to work now."

"Your brother killed her," Jessie called after him, her heart pounding as she laid the truth out. "I know he killed my sister."

Hellfire kept going, swearing to himself.

She started to go after him, but Zach blocked her, grabbing her by the arms. Straining against his interference, she spoke past him, "Please. Please, Danny. I just want to find Haley. Dead or alive, I have to find her. For my mother's sake."

Hellfire stopped in his tracks, then made a slow turn clearly designed to intimidate. Zach edged in front of her, guardian enough that she didn't call her dog. At least not yet.

"I'm not leaving until I know the truth," she told the biker, her heart pounding.

"Then maybe you're not leaving—" he began before Zach cut him off.

"Threaten her again," he said, "and you'll find out how hard it is to run that business of yours from a jail cell."

Glaring at them both, Hellfire spat on the ground then muttered something about damned Rayfords, thinking they all ran this county. But he didn't challenge Zach directly, instead telling Jessie, "Next time I hear from Frankie, I'll tell him to have Haley call. That satisfy you?"

"Only if she does." Before she could say more, he was kicking his motorcycle to life, revving the huge engine so loudly that he drowned out her demands.

Once he roared off, Clem waved them away, saying, "Just get outta here. Get off my property right now."

Zach held out a couple of twenties. "You don't want my money?"

Elam hesitated a split second before shaking his head. "I don't want one thing in this wide world except to have you two gone."

With that, he stomped back up the steps and slammed the door of the travel trailer behind him. The chained hounds took it as their cue to resume their chorus, and after that, it was too loud for Zach and Jessie to do anything but head over to the trash pit, whether or not they had Clem's blessing.

As soon as Zach parked, she bailed out and hurried toward the pit's edge, her heart sinking. For someone, clearly Clem and Hellfire, considering the dirt clinging to their clothing, had dumped and leveled fill dirt over the contents of the pit.

"They buried it," she said, despair weighing down her hope. Frustration burned and shimmered in her eyes. "They buried whatever evidence was in there. We'll never find it now."

Zach laid one big hand on her shoulder. "I know this seems impossible. Every bit of it. But we'll get it figured out. We will."

"You're not exactly batting a thousand so far," she snapped, the lash of her anger the only thing that allowed her to drive back the threatening tears.

"You okay to head over to the house now?" he asked her, holding the door open for her.

She wanted to argue with him, to tell him she was perfectly capable of driving for herself now. But the light-headedness that had begun earlier was worse now, so instead, she simply nodded and climbed up inside. Or tried to, her shaking legs forcing her to step back and let him support her waist.

"There you go," he said, reaching across her to pull and latch her seat belt.

"Thank you," she said. "And I'm sorry. Sorry for taking my frustrations out on you, when you're the only one— My only ally."

She tipped back against the headrest, her eyes fluttering closed.

"Whoa, Jessie. Here. Have another sip of water." He pressed the cool, wet water bottle from the cup holder into her left hand. "You're looking pretty pale there. You aren't going to faint on me, are you?"

"I'm not the type who faints," she protested, telling herself that no real journalist would be such a lightweight.

"I'm calling bull on that one," he said, "since I happened to be there the last time you did."

Indignant, she forced her eyes open. "I'd been *shot*. That's different. Shock and blood loss don't count."

"You're probably right," he said, clearly fighting off a smile, "so unless you want to spoil your perfect record, lean back and have that drink."

Once she had, he climbed behind the wheel and put the SUV back in gear. As the mansion came into sight, he asked her, "When was the last time you had anything to eat?"

She wrinkled her nose, nausea swirling in her stomach.

"Some fast food around lunchtime. Greasy burger, fries— not my usual, but I was in a hurry to get on the road."

"No wonder you're sick," he said. "You need something better in you."

"Not right now, I don't," she said, laying her hand on her still-churning stomach. "I'll get something tonight in Marston. I've got a room booked there tonight."

"Tell me you're not planning to poke around anymore this afternoon. You'll pass out."

She wanted to ask him, *Why should you care?* But it was clear it was his nature, the nature of a man who'd come home to take care of his mother and his niece.

His niece... What had her name been? Something unusual, old-fashioned. Edith, wasn't it? Jessie shook her head, trying to pin down the scrap of information.

Telling herself it didn't matter, she let it blow away, along with the nagging sensation that there was something beyond cuteness, something about the little girl that seemed almost familiar.

"Jessie, you still with me?" he asked as he pulled up near the barn, where she'd been parked before.

"Sure thing," she said. "Just thinking. I have a lot on my mind."

"I imagine," he said, his gaze darting toward the house and back again. "Um, you want to come inside? I'm sure I can find a place for you to lie down until you're feeling better."

"No, thanks. I'll be fine," she said. "I think I'll head to Marston now."

"It's over an hour from here. There's no way you're fit to drive that far."

"It was the closest lodging I could find, though I'm still not certain the motel manager won't freak when she sees I've brought Gretel."

"So you didn't call Margie?"

"Margie?" she asked. "Who's that?"

"Margie Hunter," he said, "my former fifth-grade teacher."

At her confused look, he explained, "She's retired now. Pension doesn't go as far as she'd like, so she rents out rooms in that big old farmhouse her husband left her. Mostly rents to land men coming through."

"Land men?" she asked.

"That's what they call 'em in the industry, even the women," he explained. "They're the ones who go around researching property owners at the courthouse and buying up mineral rights for the oil companies. There's been a lot more interest in the area just lately. Better drilling methods making what used to be worthless profitable."

"I saw something about that in the paper," she said, mostly since she'd become too jaded about television news to watch after the way Vivian had stabbed her in the back. "Read that there was oil found on your land, too."

He shot her a self-deprecating grin. "It helps support the family cattle habit."

She snorted. "So about this Margie Hunter? I never found her on the internet. In fact, I didn't find any kind of lodging here in Rusted Spur."

"Margie's strictly word of mouth. Doesn't want to get overrun by a 'bunch of out-of-town riffraff,'" he said, sketching air quotes with his fingers. "But if you and the mutt want to come back inside my office, I'll give her a call and vouch for you. The dog, too, if you promise me she won't eat anybody."

"Gretel's actually relaxed and friendly when she isn't working."

Giving the Rottweiler a skeptical look, he said, "When she's not hell-bent on ripping arms off, you mean."

Jessie rolled her eyes. "She's not ripping anybody's arms off. She's just letting you know that she's still on duty."

"Well, if you expect to take her into Margie's house, you're going to have to find the off switch on her."

"You have my word I can control her."

He eyed her, clearly skeptical. "The word of a reporter?"

Why was he distancing himself from her again like this? "You know darned well I'm not here as a reporter. I never really was, even before I got myself fired."

She forced herself to take a chance, smiling at a man whose hot- and cold-running behavior she couldn't get a handle on. But who else did she have here, or anywhere, to help her? "So how about the word of a woman who could really use a friend? Will you accept that? Or shall I try my luck in Marston, after all?"

As Zach walked Jessie to the office so he could look up Margie Hunter's phone number, he said, "So you never told me. What happened with the job?"

She winced. "Poked the wrong dragon, a *really* rich one, and lost a game of chicken with the woman sleeping with him."

"Why am I not surprised?"

"Story of my life," she said with an offhand shrug.

But he could sense the still-fresh wounds she was hiding, maybe because he had so much scar tissue of his own. Hers, however, weren't the kind that came from engaging with the enemy, but the more painful type inflicted by someone supposed to be on her side.

Before he could say more, a chiming sound from her phone interrupted. She pulled the phone from her pocket. "I'd better check to see if…"

She trailed off, her eyes widening and the color draining from her face as she read.

"What is it?"

Continuing to stare at the phone, she muttered, "That certainly didn't take long."

"Your expert already?"

She blew out a shaky breath. "I wish." Grimacing, she passed him the phone. "Go ahead and take a look."

He took the cell phone from her, tilting it to read the screen. To read the text message from a sender identified only as "Unknown Caller." The words were as simple as they were brutal, an all-caps message bristling with malice: *LEAVE BEFORE THE SUN SETS. TWO CAN DISAPPEAR AS WELL AS ONE.* No wonder she'd gone so pale.

Zach's eyes met hers. "Who saw you on the way here? Who knew you were coming?"

She shook her head. "No one, really, with my mom gone, and I don't have a boss to report to. But maybe somebody spotted me on the road as I drove here."

"Did you notice anyone? Any particular cars?"

She thought for a minute before shaking her head. "I remember thinking how light the traffic was, compared to where I came from. There were only a few vehicles, mostly trucks, on the road. Can't say as I remember anything suspicious, certainly not anyone who seemed to be tailing me or watching too intently. Don't know how they'd recognize me, anyway, since I'm not driving my own vehicle and the windows are all tinted."

"Not the windshield," he said. "That'd be illegal in this state."

"True, but I honestly didn't notice anybody in particular. Just a bunch of hats—cowboy hats and gimme caps—on drivers. And half of them were wearing sunglasses to cut the glare."

"Well, *that* narrows it down," he said irritably. "You've just described ninety percent of the people on the road around here."

She shrugged. "Doesn't matter, anyway. It's just a stupid anonymous threat. Believe me, I've seen plenty of them as a reporter. Happens every time I start making people nervous."

"Well, *this* one makes me nervous," he said, knowing it had bothered her, too, far more than she was saying. "You were shot last time you came here."

"Believe me, I'm not likely to forget that," she said, heartbreak shadowing her gaze. But a moment later, she recovered. "You have to understand, this kind of thing's gotten so common in news reporting. The station consulted with some expert in assessing the seriousness of the messages. He'd probably rate this one a yellow, at best. It's not serious."

"So you're just going to ignore it?"

"When you were in the Afghan theater," she asked, "did you marines pack up and go home every time the enemy tried to scare you off with anonymous threats?"

"Hell, no, but that was war," he reminded her.

"This isn't so much different," she said. "Only I expect there might be fewer people shooting at me here. And Gretel's got my back."

"Gretel can't stop bullets."

"A good attack dog can take a man down faster than he can pull the trigger. And Gretel here's the best."

Zach couldn't help but smile, admiring Jessie's bluster. She had to be scared as hell, but she clearly wasn't backing down. Or letting him believe she would. But despite the tough-girl attitude, he'd already seen the real

Jessie. The one who had been scared sick to think she might be going home with a collection of bones rather than a troubled sister.

"I hope you're right about this," he said before somewhere behind him, a shrill voice called his name. Turning to look, he spotted his mama hurrying his way, her thin arms crossed to wrap herself more tightly in the light sweater she had thrown on to come outside. Aside from the occasional errand and her weekly hair appointments, she mostly confined herself to indoors, preferring to call his cell phone or send someone to find him when she needed something.

What had happened at the house that she would run out here looking for him?

"Mama?" he asked, leaving Jessie to stride toward his mother. "What is it? What's the matter?"

"Nothing's *wrong,* my dear," she said, fingering her hair to check its arrangement. She smiled at Jessie, who was waiting politely out of earshot, while speaking quietly through clenched jaws. "Why should anything be wrong?"

Because something's been wrong ever since Ian died last summer...and Eden turned up on this ranch.

"I just heard we had a guest, that's all," she said, peering around him to beam at Jessie. "Why don't you invite your friend inside, dear? Surely, we can offer better entertainment than that dirty old *barn.*" Though his mother liked the lifestyle afforded by the family's oil and cattle, she had never been a big fan of the sweat and grime that went with either venture.

Zach gave her a long look, uncertain what to say. Because he realized she was far more interested in gathering information than she was in playing hostess, finding out what Haley Layton's sister really knew.

And he was afraid that he knew why, or at least part of the reason. The part he could only guess at scared him most of all.

"Jessie needed a phone number, that's all," he said. "I'm sending her over to stay at the Hunter house if Margie has a room open."

Shivering with cold, his mother asked, "So Miss Layton's in town for an extended stay, then?"

"I didn't ask," he said before risking, "Guess it all depends on how long it takes to find her sister."

At his mother's stricken look, he added, "Here you go, Mama. You're cold." He stripped off his own coat and draped it over her shoulders. "You shouldn't be out in just a sweater. You know how this wind cuts through you."

"I don't need that," she insisted, thrusting it back to him with ice-cold hands and hurrying toward Jessie before he could stop her.

"Miss Layton," she said, bussing the reporter on the cheek as if she were an old friend rather than an unwelcome intruder, "I'm so sorry you've had to return to a place that must hold such terrible memories for you. Why don't you come inside, please? I'll have Althea make fresh coffee. Or there's tea if you'd rather, even hot chocolate if you have a sweet tooth. Althea bakes the loveliest little cookies, too. I just know you'd enjoy them."

Zach ground his jaw, but before he could think of any way to discourage Jessie from accepting, she was smiling at his mother.

"Thank you, Mrs. Rayford," she said. "That's very kind of you. I think perhaps a little tea would be just the thing to settle my stomach. I've had a bit of an upset, I'm afraid, seeing where—where everything happened in November."

"Oh, you poor thing," his mother crooned. "Please, come inside, where you can—"

"Maybe you'd be better off getting to your room at Margie's so you can rest up for tomorrow," he told Jessie, prompting his mother to smite him with what he and Ian had called *The Look* when they were boys. It was, the way his brother told it, her only superpower, far more effective than their father's kicks and punches.

Too damned bad it hadn't worked on his old man, as well, though at least he had never physically hurt her, to Zach's knowledge. His father's constant putdowns and browbeating, however, were another source of battering. Not that Zach or Ian had ever been able to get her to admit it.

"Zach," his mama said, giving him a warning frown, "you heard the young lady. She'd like a little tea, and a kind word wouldn't go amiss, either, I'm sure. Now why don't you show her to the living room, while I ask Althea if she'll get a tray ready and make sure that Eden and the puppies stay occupied for a while."

Without waiting for an answer, she bustled toward the house, moving with a speed and confidence that Zach hadn't seen from her in years.

Clearly, she had an agenda. Probably to find out what Jessie knew or had guessed about Eden. His heart pounded a warning, his own blood rushing in his ears. Did his mother really believe her clumsy attempts could fool an experienced reporter, someone who'd spent years drawing information from the unsuspecting?

Jessie looked at him uncertainly. "What about Gretel? She usually comes everywhere with me, but I don't imagine your mother would understand that. And I definitely don't want to scare the little girl."

Desperate not to give away his nervousness, he

grinned, "What? You don't figure that my mama or Althea are gonna jump you over cookies? Or Eden, maybe,
with her attack puppies?"

Jessie smiled. "Puppies, huh? I'm not worried about
Gretel's training, but if you don't mind, I'll leave her in
the barn, maybe in your office?"

"That's fine," he said, and once they'd put away the
dog with a bowl of water, they both headed for the house.

"Come to think of it," he said, "that's where I left Margie's number, anyway. Haven't gotten around to program-
ming it into my new phone."

Inside the house, Jessie asked to wash up, giving him
a chance to whisper to his mother as they waited in the
living room. "I know what you're doing, Mama, and it's
a very bad idea." Bad in more ways than one, just as he
was beginning to feel about what he was doing. But how
could he know what was right, not only for his family
but especially for Eden, when he didn't understand the
situation?

A look of alarm, of fear, crossed her face, but she
quickly mastered her expression. "I have no idea what
you're talking about." She sniffed. "You act almost as
if— Why, that young woman deserves our sympathy
after everything she's been through."

"That's not the tune you were singing last time she
showed up here." He couldn't believe how crafty his
mother was.

"I was taken by surprise, that's all. I had no idea Haley
had any family, much less a twin sister. But this Jessica's
a better sort. Anyone could see that."

"You won't think that when she tears into you. She's
a reporter, Mama, with a reporter's instincts and a personal agenda." *Just like you.* "If you're hiding any secrets,
I promise you, she'll know it."

"You're being ridiculous," she argued. "What could I possibly have to hide?"

"Your *granddaughter,* Eden." He dropped his chin to look straight down into his mother's widening eyes. "If Eden Rayford is really the girl's name."

Chapter 11

After splashing water on her face and straightening her wind-whipped hair as best she could, Jessie took a deep breath and told herself, "Three, two, one—game face," before clapping on her most camera-ready expression.

Or trying, anyway, she thought, frowning at her reddened eyes and washed-out complexion. But she'd done her job in the past while sick, angry and even on one regrettable occasion after her breakup with her boyfriend, when she'd been seriously hungover. Pulling a tube of lipstick from her jeans, she tried to pump herself up, saying, "Fake it till you make it, baby."

On second thought, today called for a brand-new mantra. *Rock 'em till you shock 'em.* Because she sensed that, unlike her son, Nancy Rayford would spill her secrets with the right questions. Zach must know it, too, thought Jessie, considering his attempt to send her away rather than letting her visit with his mother. Jessie took it as a sign she'd better milk this opportunity for all it was worth.

The trouble was, Zach was no less protective toward his mother than Gretel was of Jessie. Maybe she ought to remind him of the disaster that had unfolded the last time he took loyalty too far.

Really bad idea, she realized, instinct warning her that if she brought up the loss of his wings and the reason for it, he'd shut her down fast and hard, and there would go her last hope of any help from him.

When she walked into the living room, the hornets' buzz of their conversation instantly went silent, and mother and son stepped apart. Neither one looked happy with the other, but Nancy Rayford was quicker to put on her own version of the game face, even if it looked a little plasticized.

"Please, dear, have a seat," she invited, gesturing like a game show hostess toward a cream-colored sofa with a subtle floral design. Along with the complementary chairs and coffee table, it was grouped around an expensive-looking Oriental rug in front of a beautiful stone fireplace. "I'm sure Althea will be here any minute."

"Why don't you go check on her?" Zach suggested. "I'll stay and keep Miss Layton company."

Another look passed between the two, her stubborn blue-eyed frown clattering off his subtler warning. Jessie wondered what on earth their argument could be about.

Ignoring her son, Mrs. Rayford claimed a wing-back chair. Jessie hoped for her sake it was more comfortable than the stiff fabric of the sofa.

"Your home is lovely," she said, eying a pair of beautiful—and fragile—ceramic figurines, a graceful pair of ballet dancers, male and female. "Did you do the decorating yourself?"

The older woman beamed with pleasure. "Why, thank you. Yes, I did. How could you tell?"

Jessie smiled back. Though the decor was fussy and on the old-fashioned side for her taste, she said, "It's as warm and welcoming as you are. And so neat, too. I never would've guessed you have a small child living here. Or puppies, either, from what I'm hearing."

The older woman flushed, then darted a frightened glance toward Zach. An instant later, she waved off the compliment. "Oh, dear, you clearly haven't seen the playroom. If I ever teach that child to pick up one set of toys before dragging out another, I should be considered for a Nobel Peace Prize."

Jessie smiled politely, wondering what exactly had triggered the obvious discomfort? Surely, not the mention of the puppies….

Zach's words popped into her mind, something he'd said earlier about Eden. *I figure that tiny little handful of spunk and attitude's the only thing that's keeping her afloat.*

She remembered the pain in his blue eyes when he had said it, a pain so deep that she had rushed to change the subject instead of digging for details.

"Has she always lived with you?" she probed. "Your granddaughter, I mean. She's just adorable."

Zach opened his mouth to answer, but his mother beat him to it.

"She's— Yes, Eden's always lived h-here," Nancy Rayford stammered. "Since shortly after her birth. With my son stationed overseas, it was the best solution."

"Mother, are you all right?" Zach interjected before Jessie could think of how to ask about what had happened to the child's mother. "You're so pale. It isn't another headache, is it? If you'd like, I can help you up to your—"

"I'm fine," his mother said, annoyance prickling in the two words. "Please don't interrupt, dear."

Zach sat back stiffly on the sofa, his hands interlaced, his tension a palpable presence. Jessie could almost hear him willing the poor woman to go to her room and quit talking. But why? What was the issue?

Something about the child, thought Jessie. Perhaps she'd been born out of wedlock? But that would only explain his mother's discomfort. A man close to her own age, a man who'd seen the world as Zach had, surely wouldn't be bothered about such a detail. And heaven only knew Jessie couldn't care less.

Unless...

"I was wondering, Miss Layton," Zach's mother said, as if she'd read the direction of Jessie's thoughts, "have you learned any more about your sister?"

Jessie shook her head. "I've hired a detective to help, but there's no sign of either Haley or Frank McFarland anywhere. Not a single trace."

"But then, there wouldn't be, would there, dear?" asked Mrs. Rayford. "Those two were rather adept at living off the grid."

"I imagine they'd have to be," Jessie admitted, thinking there were probably a slew of creditors who would be eager to find either one or both, and that wasn't counting any possible outstanding warrants. "But there is one new thing I found out. Every month, like clockwork, Haley found a way to visit Marston to withdraw money from the little bank there, a small stipend my mother was depositing into an account for her."

Her mother had been very ill, coughing continually with her pneumonia, when she had finally broken down and confessed about the tiny little bank in Marston. Jessie could still feel her squeezing her hand, tears in her eyes as she'd said, "No matter what your father said, I've never completely given up on Haley. She's my blood, my child. How could I possibly sleep nights worrying that she was going hungry?"

"I was told there hasn't been a withdrawal made since this past August," Jessie continued somberly. "Before then, the money had been taken out within days, sometimes hours, of its arrival. She had to have been living on it, especially since it looks like neither one of them was working."

"I do know that Frankie picked up the odd job now and again," Mrs. Rayford put in. "Always under the table."

Jessie filed away this bit of information, thinking it would make the man even harder to track down. *If* she could find some way to convince law enforcement to show more of an interest in this case than Canter had thus far.

She would need the bones for that. Or at least her source's sworn statement they were human, stomach-turning as the thought was.

"I hope you find her somewhere safe soon," Nancy Rayford said soothingly. "Maybe she went to a women's shelter. Or who knows? She might be in some nice hospital getting help with all her troubles."

As suggestions went, those were kindly meant, Jessie thought. Certainly a lot less brutal than her own suspicions about her sister's fate.

"So when my sister and Frankie left the bunkhouse," she asked Mrs. Rayford, "did you find anything they left behind? Belongings? Papers? Anything at all?"

"I'm told there wasn't much left," the older woman

answered, tensing at the question. "Just trash, mostly, a few broken items or pieces of soiled clothing."

Finally joining the conversation, Zach asked his mother, "Who was it you asked to clean it up?"

"I'm not sure who did the work, exactly." His mother shook her head. "I just asked Virgil to see that it was taken care of."

"Virgil Straughn's our ranch foreman," Zach explained to Jessie. "Been with the family for what, Mama? Maybe thirty, thirty-five years."

His mother smiled and relaxed again, a faraway look coming into her eyes. "Do you remember how he used to let you boys ride around on his shoulders and Ian used to call him Giddy Yup?"

Grief hazed her expression, and she lifted the glasses she was wearing to wipe at her eyes.

"All that hauling us around as kids, it's no wonder he's so stove up," Zach said. "I notice he's not half as limber when he stoops to pick up Eden these days."

"Why, he's just a little out of practice, that's all," his mother defended. "He hasn't been around a little child in years and years."

Jessie's pulse leaped at the woman's slip—her clear contradiction of her earlier claim that Eden had been on the ranch for years. Before Jessie could say anything, Zach jerked to his feet abruptly. So abruptly that Jessie knew he'd heard the same thing she had. Not only heard it, but was eager to cover for his mother by creating a distraction.

"There's Miss Althea," he said a little too quickly and too loudly. "Could I give you a hand with that?"

Jessie followed his gaze to the sturdily built, gray-haired woman who was bringing in an old-fashioned tea cart.

"If you really mean it," the cook said. "I have Eden in

the kitchen, and she'll be feeding those puppies tonight's dinner if I don't keep an eye on her."

"Go ahead," he said. "I've got this. It'll give me a chance to impress our guest here with my manly tea-pouring skills."

When his blue eyes turned to her, Jessie thought, *So that's what he's doing. Flirting with me just to keep me off balance.*

As Althea hurried away, Jessie looked from Nancy Rayford to Zach, whose big, work-roughened hands poured and served his mother first, without a single drop spilled.

"You're a man of unexpected talents," Jessie told him, playing along as she sipped from a cup that felt as fragile as a moth's wing. "I'm beginning to wonder, though, do all of them revolve around caffeine?"

As his mother added cream and sugar to her own cup, he leaned close to pass Jessie a plate of delicate cookies, murmuring, "Not by half, Miss Layton." His hushed tones and the wicked glint in his blue eyes giving the words a razor's edge.

An edge that knifed through grief and worry and at least ten months of sexual frustration. With a sharp indrawn breath, she looked away, warning herself not to fall for his ruse.

But when she risked glancing back at him again, he winked and said, "Tea must be agreeing with you, Miss Layton. It's definitely put the color back in your cheeks."

So she was blushing, she thought, narrowing her eyes at his comment. Because *he* was the one who ought to be embarrassed, if he thought for one moment he was going to throw her off guard.

Or keep her from ferreting out the reason he was covering for his mother's lie.

* * *

No sooner had Jessie collected her dog and headed for Margie Hunter's place than Zach turned on his mama.

She was ready for him, one trembling hand raised as if she might hold back the coming storm. "Please, Zach. I've had enough trouble and upset for one day."

"Then why on God's green earth did you invite her in for tea?"

"I was just trying to comfort the poor girl," she said, turning toward the stairwell with the clear intent of fleeing to her room.

Escaping was a strategy that had worked for her all too often. But too much was at stake here to let her play on his sympathy and concern, on his guilt for taking at least a decade longer than he should have to live up to his responsibilities.

"Don't give me that, Mama. You were fishing for information, but you ended up getting caught on your own hook."

"I—I have no idea what you mean. You're talking crazy." Paling, she swayed a little, grasping the banister as if she might fall at any moment. Though he prepared himself to catch her if necessary, he resisted the temptation to steady her and guide her upstairs to rest before dinner. He'd had enough of her manipulation, even if she was his mother.

"It all goes back to your lying about Eden," he said bluntly. "You've been lying all along."

Her blue eyes welled, and she swung around, sinking down to sit on a step. Hunched over as she was, she hid her face from his view. Her shoulders shook, making her look so pitiful, so tiny, that his instinctive need to protect her nearly had him caving. For Eden's sake, he made himself sit down on the step beside her, his strong thigh so close to her thin leg that she flinched away.

"Want to tell me all about it?" he asked more gently. "The real story, this time?"

She shook her head emphatically. "It's all legal. Eden's mine. You've seen the paperwork."

"I've seen some paperwork," he allowed. "But if the names are falsified, there's nothing legal about the guardianship. You know that."

She pressed her lips together, refusing to look at him.

"There's no Lila Germaine, is there? No mystery girl-friend who Ian never mentioned to us, no child he kept hidden and didn't bother to provide for?"

"He—he was like you. He didn't talk to me. He blamed me for not protecting you both from—" Her voice was still defiant, but her eyes begged for understanding. "Your father was raised so hard. He didn't know any other way to— He thought he was making men of you, and I couldn't… I was too weak…"

Zach banked his growing anger, appreciating for the first time that his mother's "weakness" was an excuse. A survival strategy. But at this moment it was also a method of manipulation. One he couldn't allow to get inside his head.

"Ian and I kept in touch," he told her. "Not as often as we would've liked. Whenever our assignments allowed for it, we tried to see each other. And we always touched base on birthdays and at Christmas, at least to leave messages."

"I'm so glad," she said. "Glad you had one another."

Zach grimaced, wishing that he'd made more of an effort with Ian. But there would be no more chances to amend that now. "The thing is, Mama, he would've told me about Eden. I'm sure of it."

Her gaze wandered as she considered. "Perhaps Lila

lied to me about him knowing. What if she never told him? She did say they'd already broken up by the time she learned she was expecting."

Losing patience…and sympathy…he said, "Stop. Now. Tweaking your story to make it fit the current known facts doesn't make it any less a lie."

Rising, she cried, "Why are you being so *mean* to me? Is it to punish me because of your father? Because if it that's the way you feel—"

He stood as well, saying, "It's not what I feel, Mama, it's what I *see* that's the problem. And I'd have to be stone blind not to realize that Eden has the exact same green eyes as her aunt."

"Lots of people have green eyes. And Eden doesn't have that reddish-blond hair."

Thinking of his niece's golden-brown waves, he shook his head. "Could be she gets that from her father, whoever he is. Frankie McFarland, maybe? Or another one of Haley Layton's bad-news boyfriends?"

"No, Zach. Please," his mother cried, tears spilling down her thin face. "She's Ian's. Can't you see it? In her nose, her hairline. She has the same widow's peak—just look."

"Ian wouldn't have gone within ten miles of a hot mess like Haley Layton," he said. "He liked a worthy adversary, he always told me, a woman who could hold her own with him, whether it was in terms of his athletics, his career, or—"

"Why won't you believe me about Eden? Don't you love us?" she sobbed, ducking past him and practically running up the stairs.

Feeling as big a bully as his old man, Zach stared after her. For a moment, he thought of pursuing her, but he sensed that he'd get nothing more from her today.

As he turned away, he saw a flash of movement, the white tip of a fluffy tail. Lionheart's, he thought, and sure enough, he heard the clicking of two dogs' worth of nails on the marble. But not human footsteps, which made him instantly suspicious, since the puppies followed Eden everywhere unless they were confined.

Worried she might have overheard the conversation, he called her name, loudly enough that it echoed through the entryway. But Eden didn't answer, which had to mean...

"Damn," he muttered, rushing into the rarely used formal dining room, where he nearly tripped over the freshly chewed corner of one of his mama's favorite rugs.

"Eden!" he repeated, since she'd been told a hundred times not to play in either of the formals—especially when Sweetheart and Lionheart weren't kenneled. But instead of drawing the girl, both puppies bounded in, their fuzzy round butts wagging. They looked so ridiculous, bumping off and tripping over each other, that he grinned despite his mood.

"Okay, you two. Where's Eden? Where'd your girl go?" he asked, but instead of leading him anyplace, the puppies started jumping up and down and barking at him, staring with one set of brown eyes and one blue.

Until a faint rustling sound caught all of their attention. Before Zach could figure out where it was coming from, the pups bounded to the curtain of the nearby window. The dark curtain sporting a girl-size lump near the bottom.

In two strides, he was there, but unlike that day inside Nate's barn, this time Eden wasn't sleeping but sniffling and wiping at her wet face as she sat curled up in a tiny ball.

"Why'd you make Grandma so sad!" she shouted, scowling up with all the righteous fury that a four-year-old could muster. "You made her cry real hard, and anyway, I like the new name better."

"Better than what?" he repeated. "What was your name before?" He squatted down to make himself less intimidating.

She crossed her arms and pouted, her lower lip jutting in a show of pure stubbornness. Clearly, she'd inherited more from her aunt than just eye color.

"I'll tell Grandma I'm sorry," he said. "I promise, if you tell me."

"Eden Rayford's a good cowgirl name. Eden Elibbabeth, that's what my grandma made me practice. Only I don't haf to write the hard part until I get in second grade."

Elizabeth. He recognized the name of his late grandmother. And hadn't she come from a little town in Arkansas by the name of Eden Springs?

"What was your name before?" he repeated, speaking in the soft voice of secrets. "It's okay to tell me."

Her breath hitched, and a flood of tears came. She wrapped her trembling arms about the two pups, who'd come over to wash her face with their tongues. "You can't take them away!" she cried, as terrified as he had seen her after any of her nightmares. "You can't make me leave here and go back to that bad place! I won't tell you any secrets! I never, ever will!"

All he could bear to do was gather her up in his arms and promise her that everything would be okay.

On her way to Margie Hunter's house, Jessie had to pass through Rusted Spur. At a little after five in the afternoon, the town's streets were a bit more crowded than they had been the last time she had come through, with dozens, maybe scores, of vehicles clogging narrow streets. From the looks of things, most of the town's "rush hour" consisted of what looked like cowboys and oilfield workers, nearly all of them driving mud-caked pickups.

So it shouldn't have come as a surprise when she drew a lot of stares, rolling along the main drag in the pearl-white Cadillac. She'd never felt so conspicuous, coming to a four-way stop in a chromed-out vehicle that would have passed unnoticed in her mother's Dallas neighborhood.

On second thought, maybe it wasn't the SUV they were staring at but *her,* sitting high behind the wheel. Maybe because the few women she had spotted in the area tended to be older and on the plump side, still clinging to the big hair and shoulder pads of the eighties. But, she realized with a sinking feeling, it was equally possible that those double takes and long looks had more to do with the way the sun's last rays were striking her long, reddish-blond waves—a distinctive, natural shade she shared with her missing sister. A shade that glowed when the light caught it just right.

She should've pulled it back at least, or worn a hat to cover up. Instead, she was left feeling naked as she wondered, was the handsome, sandy-haired man walking to his parked truck wondering if Frankie McFarland's woman had suddenly come into money? Was the beefy red-faced man waiting at a four-way stop leering, or trying to disguise his shock at seeing a woman thought to have been dead for months? Worse yet was the suspicion that any one of them might have been the same person who'd sent her the threatening text. A message that had rattled her more than she'd let on.

The stares sent chills rippling through her, and she didn't dare to stop at the café, now crowded with more pickups, or the tiny grocery to pick up something to eat later. But then, she didn't have much in the way of appetite, with the cookies and tea she had managed churning in her stomach.

So instead, she left town as quickly as she could before heading straight to the Hunter place. The land soon opened up, revealing slightly rolling terrain dotted with grazing cattle, goats and horses. After passing a big barn with the Texas state flag painted on its roof, she reached her destination and slowed to take in a big white Victorian, a turreted three-story that must cost the world to maintain. With its inviting wraparound porch, twin upper balconies and miles of intricate gingerbread trim, the old house was the very picture of charm—a picture that she noticed, as she climbed out of her parked vehicle, was peeling a little in some places.

Several vehicles were parked alongside the house, indicating that at least a couple of other guests were on the premises.

As she parked and climbed out of the SUV, an older woman with sparkling blue eyes stepped down off the porch to meet her. Solidly built and pink-cheeked, the woman looked far heartier and more youthful than her snow-white hair might suggest. The thought reminded Jessie so sharply of her other mother, before she'd fallen ill, that it took away her breath for just a moment.

At Jessie's approach, the woman tilted her head, looking at her oddly.

"I'm Jessie Layton," Jessie told her, heeding the prickling awareness that this woman must have seen or spoken to her twin at one point. "Haley Layton's twin sister? Zach Rayford said he called you about me."

Recovering quickly, the woman said, "Zach's friend, yes. Welcome to my home, then, Jessie. I'm Margie Hunter, but call me Margie, please. After thirty-five years in the classroom, I've heard enough of *Mrs. Hunter! Mrs. Hunter—!*" she mimed a raised hand waving for attention "—to last me a couple of lifetimes."

"If you had Zach for a student, it's no wonder you were eager to retire." Jessie added her warmest smile, wanting the woman to know that she was teasing.

"Oh, that boy and his brother both could put me through my paces," Margie said, waving off Jessie's words, "but they were both good kids at heart. Anybody and everybody but that father of theirs could see that." Frowning at some memory, the older woman quickly brushed it off. "Could I help you with your bags?"

Jessie shook her head. "I've got this. It's not heavy. But thank you, and thanks so much for letting me come on such short notice. And for letting me bring my dog along. I can promise you my Gretel won't be any trouble."

She called the Rottweiler, who jumped down from the open door, her stub tail wagging, her manner friendly but polite as she was directed.

"Don't worry. She'll fit right in with my three," Margie said, her expression melting into a warm smile. "I'm a sucker for fur babies. I'd drag them all home if I could."

Jessie gave Gretel the release command, freeing her to enjoy an ear scratch and a few moments of sweet talk. Afterward, Margie showed Jessie the house, which was decorated with a homey mix of well-loved antiques and comfortable newer pieces. Three little red dachshunds shadowed their every step—after Margie shushed them for barking ferociously at Gretel, who steadfastly ignored them.

"It's so welcoming. I love it," Jessie told her. "If I had the time, I'd spend all day on the front porch curled up with a book. And maybe one of those cute little doxies on my lap, too, if they'd let me." The moment the words were out, she shivered, taken aback that she'd feel so at home anywhere in this town of secrets, lies and murder.

Margie smiled at her, clearly not noticing her change of mood. "A girl after my own heart. And I assure you, the barking brigade would be all for it."

Gesturing toward the kitchen, she said, "I serve breakfast at eight-thirty and other meals by arrangement if you need 'em. Cooking's nothing fancy, and I'm not the place to go for any fussy special orders. But so far, nobody's starved here or called the health department."

"Works for me," said Jessie, warming to this unassuming and plainspoken woman more than ever. And realizing that the former teacher might prove a valuable source of information on this town and the people in it. Including the Rayfords, if she played her cards right.

"I was wondering," she said, "if you might've known my sister when she was staying in town."

"Haley, you said?" the woman asked.

"My twin, yes. I'm looking for her."

"Can't say as I knew Haley, but I must've seen her around town at some point. Maybe that's why you looked a bit familiar." Margie shrugged and went on without taking a breath. "Now, in about an hour, I'll have chicken 'n' dumplings with green beans and fried okra on the table. There's plenty to go around, if you care to join us."

Jessie wondered, was she being paranoid, thinking that Margie had been awfully quick to change the subject? Or had Jessie's conversation with Zach and his mother left her attuned to avoidance? Whichever the case, she politely declined the offer and was soon shown to a small second-story bedroom and provided with an old quilt especially for Gretel's use.

After Margie left to attend her cooking, Jessie fed the dog and took her outside. Before she could come back in, though, the Rottweiler went on alert, her teeth bared and her growl a low rumble.

Turning, Jessie took in a tanned and handsome jeans-clad man about her own age, holding a covered cake plate in both hands. "Pardon me, Miss Layton. I'd tip my hat, but if I drop my mama's apple-pecan cake, she 'n' Margie'll have to flip a coin to see who gets to tack my hide to her barn wall. It's tonight's dessert, I understand."

Marking his use of her name, Jessie gave Gretel the command to remain watchful but quiet. "Do I know you?"

"Sorry. No. I'm Nate. Nate Wheeler, friend of Zach Rayford's. I'd offer you a hand, but…"

"Your hide on a barn wall. Got it," she said.

"Zach told me all about your… What happened at the bunkhouse. Just wanted to tell you, I'm sorry about your friend, and I—"

"Did you know my sister, Mr. Wheeler?" she asked, thinking that he'd recognized her awfully quickly. .

He nodded, telling her, "I knew the family—her and Frankie, anyway—enough to say hello. Not well or anything, but it's a small town. You tend to run into people, and I've been around most of the past year trying to get back in shape for the circuit."

At her puzzled headshake, he elaborated. "Pro rodeo. I'm a bull rider—though just lately, my back and those bulls haven't been on the best of terms."

"Sorry to hear it," she said. "But about my sister—"

"Let me take this cake inside. Then we can talk out on the side porch."

"I'll get the door for you," she said, her heartbeat racing as she fought to disguise her excitement. Because, just as Nancy Rayford had slipped up not an hour earlier, so had this man.

I knew the family, he'd said. Not *couple.* The words pulsing through her brain, she stifled a loud gasp, her mind filling will a pair of green eyes she'd seen earlier today.

A pair of green eyes that confused, excited and terrified her all at once.

Chapter 12

From the time he'd been old enough to sling a bucket of grain or muck out a dirty stall, Zach had been an early riser. His days as a marine corps pilot had only reinforced the habit, so that even after a nearly sleepless night, he was up and around by his usual five a.m. the next morning, meaning to head out to his barn office and crunch some more numbers to convince Virgil the switch to a cow-calf operation would be a smarter, more efficient way of doing business. Not that the long-time ranch manager had much interest in the opinions of some Johnny-come-lately who'd turned his back on his heritage until fate—and a Kabul disaster—had finally dragged him back.

Though Zach had listened to the more experienced man's objections, most of Virgil's "Grand Rayford Tradition" talk had boiled down to nothing but "This is the way we've always done it." But judging from the past few years' worth of figures, that way hadn't been cutting it in quite some time.

A lot of men in Zach's position might have ignored the recent drought's high toll on the cattle business, especially since the oil revenues had more than made up for the loss. But if he'd learned one thing from his old man—other than the necessity of a good escape route—it was that both beef and oil prices fell as often as they rose, bankrupting a lot of good people in the process. Including old families like his, more and more of which had sold off or broken apart their massive holdings over the past few decades.

Though as recently as a couple of years ago, he'd have said he didn't give a damn whether the place fell to pieces and went to strangers, his father's death had given him pause and somehow the work itself, the grit and patience it required, had gotten under his skin. Or maybe it was the idea of passing it along to the next generation someday, of teaching Ian's daughter to be the land's caretaker, teaching her with gentle patience instead of harsh words and brutal blows.

The thought of the child who had breathed new life into his dying legacy hacked at him like a machete, and he wondered how he'd stand it, how he'd bear the burden of a life he'd never asked for, without her to blunt its harsher edges. And how he could possibly explain away his mother's failure to come clean from the start.

Not that she exactly had, as yet, he thought, wincing with the memory of how she'd claimed to be too ill and exhausted to come down to last night's dinner. But now, she knew that he knew, so it couldn't be much longer before he pried loose the whole story.

The problem was, once he had it from her, he'd have no choice other than to take the truth beyond the safe confines of the family mansion. To Jessie or George Canter? Zach broke out in a cold sweat at the thought.

Groggy and distracted, he took longer than usual to shower and dress, and he was tossing back his second shot of espresso when the phone started ringing. Not his cell, which he used almost exclusively, but the house phone, so he rushed to pick it up before it could wake his mother, who had rarely been known to get up earlier than eight.

To his surprise, however, she had already picked up and was speaking, her voice threadbare as it was shaky. "He's always out of the house by now, yes. Now, stop worrying and just tell me, what am I going to do? He *knows*."

"Knows what?" a gruff voice answered, male and aggravated.

Familiar, too, Zach thought, though he could not immediately place it. Virgil?

"He knows about Eden," his mother answered, fear tightening her voice like old guitar strings. "And what's more, he's been talking to that reporter again, that other Layton girl, her twin. What if the two of them put it all together and they take my baby from the only happy home she's ever known?"

My baby. Those two words pounded at Zach's temples in time to his surging pulse.

"You don't have to worry about the Layton woman," the gruff voice reassured his mother. But Zach was no longer certain it was the ranch foreman on the other end. Then who? He racked his brain for an answer before his mother shut it down cold.

"What do you mean, I don't have to worry? If she finds out somehow, if she even guesses, the Rayford name will end up smeared all over the news. I could go to jail, to prison for the rest of my life! Or maybe even worse, since this is Texas. I could even— I could be put to— They could send me to the death chamber."

Nausea hit Zach like a gut punch, and it was all he could do to keep from shouting. What the hell had his mother done? Had she stolen Eden rather than accepting the child who Haley Layton had voluntarily left in her care? Or could—and he could barely draw breath as the thought struck—could his gentle, fearful mother have killed the person whose bones he'd photographed?

"Nobody's putting you in prison, much less executing anybody," the gruff voice said. "I swear on my life. And I promise you, too, this Layton woman will be gone from here today, if I have anything to say about it. Either that, or she'll be spending the night inside my jail."

The barking broke in the frigid predawn silence, giving Jessie away. She should have figured Zach would take Eden's pets out first thing in the morning, should have remembered that even puppies were capable of sounding the alarm.

Too well trained to respond in kind, her own dog remained silent as a shadow at her side.

"Who's there?" Zach called, swinging a flashlight's beam to illuminate the spot where she was standing, not far from the entrance to the barn.

"It's me, Jessie," she said over the pups' racket. "I was having trouble sleeping—" mostly because of a second, even more frightening, anonymous text she'd received at three a.m. "—and I figured anybody who takes his coffee strong as yours might be, too. Besides, don't all you farmers get up with the chickens?"

"*Ranchers.* I'm a rancher. We grow beef here, not beans and barley," he said irritably. "And what the hell're you doing sneaking around here, at this hour, without an invitation? But wait. Why should today be any different than any other time you've trespassed?" Glaring down at the puppies, he said, *"Quiet."*

The two balls of fluff fell silent but couldn't be still, bounding up and play-bowing toward Gretel. Head lowered, the Rottweiler gave a warning growl that sent them slinking off to hide behind the rancher's long legs.

"Get out from under my boots, you big babies," he scolded, but there was more exasperation than heat in his voice.

"I wasn't *sneaking around,*" she told him. "Like I said, I was waiting to see you."

He shook his head and then sighed. "Might as well come in, I guess. I'll get the coffee started. Then you can tell me what you came for that couldn't wait until the sun's up."

Once he had rolled back the large metal outer door, she followed him into the barn, where he put the two pups in a kennel with a bowl of kibble.

"This way, we can talk in peace," he explained, "though I expect you're bringing your monstrosity inside again."

"I was about to say how adorable your puppies are, but if you're going to call my sweet Gretel names…"

"If that dog has a sweet side, I sure as hell haven't seen it."

"You're really grumpy before caffeine, you know it?" If he thought he was in a bad mood now, wait till she hammered him with what she'd figured out last night.

"The caffeine's not the problem. I've already had two cups."

She threw up her hands. "What do you have, an IV drip by your bedside?" Light as her tone was, an image of Zach, in bed, stole into her thoughts. And she would bet her bottom dollar he wasn't the kind to wear pajamas. She winced, reminding herself that the last thing she should be thinking of was his naked body.

Judging from his smile, he didn't notice. "That'd be a real timesaver, but I think I'd miss making it myself."

Inside his office, he washed his hands and started up his espresso machine before pulling out a small bag of beans, which he measured carefully and ground.

"I'm really not that picky," she said. "Just plain old instant would've been fine."

"I'm going to pretend you never said that," he said, and went back to the precise moves she found so fascinating to watch.

She found it oddly sexy, the idea of such raw power tempered to create something for her enjoyment. Would he be as painstaking, as thoughtful, as a lover? The question sent fresh heat rushing to her face, rising like the fragrant steam off the espresso.

As hard as she was trying to keep her mind out of his bedroom, her thoughts relentlessly dragged her back there, leaving her wondering what it might be like to see those blue eyes staring down into hers. To run her fingers through the shiny black hair, or slide her palms over the roughness of his dark, unshaven jaw…

She jerked her gaze away, telling herself it was only lack of sleep that had her brain skidding off the rails. Lack of sleep and stress, coupled with the memory of him lifting her into his arms and telling her to close her eyes before he'd carried her past Henry's body. He had stanched her bleeding, too, wrapping her hand after calling an ambulance to come and help her.

That was when it hit her. "I never thanked you, did I?"

He took a seat near hers, passing her the cup.

"For this? There's no need."

She shook her head. "For finding me, that night in the bunkhouse, when you'd already been injured in your truck. For saving my life."

He shrugged. "That might be overstating it, don't you think? You had your car, a phone."

"I was in shock when you showed up. I'd already passed out once, and my old cell had no signal. I would have bled to death there, would have left my mother all alone. Thank you for that," she said, and meant it. "And thank you for being so kind about Henry."

"I warned you before, don't mistake me for a kind man."

"I've seen you with your mother and with the little girl, too, so I'm afraid your secret's out."

"They're family. That's different. I protect my own."

She speared him with a look. "Even when they're not yours, really? Not Eden, at any rate."

He went very still: no questions, no denial, no emotions on display. But the reporter in her noted the way his blue eyes dilated slightly and a vein pulsed, creating a flutter at his forehead.

"Whatever you're trying to say, just come on out and say it," he said flatly. "So I can get on with my day."

Her own blood surging, she said, "Let's all stop pretending, please, Zach. Because I know, and it's obvious to me that you do, too. Eden's not a Rayford—in spite of what you've told me."

He banged his cup down so hard, half of the espresso sloshed onto the top of his desk. "I haven't lied to you. Not once."

Heart racing, she burst out, "That's garbage and you know it. You sat and listened to your mother tell me Eden's lived here nearly all her life. And you said nothing, not a single word, to correct the statement. And a lie of omission's just as bad as—"

"What the hell would you have me do?" He threw up his hands. "Make out my own mama to be a liar before I even had the facts myself? You forget, I've only been back for a few months."

"Did you come before or after Eden? If that's really even her name."

"That child—that little girl's my mama's *life*. You understand that?" He came to his feet so suddenly that there was a flash of black and tan and white as Gretel leaped between them, showing him her teeth.

Jessie gave a hand signal, and the dog lay down beside her, where she was told, *"Bleib,"* to stay in place. Because as angry and upset as Zach appeared, Jessie didn't fear him.

Maybe it was because she recognized the struggle behind the bluster, along with the pain and fear that had provoked it. How could she blame him? In his shoes, she knew she might have felt the same way.

"After Ian— After Mama got word of my brother's death, I took leave and came home, quick as I could." He sighed. "I barely recognized her. She was all but catatonic. She wouldn't eat or drink or *move,* and she barely reacted to my presence even though I hadn't seen her in years. Some stupid grudge over what happened with my old man, before you ask. But when I saw how thin, how worn down, she'd gotten, I finally realized what a damned cruel thing I'd done, not reaching out to her in all that time. And I was scared to death I'd lose her before we had the chance to make things right."

Jessie pressed her lips together, trying to hold on to the fury that had kept her awake much of the night. But part of her couldn't help feeling compassion for the abused and angry boy who had returned a grieving man. A man mature enough to acknowledge his own role in a family torn apart by violence. A man who cared about his frail mother, just as she'd cared about hers.

Not that that excused either of the Rayfords' actions, but it did help to explain his.

"When they offered me the discharge," he said, "that's when I knew I had to head to California, muster out and pack up a few things. I wasn't happy pushing papers, anyway, and you and I both know, there was no way I was ever getting to fly again, not with all the publicity."

"But what happened in Kabul wasn't really your fault, was it? In spite of the early reports, you weren't really the one who caused the—"

"I might not have been the one to bump *his* wing, but it was never about what I did, not to anyone that mattered," he said, pain deepening the creases on his forehead. "It was what I failed to do. And what I let friendship blind me to, until it was too late."

"It wasn't a cover-up, then, was it? Not like that reporter—"

"One of the many 'facts' she got wrong. There was no cover-up, never even for a second. Just loyalty to a man I figured I could help on my own."

"I'm sorry," she said simply, going quiet as she imagined how terrifying it must have been, that moment when Marc Hernandez, a younger pilot Zach had taken out on a maneuver, had clipped Zach's wing before spiraling down out of control into an apartment building. The moments after, when Zach had somehow managed to steer his own jet toward the surrounding desert before ejecting, and watched helplessly as his fellow officer exploded in the fireball that had destroyed so many lives.

How much worse it must have made things to be publicly blamed for causing the crash—a crash later attributed to a substance abuse problem Hernandez had taken great pains to hide. No wonder Zach had such contempt for reporters. And here she was, trying to tear apart the new life he was building.

"When I came back home," he told her, "there was my mother, with this child of my brother's that neither of us had ever guessed existed. My mama gave me some story about a girlfriend, a woman who was overwhelmed and desperate, showing up out of the blue and handing Eden off. A wild, crazy story—but if you had seen my mother's eyes, all lit up, the life in them, the hope and purpose…"

He shrugged his impossibly broad shoulders, the fabric of his shirt pulled by the hard muscle. "Marines sent me to survival school, where they teach you that if a man's lost in the desert long enough, he'll walk ten miles just to get to a mirage. Sometimes, he'll even kill himself trying to drink down the illusion. Only in my case it wasn't hot sand, but a sweet, funny little kid who filled that big empty house with all her chatter. Unhappy as I was at first about getting stuck here to do my duty, it took me a little longer than my mama, but pretty soon, I fell in love with Eden, too."

Jessie felt a pang, deep inside. But she couldn't let compassion, along with an attraction she realized was more than physical, keep her from following through. Not until she had the whole truth—and maybe even the miracle she'd come here seeking….

Not the miracle she'd prayed she might find, she thought as her gaze sought out the grinning little girl in the frame on Zach's desk. But something as unexpected as a butterfly in winter.

"I can't believe I didn't see it the first time I set eyes on her," said Jessie. "The hair may be a little darker, but otherwise, it's like looking at my sister, back when Haley was her age."

"Like looking at yourself, you mean. That's when I first suspected, when you showed up the first time. Before then, you have to believe me, I had no idea. Zero."

The coffee suddenly bitter, she slammed her cup down, too, her sympathy abruptly morphing into anger. Coming to her feet, she paced the room like a caged wildcat. "And yet you never told me. You blame yourself for keeping your mouth shut about Hernandez? Well, *I* blame you for this. And so would any judge or jury."

He shook his head, his eyes pleading. "You have to understand. My mother showed me guardianship papers. They're notarized and everything. The woman signed away parental rights."

"*What* woman?" Jessie challenged, feeling lightheaded as the blood drained from her face. "Not my sister. Haley wouldn't have permanently given up her—"

He rose and stood in her path, stopping her in her tracks. "How would you know what she'd do? You didn't even know your sister *had* a child, much less how she felt about that. You had no idea what was going on with her, whether she was worried about her kid going hungry or if Frankie was pounding the snot out of them both every night. So don't be telling me what your sister would or wouldn't do. Because you have no idea."

"You're the one who has no idea," she argued, wanting to explain how clearly she had felt her sister, how she still sometimes imagined she could feel her even now. "So don't presume to tell me what I know or feel about my twin. And don't you dare use it to try to justify kidnapping."

"That's a hell of a harsh word," he warned. "Harsh

as *abandonment* and *neglect.* All I know is that we have the papers."

She opened her mouth to argue, feeling a stab of despair to realize he was right. "With my sister's name on them?"

"It wasn't her name," he admitted, his tone softening a little. "Or I'd have definitely told you. I swear I would've, Jessie."

"If it's not her name, then it can't be legal. For all we know, your mother forged the signature—or paid off someone to do it for her. While you knew and did nothing."

His gaze slanted down to study her eyes, and she fought to still her trembling, to quiet the sense of betrayal roiling inside her.

"I couldn't really admit it to myself until last night," he said. "Instead, I told myself a lot of people have green eyes, tens of thousands of 'em, maybe. I let Mama convince me, and Eden seems so happy—and so upset at the thought of leaving. Heaven only knows what that poor kid went through before she came here."

"Of course she's happy here." She blinked back threatening tears. "You've bribed her with puppies and a pony and heaven knows what else."

"It's not bribery. It's love. And I blame my friend Nate for the puppies."

She snorted, almost as angry at herself for beginning to trust him, to care for him, as she was at Zach. "I've met your friend Nate. Just last evening. You should've gotten your story straight with Mr. Rodeo if you hadn't wanted him tipping me off."

Zach swore under his breath. "This was no conspiracy. I swear it."

"Your mother lied to me about when Eden came here

for a reason, just like she freaked out when she saw me the first time. What Eden said when she saw me yesterday, telling me she wouldn't go with me—it all makes so much sense now. She was afraid I was her mom at first, come to take her back."

Though his eyes remained dry, grief passed across his handsome features, a bottomless heartache that made him hang his head. When finally he spoke, his voice was rough and raw with emotion. "I know," he admitted. "I heard and saw it, too. I swear, I saw the moment it sank in that you weren't her."

She took a step nearer, looking up at his face. And unable to keep herself from reacting to the misery etched in it. From feeling for the impossible situation he'd been put in, and the innocent child whose future was at stake. "So how are we going to handle all this?" Jessie asked him, her voice softening a little.

He shook his head. "Not with lawyers, *please.* My mama—she's never been strong. Not strong enough to stand up to my father's bullying and not strong enough to deal with his death, let alone her younger son's. She was a drowning woman, not even in her right mind, when that child showed up. For all we know, she's convinced herself that Eden's really a Rayford, that a part of Ian lives on through her."

Jessie raised her palms, and then, on impulse, laid them against his broad chest. Bandaged though her right hand was, she felt the pounding of his heart beneath it, the heat pouring off him, though the room was cool. And she ached to bury her face there, to comfort him as she accepted comfort. Resisting, she instead assured him, "I promise you, Zach, I'm not out to put your mama in a cage or tie us all up for years on end with a bunch of litigation. I know you don't think a whole lot of reporters, and I know you have good reason to suspect me. But I swear to you, I'm not that kind of person."

He studied her face, searching its depths for... something. Sincerity, perhaps, but between them, something else ignited, the spark of something far too dangerous to contemplate.

Or so she told herself, but with temptation arcing through her body, her eyes refused to obey. One glance at his lips, and it was too late to step back. Too late to do anything but tilt back her head when he whispered, "I believe you."

To do anything but part her lips when his mouth fell upon hers.

His taste was bittersweet: the mint of toothpaste mingled with the darker notes of coffee. But this sensation submerged completely beneath the unexpected pleasure, her every nerve ending flaring, awakening to his touch.

Some slim margin of her brain warned, this kiss, this passion, was too sudden and too needful, and flung at her like a net....

A net that he could use to save his family.

Swept up in the moment, though, she didn't struggle to get free, didn't make a sound to stop him. Her mind's warnings fell away, and she became aware of nothing else except the power of his embrace, the explorations of her own hands, the kiss that sent pure desire pulsing in parts of her that had gone wanting far too long.

Yet on the frayed edge of her awareness, she recognized the urgent trilling of her cell phone, a sound programmed to escalate the longer she ignored it. But not even that would have brought her to her senses, had Gretel, trained to think for herself rather than blindly obey, not come over and nudged her hard, then reached up to push her damp snout under Jessie's top.

"Yuck," she said. "Go lie down. *Platz!* And no more cold-nosing my stomach."

Looking chagrinned, the dog whined once before complying, and her call rolled to voice mail.

Zach cleared his throat. "Your dog clearly hates me."

"Gretel doesn't hate you. She's probably confused, that's all, wondering if you were attacking me."

"You mean, she thought we were *fighting?*"

"Oh, no. If you'd done something she's been taught to recognize—pulled a weapon, put your hands around my throat or struck me—she would've ripped your arm off."

He gave the dog a sidelong glance. "Is that supposed to reassure me?"

Jessie shook her head. "No. It shouldn't. Because this isn't a good idea, not on any level." Regret welled up inside her, a desperate wish to touch him again.

He turned his gaze directly to her, those blue eyes blazing. "Felt to me like a very good idea, Jessie, maybe the best one I've had in a long, long time. You didn't feel it, too? I thought you—I could've sworn you—"

I'm still feeling it, still wanting... "It doesn't matter what we both felt, not when you and I have such a huge conflict of interest. We don't even know if my sister's still alive, or if she's..." Her throat tightened. "I thought— for a moment, I could've sworn I felt her last night—"

"Felt Haley?"

"You'll probably laugh at this," she said, "but sometimes, we used to know things, things we shouldn't have. Back when we were just eight, I stayed home sick while a friend's mom picked up Haley and took her to a roller-skating party. A couple hours later, I started crying, telling her my arm hurt. I could hardly move the elbow. But it was Haley who had broken hers."

"Coincidence?"

"It happened other times, too. When *I* got poison ivy, *she* itched. When some creep broke her heart, I cried. And those last two years, before she ran off with another loser, it was so hard for me to stay on course. Her emotions were like a big tornado outbreak, slamming into me so hard that I had to run for cover to survive it."

His forehead creased, his gaze sympathetic. "How'd you manage that?"

"I distanced myself from her," she said quietly, "threw myself into my schoolwork and the debate club I'd joined. It was self-defense, that's all, pushing her away in an attempt to save myself from being smashed to pieces, but in the process, I lost the connection. And I lost my sister, too."

The old regret resurfaced, the idea that she should have fought harder for her twin. Should have found some way to make her dad lay off Haley, rather than trying to appease him by being the "good daughter." Not that he had ever praised Jessie to her face.

"Self-preservation's a hard-wired instinct," Zach said, as he gently touched her arm. "You have nothing to feel guilty for."

"Tell me that if it turns out my sister's—" She sucked a breath through her teeth. That call she'd missed. It might have been Andrew Pollard, from the body farm in Huntsville.

To Zach, she said, "Excuse me for a second. I need to see who called me."

Sure enough, when she looked at her cell, she saw the call had been from Dr. Pollard. Instead of calling back, she listened to the voice mail he'd left for her.

As the forensic anthropologist spoke, his words chewed through her strength like a strong acid. Her vision dissolved into blackness and her knees wobbled so severely that she might have fallen if Zach hadn't helped her to a chair.

Chapter 13

As Jessie let the phone sag, Zach squatted down beside her to take it out of her hand.

"Lean forward and put your head between your knees," he said. "Otherwise, you're going to pass out."

"I—I told you, I'm not the kind who faints. I was on the night beat. I saw e-everything, s-so much of it—"

"Just humor me, okay?" Was arguing her defense for everything?

"Forget it," she said, her fair skin flushing. "Go ahead. Replay the message. But put it on speakerphone this time."

He did, and they both listened to the recorded voice speak, *"This is Andrew Pollard, about those photographs you sent me. I know I told you I was backlogged, but I was thinking about our conversation, and it got me curious.*

"Before you put much stock in this, remember that without the actual specimen to test and measure, noth-

ing that I say would be admissible in court. There wasn't anything in the photos to give the sample scale, but I can tell you that the shape of the femoral head in photo three and pattern of heat fracture—from where the steam from boiling marrow creates its own escape route—has me convinced this is bone tissue. And the chunk of mandible in photo five leaves me no doubt it's an adult human.

"Get me more, Ms. Layton, and I may be able to determine race and gender. If you can get me properly handled samples, I might even—and here, I emphasize the word 'might,'*— be able to gather enough mitochondrial DNA to—"*

The message stopped abruptly, probably because the recording time had been exceeded.

"I was praying those were pork bones," Jessie whispered to Zach, "or beef or something like that. Anything but human."

"You're not the only one," Zach said, feeling as troubled as the reporter looked. "But we still can't say for sure it was your sister."

Taking a deep breath, she pushed herself up from the chair. "No, but we *will* get a positive ID. And she'll have a proper burial—if I have to go dig up Clem Elam's dump by hand."

Zach nodded grimly. "It could take months for us to find those bones, even if we knew for sure they buried the grill there."

Her gaze locked on to his. "You said *we*," she pointed out, "so does that mean you're finished interfering, no matter where the facts lead?"

He wanted to say, *Hell, no,* wanted to tell her there were certain lines that he could never cross, as he recalled his mother's terror in the call he'd overheard. A wave of paralyzing sickness washed over him at the thought that she might have somehow been involved in Haley Layton's murder. Was it possible? In her grief-stricken state, could she have seen a child in need, a child suffering the kind of abuse he and Ian had both endured, and done something—something terrible—to stop it from happening again?

"You're not answering," Jessie pointed out, "and I can see wheels turning in that head of yours. And I know you're thinking about *her*. Your mama."

He nodded and admitted, "I can't do anything to hurt her. But whatever's going on, whatever she and Canter both know, I can't just let something this big lie."

"Maybe she found Haley," Jessie suggested. "Found her abandoned after Frankie'd killed her. That makes sense, doesn't it? That your mother would take in a child she thought was an orphan? That she'd fall in love so quickly, especially after losing your brother, that she'd make up a new identity, a way to keep Eden for her own."

He let it sink in, trying it on for size until relief cascaded through him. "Yeah, that has to be it. It makes a lot more sense than anything else I've come up with. Except why would Canter know about it?"

"Maybe she called him when it happened. Could be they decided together to temporarily leave her with your mama. And then, when she got so attached…"

"Canter definitely has a soft spot for my mama," Zach agreed, "maybe a bit too soft."

Jessie's head tilted, her delicate reddish brows rising. "Surely, you don't mean there's some kind of— That's an awfully big age difference."

"Maybe not so much when the widow owns a big chunk of this county," he said, anger coiling low in his gut. "Especially when that chunk is about to see some serious new drilling."

"I thought you told me that the oil wasn't a big deal. Just a little something to help your cattle business."

"My mama always told me, a man ought not to brag on what he's got. But the truth is, if the geologists' predictions are on target, the ranch is about to be worth a whole lot more."

She thought about that for a moment. "Maybe that explains the way Canter's acting toward you. If his plan is to catch a widow, he can't be happy you've come home."

Zach shook his head. "There's no way. I can't see it. My mama and a big strapping sheriff in his forties?"

"Stranger things have happened," Jessie said. "Which means he can't be happy to have you back in the picture. I'd watch my back if I were you."

"Me?" he burst out. "You were the one shot. You're the one who ought to worry."

She opened her mouth to argue, but the dog interrupted, coming to her feet, growling. Bounding to the door, she looked to her mistress for instruction, every canine muscle tensed.

"Ruhig," Jessie whispered, quieting the animal before turning to look at Zach. "There's someone out here. I heard an engine. And do you smell something odd?"

"Don't set her loose. It's probably just Virgil talking with one of the cowboys," Zach warned, as Jessie went to the Rottweiler. "We usually meet here around this time for coffee, and I'd hate to get my foreman chewed up."

But outside, the puppies raised a fuss, their noise sounding more like true barking than the friendly yips they would use to beg attention from anyone they knew. He found Jessie's worried eyes at the same moment he identified the odor that she had—a smell that every barn or stable owner feared above all others.

"Fire!" he shouted, hearing a rumble like rolling thunder. "Hell—the horses! We have to get them out, now—all the animals."

He threw open the door and immediately sucked in a choking lungful reeking with the odor of gasoline. Cinders floated on the dark air, and flame lit the wall above the bin where the wood shavings they used for stall bedding were stored—shavings he knew instantly must have been intentionally soaked with fuel.

As they moved out, horses whinnied, instinct causing them to kick at their confines. The puppies' barks turned to yelps as they pawed frantically at the chain links of their kennel door.

"Look!" cried Jessie, gesturing toward the sound of thunder, the narrowing gap where the outer metal door was closing.

"Gretel, *Voraus!*" she shouted, followed by another, indecipherable command. The Rottweiler bolted past Zach, launching herself at the narrowing gap with a terrifying snarl.

A thud rattled the metal as the animal struck it, hitting the closed door hard enough to dent it. Undeterred by the collision, the animal ran around searching for another exit, her muscular body silhouetted by flame.

"It's up above us, too," Jessie cried, pointing toward the open hayloft—an insulated hatchway that was supposed to stay closed. Smoke was spilling from the opening, the pull-down staircase dangling halfway to the floor.

Zach ran to the door but could barely budge it. It scarcely opened an inch before it slammed hard into something. He tried several times to rattle it open, but there was no budging it.

"Jammed shut!" he shouted, knowing now for certain that the arsonist had meant to trap them inside.

"I've got the pups," Jessie called, bent low as she unlatched the kennel. The pups burst out, whining and cowering.

"Take them into the office," he yelled, coughing on the thickening smoke, "and see if you can break out one of the windows behind my desk and get out that way."

"Come with me," she pleaded. "We'll get outside and call for help."

"Be careful out there— Take your dog," he said, "and I'll meet you soon as I can. I have to get the horses out."

"Get them out *how?*" She panted as she spoke, checking the advancing flames with a terrified glance.

"Just get in there and get going," he said, pushing her toward the office. "And close the door behind you, or the fresh air from the windows'll blow this fire all to hell."

Heart punching at her breastbone, Jessie called to Gretel. The Rottweiler responded instantly, but it took several frantic moments for Jessie to coax, then drag the terrified pups into the office with them. Before she closed the door behind them, she searched the smoke for Zach, who had disappeared down the aisle where a dozen stalls faced each other.

Was there another exit back there? A way out for him and the horses?

All she saw was a silhouette, the faint suggestion of a figure moving. Praying for his safety, she closed herself inside the office with Gretel and the dogs.

Though the air was better inside, she soon saw she had her own problems. The windows behind Zach's desk were higher off the ground than she'd remembered, and their narrow height would make it a challenge getting the dogs and herself out. And what if they were waiting outside for her—the monsters who had set this fire?

The lights flickered and went out, plunging the room into a darkness broken only by the dawn-lit windows. A pair of small windows, each one barely tall enough for her to squeeze through, that now offered her sole chance of escape.

With no other choice, she knocked aside the chair, then shoved the desk against the wall, her strength fueled by the adrenaline pounding through her body. As she climbed up onto the desk's surface, she realized she would need the chair. The window was a single pane, not designed to open.

As all three canines milled about nervously below her, she swung the chair against the glass, only to have it bounce back, jarring her shoulder and sending fresh pain through her healing hand. But there was no time to worry whether she'd reinjured it. No option to do anything but clench the metal chair legs harder and try again.

With the third direct hit, cracks formed a spider's web in the glass. With the fourth, the window shattered, and the air rushed in, fresh and cold but welcome, though she was coughing as she pulled off her jacket.

Wrapping it around her arm, she knocked away the worst of the shards and looked to Gretel, then repeated her earlier command, *"Voraus!"* and stepped aside.

The Rottweiler clambered through the window, where she would range widely, searching for anyone who might be lurking. Where she would take down an armed man if she found one, waiting to pick off those emerging from the barn.

With Gretel gone, Jessie jumped down and collected the fuzzy blue-merle puppy.

"Sorry about this, cutie," she rasped as she shoved the struggling animal out the open window. The puppy yelped as it tumbled five feet, but immediately jumped up and started barking.

The larger male pup was a little tougher, since he had seen his sister's treatment and wanted no part of it. "Come on, boy," Jessie huffed, tiring as she cornered him before sending him after his littermate.

Next, she pushed herself through, gritting her teeth as a remaining shard of glass bit through her shirt. Taking a deep breath, she rolled out the window, slamming down hard enough to send the air exploding from her lungs with a noisy grunt.

Lying on her back, she looked up at the smoke darkening the dawn sky. In some places, an eerie glow broke through the blackness—fire breaking to curl around the edges of the structure's roof.

An awful chorus paralyzed her: the crackling and the hissing, the whining groan of burning timber. From inside, she heard the desperate neighs, a pounding and a gut-wrenching scream she feared might be a horse's.

What if it's Zach? He had seemed so certain of himself, so commanding when he'd given her instructions, that she'd more than half expected him to be here waiting when she got out. Instead, she felt his absence like a hollow in her heart.

Call for help, and get the door, she heard him tell her, in a voice so clear and present he might have been speaking right beside her instead of in her head.

The thought snapped her out of her daze, along with the licks and small nips of the two puppies and the twisting and popping of old lumber in the heat. Rising, she pulled out her phone and thanked her luck to find that she had enough of a signal to place a 9-1-1 call.

As she waited to connect, she coughed her way toward the front of the barn to reach the stuck door. At the corner, she froze for an instant, fear seizing in her chest at the thought of what—or whom—might be waiting for her. Waiting with another bullet, a bullet that would kill her this time.

Her brain flashed a reminder of Henry falling, bleeding, dying, a warning on his lips. It wasn't Henry, but Zach that she thought of now. Zach, who might be in there dying, just as the second anonymous text message had warned her.

WHICH IS WORSE, FACING YOUR OWN DEATH OR THE KNOWLEDGE YOU COULD GET ANOTHER GOOD MAN KILLED?

In her ear, a woman's voice spoke. "9-1-1 center. What is your emergency?"

"I'm at the Rayford Ranch off West Road," she said, flinching at the sound of a loud bang from inside the building. "The barn's on fire! There's a man trapped inside! Hurry, please!"

But she already knew that waiting for a fire truck was hopeless, as far from town as the ranch was. Terrified as she was, there was no one else around to help. So instead of answering the operator's questions, she shoved the phone into her pocket and forced herself to rush toward the rolling door, her frantic heart pulsing its way into her throat.

Between the dim light and the choking smoke, she didn't see it at first. But as she felt around, her kneecap struck the jutting end of a metal crowbar that had been used to block the mechanism. It stuck out at an angle, jamming the door against the frame near ground level. She knelt to grasp the end with both hands, ignoring the pain that made it feel as if the small bones of her injured right hand were twisting apart as she jerked and pulled for all she was worth.

At the sound of Gretel's deep bark, she glanced over her shoulder, some instinct making her duck her head—or maybe it was the whoosh of something solid swinging at her like a thick club.

What followed next was chaos, so fast and confused in the smoky darkness that she had little idea what was happening. Pain splashed across her vision in blue-hot bolts as a dark shape grabbed her hair and jerked her head back. The club rose over her skull, but everything was knocked aside as the Rottweiler slammed like a snarling twister into her attacker.

Thrown to the ground, Jessie crawled clear of the struggle. Barks, shouts and a rough curse ripped through the swirling smoke—all punctuated by a booming crack and Gretel's yelp of pain.

"No!" Jessie shrieked, rising with the intent of hurling herself at the gunman. But he was gone already, running amid several shouting voices, and moments later, a man's strong arms wrapped around her neck and shoulders and swung her back away from the door.

"Zach!" she cried, relief exploding through her terror. "He's got a gun! He's—"

"He took off! Leave him to Virgil and the others. I've got to get this door open for the horses!" he rasped, triggering a round of coughing.

"I thought you were trapped. How'd you get out?" she said, but he was too busy throwing his every bit of brawn against the crow bar to answer.

With a squealing noise, it finally pulled free, and he yelled at her. "Get out of the way!"

She stumbled back and, as he yanked open the door, a small herd stampeded out through the thick smoke.

Still too close for safety, Jessie took a step back, but one panicked animal abruptly wheeled around, slamming her hard with one huge shoulder.

The last thing she remembered was pitching sideways, followed by a sickening jolt of pain.

Chapter 14

Jessie's head was still pounding when she woke up, the light exploding in her eyes like shattering glass. She raised an arm to block it out, groaning with her body's stiffness, abruptly aware of where she still must be. But how had she gotten to this bedroom? Had Zach carried her here, just as he had carried her to safety before the roof of the barn collapsed?

She racked her brain searching for an answer, but couldn't recall anything beyond an EMT checking her over while an ash-coated but uninjured Zach went to help corral the frightened horses while volunteer firefighters worked to keep the blaze from spreading.

The EMT had urged her to let them load her in the ambulance to get checked out at the E.R. Though she was aching everywhere, she'd argued, she remembered, thinking how upset her mother would be to learn she was in the hospital again. Forgetting for a few merciful moments that her mother was no longer around to worry about her well-being.

Her other memories of the fire were no more than a swirl of smoke, hot ash and a jumble of emotion. She remembered her relief that Zach had safely escaped, her gratitude that Gretel had driven off her attacker and her horror at the scope of the destruction. There had been grief, too, when she'd spotted the Rottweiler on her side, panting, her black hair matted with the blood that pumped from her side. Her big brown eyes liquid with pain, Gretel had whined and tried to crawl to Jessie when she saw her. Tried to lick the hand of the person who'd become her caretaker this past year, who had slipped her treats from the table and secretly wrapped pale arms around her thick neck, weeping into her fur after Jessie's mother's death.

Jessie felt her breath hitch, her eyes burn. Had Zach had her poor baby, who'd fought so hard to protect her, put to sleep already? Or had Gretel bled out just like Henry—another life she'd been responsible for bringing to this awful place?

Overwhelmed as she was, she barely noticed the child slipping into her room and moving to her bedside, until the piping little voice cut through her daze.

"I made you a picture. To help you feel all better."

Jessie's heart sagged at the sight of Eden, looking so much like her sister she couldn't believe she hadn't seen it earlier. A tear leaked out, rolled along Jessie's face, but she moved to wipe it.

Eden stroked her arm with one small hand. "It's okay. My grandma cries a lot, too. She gots a real bad hurt place on her heart 'cause of Ian."

Jessie turned her eyes to look at the girl, only to see brilliant crayoned colors only inches from her face. Colors that seared her eyes and intensified the throbbing in her head. In self-defense, she accepted the page and croaked out, "Th-thank you, Eden. This is very pretty."

Holding it farther back to see it, she tried to focus on the wash of colors. Mostly oranges and yellows, with dark clouds that resembled— She squinted, making out the houselike shape of the barn with fire shooting out of it. And a stick figure with flames for hair.

Surreptitiously, she felt her loose waves, relieved to find them smoky-smelling and gritty but still present. "I like the way you made it sparkle."

Eden nodded, regarding her with a serious expression. "Glitter makes everything better. Only Uncle Zach doesn't like it 'cause he's a boy."

"What do boys know?" Jessie said, faking a smile and poking playfully at the child's tummy. And aching as she wondered if, when in Haley's care, the girl had ever known even a fraction of the stability, the love and family that she'd found on this ranch.

Eden giggled, covering her mouth, and Jessie's heart broke wide-open. For this tiny creature, this lively little sprite was *her* flesh, *her* blood, as close a relative as if Jessie herself had given her life. Just the thought of it brought tears to her eyes.

How, then, had Haley been able to simply walk away from a miracle like this? Had she done so with as little thought as when she'd turned her back on her twin and parents? Or had it happened as Jessie had guessed earlier? Had the little girl been found—or given into Mrs. Rayford's keeping—after Haley's murder?

"Eden!" scolded Mrs. Rayford as she fluttered through the doorway, wearing a neat lilac-colored pantsuit and a frown. "What are you doing in here? I told you to not to bother Miss Layton while she's resting."

Eden nodded, looking serious. "I fixed her hurt place with a picture."

Jessie pushed up on her elbows, struggling not to wince at the flare of pain in her head. "It's all right." *More than all right. She's my family. My family, not yours.* "I needed to get up, anyway. I'm getting your poor sheets and blankets filthy, for one thi—"

"Nonsense. You lie back and rest, and I'll bring you some water—or anything you need."

"I'll be okay, but where's Zach? I mean Mr. Rayford," she amended, seeing a flicker of unease cross the older woman's face. "Is he all right?"

Mrs. Rayford nodded. "The barn's a total loss, an awful thing, but I thank God that my son came through it unharmed. The firefighters, too. They still have one truck out there, spraying water to cool the ruins."

Jessie realized she must have been out much longer than she'd imagined. Probably as much from exhaustion as the bump on her head.

"Zach will want to talk to you as soon as he's able," Mrs. Rayford said. "But he had to take a couple of the injured horses to the vet's. Your poor dog, too. He was worried."

Jessie sat up straight to hear it. "My Gretel? She's still alive?"

The older woman shook her head, her blue eyes sympathetic. "I'm not sure, dear, but I do know Dr. Burton is a good man. If the animals can be saved, he'll do it. If not—he's a kind man. He won't let them suffer."

"What about the puppies?" Jessie blurted, then darted a guilty glance at Eden as she realized she should have never asked in front of her.

"Grandma won't let me play with them," Eden said cheerfully, "till they get a bath 'cause they're all stinky."

"They both seem fine," Mrs. Rayford assured Jessie before turning to Eden. "Miss Layton needs her rest. But first, could you please go downstairs and get a glass of water for her? Ask Miss Althea to help you."

There was a definite edge to Zach's mother's voice, even though she had tried to disguise it. She definitely wanted Eden as far from Jessie as could be managed.

"I can do it!" Eden shouted, speeding out of the room and clattering down the staircase.

"Before you go," said Jessie, as the older woman turned to follow, "did the sheriff catch the man who set the fire?"

With a gasp, Zach's mother stiffened. "Do you mean it wasn't accidental? This—this person tried to burn the barn while the two of you were in it?"

The horror in her shaking voice made Jessie wish she could take back the question. But Nancy Rayford wasn't four years old, and besides, the truth was out now.

"I'm sorry to be the one to tell you," Jessie said.

"At least you *did* tell me." Mrs. Rayford shook her head, tears welling in her blue eyes. "Unlike some people, who want to wrap me up in cotton and hide me in a closet somewhere. My son hasn't said a word to me about this, not a single word, or the sheriff, either. No one has."

"With everything that's happened, I imagine Zach hasn't had a chance to tell you." Jessie wondered what she was doing, making excuses for him.

"He's trying to protect me, and I hate it. How can I hope to keep *my* granddaughter safe if I don't know what's going on?"

Jessie winced at her use of the word *granddaughter*, at the emphasis that convinced her that the woman more than half believed it. That she was desperate to keep believing the child that she clearly loved was her own flesh and blood.

"Zach worries about you," Jessie said gently, "the same as I worried about my mother."

"Zach told me about your mother, and I'm sorry. But don't you think, if she were here, she'd encourage you to go get medical attention?"

Jessie shook her head and closed her eyes as the world spun around her. When the carousel ride stopped, she managed, "I'll be fine. Everything will be fine." Though how in the world would anything ever be fine again?

"You're sounding like my son, trying to convince me." Mrs. Rayford pouted, folding her thin arms in front of her. "You young people forget we older folks have known our share of heartache. We persevere. We have to, no matter how terrible the pain is."

"Except my mother wasn't just playing the frail prairie flower," Jessie said abruptly. She immediately regretted her rudeness, but chances were, she'd never get a better chance to shock the woman into giving her straight answers. "She had stage-four metastatic cancer. And she died without knowing what happened to her other daughter, died before she ever had the chance to meet her only grandchild."

Mrs. Rayford's head cocked, reminding Jessie of a bird considering whether to risk pecking at a tempting morsel. Behind those glittering eyes, Jessie sensed the rapid-fire calculations as the woman tried to decide whether to play dumb or take flight.

Frowning, she went for the first choice, "So your sister had a child at one time? How odd, she never mentioned it to me."

Though pushing here and now probably made Jessie the world's most ungrateful houseguest, now that she'd tipped her hand, she had no choice but to play it. "What I want to know is this— Did my sister *give* you Eden? Of her own free will?"

Nancy Rayford staggered a step or two and grabbed the doorjamb as if she needed it for balance. "I—I have no idea what you're talking about. What does any of this have to do with my son, Ian's, daughter?"

Jessie came painfully to her feet, taking an unsteady step nearer as the world did another slow roll. But that didn't stop her from pushing even harder. "The one you lied about, you mean?"

"I didn't! I would never." An age-spotted but well-manicured hand went to Mrs. Rayford's forehead and her eyes scrunched as pain flashed over her expression. "My head— I'll need my pills. I have to have my medication."

Though Jessie's every instinct urged her to rush to the older woman's aid, she forced herself to stand her ground. "Convenient, isn't it? How you come down with a headache every time somebody asks you a tough question."

Zach's mother covered her eyes with both hands, tears sliding down her face. "A migraine. I'm sure of it. Please, help me to my room. Or call Althea if you would, dear."

This close to the truth, Jessie wasn't about to let Nancy Rayford off the hook. "Did you. Take. My sister's child? And do you know who killed her?"

The older woman wept piteously, collapsing against the door frame. But she did not let herself fall.

"Tell me," Jessie pleaded, "tell me right now. Because whoever hurt my sister meant to kill again today. And next time, they could kill your last son. Is lying worth that risk?"

A stair creaked, and she heard the sound of boots stalking down the hallway. She braced herself for the coming confrontation with Zach Rayford. But it wasn't

Zach who appeared, glaring as he grasped Mrs. Rayford's shoulders to support her.

It was Sheriff Canter, red-faced and so furious that Jessie half expected he would shoot her on the spot.

"What the hell is going on here?" he demanded. "What are you doing to this poor woman?"

"She *attacked* me in my own home. That's what she did!" Mrs. Rayford cried.

Before Jessie knew what had hit her, she found herself roughly spun around and cuffed.

"What?" she cried. "I didn't do anything to her! You can't do this!"

"Watch me," Canter growled through clenched teeth, marching her out of the room and down the staircase so quickly that it was all she could do to avoid being dragged along.

When a female jailer escorted Jessie out of her cell the next morning, Zach stood with his hat in hand. He had no idea what to say, or how to make what had happened up to her. Considering that she still wore smudges of ash and had only been allowed to dress in her filthy clothing she'd worn the day before, bailing her out wasn't going to cut it. With the rings of fatigue beneath her green eyes and the red-hot anger in them, he wondered if she'd toss the insulated mug of strong black coffee he had brought her in his face simply because he was a Rayford, but he took a chance and handed it to her, anyway.

She accepted it and stared up at him suspiciously, the hair that had escaped her messy braid framing her face. "Are you sure this isn't poisoned? Because if your mother had her choice…"

"Not here," he said, for the shabby waiting area contained a motley collection of those waiting to arrange bail or waiting for a friend or loved one to be processed out. Bored and restless as they were, they would hang on every word. As would the jailer and the deputy behind the counter. Besides, Zach's heated discussion with Canter had left no doubt that the sheriff would be happy for another excuse to arrest her.

Though yesterday's had been so flimsy, anyone with half a brain could see right through it. Even his mother had been horrified by the speed at which her accusation had snowballed out of control. Or so she'd claimed when Zach had demanded to know why the sheriff, who'd allegedly come to question Jessie about the man who had attacked her, had arrested her instead.

"Let's get out to the truck," Zach said now. "But first, here's your jacket. I brushed it off as well as I could." Seeing her looking so exhausted, so vulnerable, he wished he could do more. Wanted to wrap her up and carry her out of here. To take her home and tuck her into bed. His bed.

She drank down half her coffee and then handed him the mug. As she slipped into the jacket, she asked, "You bring my shoes, too? I wasn't wearing any when the sheriff—"

She darted a look at their audience and then gestured down at the cheap canvas slip-ons she'd evidently been provided. "Or do I get to wear these lovely parting gifts?"

"Sorry. I'm afraid it's jail shoes. I didn't know about yours. But I have your keys and cell phone in the truck."

Her face flushing, she reclaimed the coffee before making a beeline for the door. Outside, heavy clouds darkened the morning, and the temperature had dipped into the upper twenties, thanks to the Canadian air mass that had rolled in. Judging from the bitter winds, the forecasted ice storm might be coming sooner than the weather people had predicted.

Inside his pickup, the atmosphere felt even colder, even after Zach had started up the engine and turned the heat up high.

"I fought like hell to get you out last night," he offered, still frustrated over Canter's arrogance, along with his unwillingness to turn her loose in spite of Zach's mother's refusal to press charges. Not even the explanation that Jessie might need treatment for a concussion had moved the stubborn SOB. "Best I could do is get you bumped up to the head of the line for your arraignment and be here waiting once the bail was set."

"She lied," Jessie blurted, hugging herself in an attempt to warm up faster. "Your mother *lied* to get rid of me because I confronted her about Eden."

You're right, he wanted to say. The habit of defending his frail mother was hard-wired. Or defending family against outsiders—but was Jessie really an outsider anymore?

"My mother was upset," he said, hating himself for it. "She was overwrought about the fire. My great-grandfather built that barn. It had been standing longer than the house has. Longer than my mother's been part of the family."

He pulled into the street.

"That doesn't excuse what she did for a second, but I am sorry about your barn," Jessie said. "What about the animals? Did all of them make it?"

Hearing the fear in her voice, he was quick to answer, "Lost one of the horses. It was that mare that panicked and knocked you down. Headed back for what she probably figured was the safety of her stall."

"Oh, no. I'm so sorry."

He nodded, knowing that she really meant it. That she cared about the animals every bit as much as he did.

"Another has a crisped tail and some minor burns, but the rest are gonna be fine. And your Gretel's hanging in there, too, after a blood transfusion. I told the vet, do whatever you need to. Anything to save her."

Closing her eyes, she sighed. "Thank God, and thank you, Zach. I was so afraid— I know this might seem crazy, but that dog's the best friend I have."

His heart ached for her, that she had no one else to turn to. But then, no human friend could have done what Gretel had to save her mistress. "Darn good friend to have. Whoever hurt her, she returned the favor, judging from the blood trail your attacker left. But I have to tell you, Doc Burton says she's not out of the woods yet."

"In the last few months, I've lost my mom, Henry, my job—and now probably my sister. I can't lose Gretel, too, or I swear I'll lose my mind, Zach. You understand?"

"Better than most people, I imagine," he said, wishing there was more he could do to ease her pain. "That's why I told the vet I'm picking up the tab on this one."

"Thank you," she repeated, wiping at her eyes. "And thanks so much for coming here to get me. Last night was—it was awful."

"I'm sorry, and I know you won't believe this, but my mama's been beside herself with worry. She says things got away from her, that Sheriff Canter misunderstood what she said."

"Canter's nothing but a two-bit bully," she said bitterly. "By the time I get through with that jackass, he can kiss that badge of his goodbye."

"That's the spirit," he said, figuring she must be feeling better if she was fighting mad and ready to set the world right. Or Rusted Spur, at least.

"Where are we heading?" she asked as he slowed down to make a turn.

"Straight to Margie's. I figured you'd want a shower and to get some real sleep. I'm betting you didn't get a whole lot of it last night."

She grimaced. "The one time I nodded off, one of my cellmates swiped my blanket. That's in addition to the dinner tray and breakfast they snatched out of my hands, too. Right down to the sour milk."

Zach swore, imagining what a shock it must have been to a woman as classy as Jessie to rub elbows with life's rougher elements. "They hurt you? Anybody touch you, Jessie?" He'd personally take care of anybody who had dared, right up to the jailers and Canter himself.

She favored him with a wan smile. "Seriously? You think I was going to *fight* a couple of drunk tank frequent flyers over some stinky, threadbare blanket and a couple of meals I couldn't identify on a bet?"

He shook his head, admiring her sass. "I hope not, and anyway, I'll sweet-talk Margie into making you something a lot better."

"Why? You feeling guilty about what happened to me? Because you're not the one to blame here."

"Really? I figured you would want to slug me. 'Sins of the mother,' or something like that."

Jessie laughed, and he smiled, relieved to know that she could find anything about this funny. But Jessie sobered quickly, uncertainty in her eyes.

"You think it's okay for me to stay here? I wouldn't want to bring down any trouble on your friend Margie."

"I can tell you, she'd never turn you away."

"Even considering where I've been?"

"She's never judged me, not once," he said, "even when I spent half my high school years stirring up trouble."

As it turned out, Margie was a lot more understanding than even Zach would have imagined.

"Trust me," she said after Zach quietly explained Jessie's issue while she was upstairs getting cleaned up. "It's not the first time someone innocent's run afoul of good old George."

"You?" he asked, incredulous.

Laughing, Margie slapped her plump thighs, causing all three dachshunds to bark until she shushed them. "Me? Canter wouldn't dare, not if he doesn't want everyone in town to know why he never got invited to boys' slumber parties back in the fifth grade."

"Why not?" Zach threw up his hands. "On second thought, that's probably one of those things I don't really want to know."

She smiled and headed for the kitchen, leaving him to follow. "You hungry, too? I can make omelets for two as easy as one. Or do you think Jessie would rather have some of my banana pancakes?"

"The kind with the real maple syrup?" He hadn't forgotten her whipping up a batch when he'd stopped by to say hello a few days after his return to Rusted Spur. But his gratitude went deeper, dating back over the years she'd cooked him other meals, too, on other mornings when he'd been too damned scared to go home.

When she nodded, he said, "Absolutely, and I'd love some, too. Thanks."

"Good," she said. "Now why don't you go and set the table in the breakfast nook, where you two won't be disturbed."

"You sure you won't marry me?" he asked with a loopy grin.

"I'm pretty sure I dodged a bullet the first time you asked me," she said, laughing at the memory of a ten-year-old boy's gratitude when she'd relented on her threat to call his father about his forgotten homework.

Mainly, Zach understood now, because she'd had an inkling he'd be beaten for the foul-up. Just as he understood that she must have been the one who'd sent a Children's Protective Services worker snooping around, that she hadn't believed the stories he'd come up with to explain his bruises.

Though Zach had been horrified—and nothing had come of the investigation except sore rears for him and Ian for "spreading lies about the family"—it had given him courage to know someone cared about them. Had given him the confidence that another adult believed what was happening in their house wasn't right. If he hadn't had at least that, he might have believed what his dad said about his and Ian's treatment being normal. Might have bought all that bull about the Bible itself demanding that his father not "spare the rod."

With the perfect timing she must have developed keeping one step ahead of kids as rowdy as he'd once been, Margie was just bringing out the pancakes and some bacon she'd fried when Jessie came downstairs wearing a pair of form-fitting black jeans and a nubby violet sweater that made the green of her eyes stand out. In spite of her ordeal, she looked far better than she had any right to, her red-gold hair gleaming and her skin glowing.

The thought of her, scrubbing off the layers of ash and county jail under a hot shower, sent pure need spearing through him. Desire for the one woman in the world he should stay farthest from.

But painful as the decision to help her had been, his sense of honor wouldn't let him step back, no more than his ill-timed lust would leave him alone.

"I was coming down to thank you, not to bother with the brunch because I'm so tired," Jessie admitted. "But the moment I smelled that coffee and bacon, I mysteriously got my second wind."

"And wait until you taste these banana pancakes," Margie said. "Now, Zach, you be a good boy and go get that syrup I just heated while I pour the coffee."

Jessie caught his eye and grinned. "Yeah, Zach, be a good boy," she said before turning, all innocent, toward Margie. "You don't need to go through so much trouble. Let me help, please."

"Nonsense," Margie told her. "You were dead on your feet when you came in, and no wonder, after what that tin-star tyrant put you through."

"I'm only glad your other guests were all out, so they didn't have to see me taking the walk of shame in my fabulous footwear." Jessie looked down, her expression pained, as if she were still seeing the grungy canvas jail shoes instead of the stylish black boots she now wore.

Utterly impractical boots, with their mile-high heels and the straps across the ankles, thought Zach, except he liked them. Liked them enough to wonder how she'd look wearing them and nothing else. As he headed for the kitchen, he thought of sticking his head under a cold faucet. What the hell was wrong with him?

"Huh!" Margie said emphatically, her voice loud enough for him to make out. "If you ask me, if anyone should be ashamed, it's George Canter. See if I vote for that bully next November. Well, not that I voted for him last time, either, after he harassed my poor lost boys the way he did."

Jessie murmured a question Zach couldn't quite make out.

"No, not my sons. My husband and I were never blessed with children," Margie answered. "I meant those boys I taught, the ones who had so much trouble in their home life. You ride a child like that too hard and too early, you'll break him down—or drive him miles from home. The girls, too, so many of them, I tried to take them under my wing over the years."

Troubled—and somehow ashamed—to be lumped in with Margie's other "projects," Zach stalled, washing his hands at the sink before returning from the kitchen, tiny pitcher in hand. But he hesitated in the doorway, seeing Jessie seated with her head bowed as Margie leaned over to hug her and speak quietly in her ear.

"Should I go back out?" he asked, feeling nine kinds of awkward.

"You're fine," Jessie said, dabbing at her eyes with a cloth napkin. "I'm fine. Just a little tired, that's all. And Mrs.—I mean, Margie, here—reminds me so much of my mother, back when she was still well."

Looking up at the older woman, Jessie added, "You'd have loved her if you ever had the chance to— And I know she would have loved you, too."

"I'm sure she was a good woman," Margie said, giving Jessie a squeeze. "She'd have to be, to've raised a daughter like you."

"She raised *two* daughters," Jessie said. "Only she never got the chance to see the other one again. And I might never, either."

"What do you mean?" Margie pulled away to ask.

"I think my sister's dead." Jessie glanced at Zach, her gaze seeking his permission.

"I found some burnt bones, out at the old bunkhouse," he explained. "I took some pictures of them before they disappeared, and Jessie here sent the photos to an expert."

"The bones were definitely human," Jessie added. "But we'll have to find them if we want to prove they belong to Haley, who disappeared back in August."

Margie stiffened. "You're saying these bones are your sister's? That she's been dead since last summer?"

Jessie drew an audible breath, her beautiful face pinched with worry. "I hate to admit it, and I'd give anything to be proven wrong. But all signs point in that direction."

Margie turned her back to pour each of them a cup of coffee.

But Zach would swear he'd seen something indecisive and troubled in her blue eyes. Did she know something she felt conflicted about sharing?

"Margie," he said, "if you've heard something about Haley, you can tell us. We really need to know."

"Why, what on earth would give you the idea that I know anything?" she asked as she put down a cup in front of Jessie's place, sloshing a little into the saucer. "I never taught the girl."

Jessie pushed back from the table, her eyes pleading. "You're not protecting Frankie McFarland, are you? I don't care whether he's one of your lost boys or not. If he killed my twin, I need to know about it. No matter how I failed her in life, I need to find her—what's left of her—and give her a decent burial. And I need to know that Haley didn't intentionally turn her back on our mother at the end."

"I truly wish I could help you," Margie said, splashes of color coming to her cheeks. Shaking her head, she backed toward the door.

Wondering whether Jessie might be right, Zach asked Margie, "If you could tell us something, you wouldn't just be helping Jessie and her family. You might be keeping both of us alive. Because we're not stopping until we know everything, and whoever burned my family's barn down isn't about to give up, either."

"I'm sorry I can't help you, and I really should be going," Margie told them, checking her watch. "I want to pick up some supplies before this storm gets any uglier."

"Maybe you should wait. It's already getting nasty out there," Zach said, gesturing toward the window, where the morning seemed to be reversing itself, rolling backward into nightfall.

"My little wagon's half four-wheel drive, half mountain goat. Don't worry," she said. "You two go ahead and eat while everything's still warm. And don't worry about the dishes, either. I'll get all that when I come back."

"Margie, please. Don't let us run you off. Stay and talk to us," Zach said before Jessie touched his arm and shook her head to shut him down.

"Thanks for everything," Jessie said politely. "It was kind of you to go to all this trouble."

Margie assured them she'd been glad to do it before fleeing toward her little office with her dachshund entourage. After crating the animals and grabbing coat and purse, she hurried out the door.

Zach looked at Jessie.

"Why'd you let her off so easy?" he asked.

"So she could go meet with whoever it is that's running all this," Jessie told him. "Because she's not telling us a single thing until they get their story straight."

Chapter 15

Zach's blue eyes bored into Jessie's, setting off a flutter just beneath her stomach, a reminder of the searing kiss they'd shared before the fire. Maybe it was the knock to the head, but she could swear that she still felt it, that she felt, too, a tingling in all the places where their bodies had pressed together. Or maybe it was the absence of that pressure that had her aching to repeat it, even though she knew getting any further involved with this man was a terrible idea.

But despite the kindness he had shown her and the look she'd recognized—pure, male appreciation mixed with speculation—in his gaze when she'd first come downstairs, his look promised an argument, not passion.

"Getting *her story* straight?" he asked her. "I'll grant you that she was acting a little odd, but I'm not buying that my fifth-grade teacher would be involved in some kind of conspiracy. Especially a conspiracy involving murder."

"She really seems like a nice woman, but she's a re-tired teacher, not an active-duty saint," said Jessie, who had reported on enough bad acts from doctors, ministers, cops and educators to know that anyone could slip up, no matter how respected. Especially if the person in question could somehow justify her actions. "You might not want to see it, but it's obvious to me that she knows something. I didn't think much of it before, but the way she looked at me when I first came here—she had to have known Haley, just like your friend Nate did."

"So now you're accusing my best friend, too? Good try. But Nate Wheeler couldn't keep a secret if his own mama's life depended on it."

She shrugged. "He sure did clam up and take off in a hurry when I started drilling him with questions."

"I can see why that would be suspicious," Zach scoffed, "because otherwise, people around these parts love nothing more than a good inquisition. Anybody else you want to point the finger at?"

"Your mother has to be involved. Plus, we'd better not forget the sheriff."

"And what about Danny McFarland? You really think all these respectable people are in league with a lowlife like Hellfire?"

"Reformed lowlife," she corrected, "according to him, at least." Something in the statement triggered an idea, but before she could grasp the thought, her stomach rumbled a loud reminder about the delicious-smelling food cooling within reach.

"Apparently, your sarcasm makes me hungry," she said, dropping back into her seat and spearing a bite of her first meal since the cookies she'd had with tea the day before. "So if you don't mind, I'm going to eat while we talk."

Before he could respond, she popped the forkful into her mouth. Even lukewarm, the pancake was fluffy and delicious.

"Good idea," he said, lowering himself into the opposite seat and pushing the syrup toward her. "You'll definitely need your energy to spin this wild theory of yours. Bonus points if you can somehow tie it to the Kennedy assassination."

Ignoring his comment, she occupied herself with the food for the next few minutes. "This is wonderful," she commented when she had eaten as much as she could manage, lifting her coffee cup in tribute. "Almost makes me glad my new pals in the drunk tank helped me whet my appetite."

"If you want, I'll take you back there so you can thank them personally."

Buzzing with the burst of caffeine and sugar, she smiled. "I'll pass, thanks, but you'd probably like to turn me in and get your money back."

He swallowed a mouthful and then shook his head, his expression serious. "Maybe I ought to. You really are a lot of trouble."

"You think I'm a hassle now, you just try dragging me back to that jail."

"*Pure* trouble," he amended, "but for the time being, I think I'll keep you around."

Their eyes locked, the blue-to-green connection sending an electrical charge straight through her, and a jolt that made her smile. Because she liked this ex-pilot-turned-rancher, too, far more than she ought to, and the more time she spent with him, the stronger the attraction grew. Along with the suspicion that something far more dangerous than a searing physical connection might be brewing. And far more likely, in the long run, to reduce her heart to ash.

Outside, the wind whistled past the old house, and icy pellets tapped like grains of sand against the windows. But cold as it was outside, Jessie felt nothing but the heat that burned in Zach's gaze, along with the awareness that they were here alone.

"You know, this isn't going to end well between us," she said, warning herself as much as him. "Not if we're guessing right about Eden. And especially not if your mother's guilty of doing something she shouldn't have to keep her."

"I know it," he said miserably, "and part of me feels like a traitor—and the worst son in the world—for even talking to you, much less digging into this business with your sister."

"So why are you?" she asked him.

He let out a breath before shaking his head. "Because this kind of secret can't—won't—stay buried, not forever. Whatever happened to your sister, however my mama ended up with Eden, it's going to come back to hurt that child. And I can't have that. I won't. She's just a little kid. A little girl who needs someone to put her interests first, no matter what."

"You really do love her, don't you?"

He looked down at the tablecloth, his callused finger running along a hand-embroidered detail. She realized that this strapping, powerful man, a veteran fighter pilot and wealthy head of one of the most influential ranching families in the state of Texas, was too choked up to say the words aloud.

And that was when she felt her heart give way completely. Realizing that, even if it meant losing Eden—and possibly his fragile mother in the process—he loved her niece so much that he was willing to do whatever it took to do the right thing by her. To offer up the strength she needed, no matter what price.

Can I really do that to him?

Putting down her fork, she reached across the table and laid her hand atop his, stroked those work-roughened fingers with her own. "I can tell that Eden loves you, too. She loves both you and your mama. You've been good to her, probably far better than my sister ever managed—if we're really right and she was hers." Even with everything she'd heard and seen, Jessie was still having trouble wrapping her brain around it.

"Any fool could see it, if they looked at the two of you together, but we'll do one of those DNA tests just in case. Pretty sure they'll be able to check a swab from Eden against yours for a match."

Jessie nodded. "We should probably check yours, too, or maybe your mother's, just to rule out any other possibility."

"Can't say I see my mama cooperating," he said grimly. "She has ways of getting out of things she doesn't want to deal with."

"So I've noticed." Last night's demonstration had driven home how far Nancy Rayford was willing to go to avoid being confronted. "Tell me, has she always been this evasive? Or did it just start after she lost your brother? Or maybe with your father's death?"

"She seems worse now, but to some extent, yeah. She's the same old mama I remember, either making excuses for the old man or retreating to her room with one of her 'sick headaches.' But it couldn't have helped that I abandoned her and Ian, and without me there to help deflect my father, my brother took off, too. Didn't even wait till he was eighteen. We left her there alone with him. All by herself in that big house."

"Did—did your father hurt her, too?"

"I never saw him touch her, but then I never saw any affection, either, just cold demands—and blame, too, for giving him a couple of sons who never measured up, let alone appreciated the Rayford legacy." Zach shoved his plate away, his mouth curling as if a bitter taste had filled it. "I should've toughed it out awhile longer. Should've stayed for Ian and my mama, too. Could've stood up to the bastard. Could've made it stop."

"Your mother was an adult. You were an abused kid." The thought of it had her aching for him. "*She* was the one responsible for taking care of *you*."

Zach shook his head. "I thought that for a long time, but I'm the eldest son. I should've found some way to help her—or tried harder to make peace once I'd gotten myself settled. It's taken a toll on her, make no mistake about that. And now I'm about to go and break her heart again. Only if it costs her Eden, I don't know if she'll survive it."

"Are you sure about that? Or is that just what your mother's wanting you to think? What she's relying on to get you to let her have everything just the way she wants it?"

"What do you mean? That she's faking? Because if you ever saw the way that she gets with her headaches— the vomiting, the need for darkness, you'd see—"

"So these are migraines, right? I've had a couple, and I wouldn't wish them on my worst enemy." *Except for maybe Vivian,* Jessie thought, still fuming over how neatly she'd been maneuvered—pushed into violating the no-compete clause in her contract so she could be threatened with a lawsuit if she didn't go quietly. A lawsuit she couldn't deal with, with her life crumbling around her. "But as horrible as they are, people don't die from those. And they don't die, either, from not getting their own way."

Zach grimaced. "But she *cries*. My mother cries, and I can't stand it."

"Do you give Eden what she wants every time she turns on the tears?"

At his chagrinned look, Jessie winced. "Oh, boy, do you ever have a lot to learn about women."

"I think maybe you could teach me," he said, his voice as low and rough as the hiss of ice against the window, "all sorts of things about women."

"I'm thinking that's not a good idea," she said, no matter how sexy she found the blue eyes blazing above his stubbled jaw.

A gust shuddered around the old house, and the lights flickered and went out.

"These old power lines around here are no match for a really good blue norther," Zach said as he rose and lit a pair of candles in brass holders sitting out on the buffet. "I only hope that Margie's safe, wherever it is she went."

"I hope so, too," Jessie managed, though she couldn't take her eyes off the flickering light against his skin. Couldn't get beyond what she saw whenever their eyes chanced to meet.

Rising from her chair, she started stacking up the dishes. Without a word, Zach rose to help her, carrying the candles to the kitchen. There, the two of them took care of the cleanup so Margie wouldn't have to deal with it on her return.

Or maybe they were only stalling, immersed in the warmth of a companionable silence, with Jessie's gloved hands down in the water, Zach's big hands occupied with the linen towels he used to dry.

Or so she thought, until she sensed his presence, close behind her.

"Why don't you let me finish here and you go on up to bed," he murmured, the warmth of his breath stirring silky hairs that tickled her ear. "Your hands are barely moving, and your eyes keep sliding closed."

She jolted fully awake, awareness of his nearness crackling through her.

"Maybe I don't want to go to sleep," she said. *I want you to touch me.*

She shivered with the thought, and the desire shuddered through her body with the stark awareness of how long it had been since she had allowed herself to shed her worries, even for a little while, in a man's arms.

Her heartbeat revved, a feeling of panic tightening her stomach. She couldn't afford to lose control here, not in Rusted Spur. Couldn't afford to lose another piece of herself, with all she'd lost already.

"I should check on Gretel." She pulled the sink's plug to drain the water.

"Dr. Burton promised he'd call right away if there was any change. Besides, this storm's going to get a lot worse before it gets better," Zach said, still standing so close, she felt the heat of his body behind her.

So close, that if she turned around and stood up on her toes, she could find out if what she'd felt in the barn office, what she was feeling whenever she heard him speak of family and duty, might be real.

But she had family, too, and duty. A duty she could not ignore. Her jaw tightening, she rinsed away the last of the suds before pulling off the dishwashing gloves and laying them across the rack.

He placed a hand on the curve between her neck and shoulder. "You're all tensed up," he noted as he began to knead the muscles. "Am I bothering you, Jessie? Because I can leave if you want, grab one of the cowboys and drop your SUV by later."

She shook her head, "It's not that. It's just—I was thinking about Haley out there somewhere, wondering how I'm ever going to bring her home."

Taking her shoulders in his strong hands, he turned her around to face him. "*We'll* find her, and we'll get answers," he swore. "You see if we don't."

And just like that, she felt the weight lift, knowing that this honorable man, a man willing to step up and return to a family that had brought him so much pain in his youth, had given her his promise. A promise she knew instinctively he would never willingly break.

With his vow, the world seemed suddenly more bearable…especially while she stood at eye level with those sensuous-looking lips.

Outside, the icy rain lashed at the windows, scouring away her memory of all the reasons that leaning forward would be unthinkable. Judging from the harsh scrape of Zach's breathing, the intensity of his gaze, he was having as much trouble as she was trying to resist the tidal pull.

"Like I said before," he told her, "you need to get yourself up to bed."

"And like I told you," she said stubbornly, "I don't want to sleep." *Alone, at any rate.*

"Who the hell said anything about sleeping, Jessie Layton?"

Wrapping his arms around, he pulled her tight against the hard contours of his body. Including the impressive evidence that he was every bit as aroused as she was by their nearness.

His voice turned rough as he added, "The question is, do you want company or not?"

An instant later, his mouth slanted over hers, his kiss hungry and insistent. Demanding in a way that threw gasoline atop the fire she'd been trying so hard to dampen. With the parting of her lips, the kiss deepened, the heat of his thrusting tongue and the strength of his questing hands vaporizing the unbearable pressures weighing on her.

Desperate to keep the world at bay, she pulled out his neatly tucked shirt, sliding her palms underneath it. Feeling the taut ripples of a set of abs that wouldn't stop.

He groaned, and followed suit, one hand finding and then cupping her breast. Squeezing and groaning, then breaking the kiss to growl, "I need more. Need all of you. If that's not what you want, too, you'd better not set one foot on that staircase."

"This is what I want," she murmured, standing on tiptoe to mouth his neck. "What I need," she breathed, molding her body against his. "And probably even some of this, as well."

He gasped in surprise and excitement when she reached down to cup and squeeze him. A wanton move, and one that left no lingering doubts about where this was heading.

"You better get me to your room," he told her, "unless you want me to take you on my old teacher's kitchen counter."

Taking his hand in hers, she said, "Sounds a lot less comfortable than the featherbed upstairs…."

Within minutes, Zach had her there, pieces of their clothing strewn all around the room's floor. After blowing out one candle, he'd brought the other upstairs with them. Now its soft glow flickered in the dresser mirror, the reflected warmth a perfect counterbalance to the icy rain pelting the windows.

"Anybody ever tell you you have a body made for candlelight?" he asked, his voice a low growl as he took in the blush of her fair skin, the play of shadows across her silky hair and the way it fell across the soft swell of her breasts.

Her gaze raked over his shoulders, his chest…and lower. "Anybody ever tell you you talk way too much?" She grasped his wrist and pulled him to her.

After that, there were no more words between them, nothing but the sound of rain and breath and quiet gasps, the heat and moisture of their kisses, the taste of her as he made his way down that slender body, pausing to run his hands, his lips, his tongue over every curve. As hot and hard as he was for her, he lost himself in bringing her pleasure, and it was not until he'd teased and touched and wrung a second and a third cry from her that he finally allowed her to pull him up over her.

"Please," she begged, the desire in her green eyes nearly making him forget caution—nearly, but not quite—before he reached for the condom he'd taken from his wallet when they first came upstairs.

Ripping it open, he groaned when she insisted, "Let me," and put it on him with a flurry of teasing touches.

In moments, he was inside her, spearing her with a deep thrust that made her moan louder than the wind beyond the walls. Biting his lip to make himself last, his closed his eyes and focused on a steady rocking motion, not counting on her damp heat and her own thrusts breaking down whatever self-control remained.

Giving way, he lost track of the guilt and worry he'd been feeling, of the grief and pain of his past—forgot everything except the smart and sensual woman moving just beneath him, and the hot fuse of pure pleasure burning toward completion. When she threw back her head, her body pulsing all around his, he finally exploded inside her, her name on his tongue as he came.

Only when it was over, and he held her in his arms beneath the tangled sheets, did he allow himself to consider the relief washing over him. And to wonder if he was being honest with himself about the reasons he had seduced this woman…

Or if he was, even subconsciously, trying to save his family the only way he might.

For the first time in days, Jessie slept well. Nestled against Zach's powerful chest, she felt secure for once in this place, safe from all the hostility Rusted Spur had heaped upon her. Or perhaps exhaustion was only physical, heightened by the afterglow of a sexual encounter she knew she'd never forget.

Hours later, she finally stirred, wondering if lovemaking had ever felt so good before, so right, so inevitable. Certainly, she'd never met a man like Zach, who made her feel as if her pleasure was more important than his own.

Or maybe her attraction had more to do with her instinctive need for an ally to get her through this nightmare in one piece. Troubled by the thought, she rolled to her side, wondering if her subconscious could be so devious. So mercenary as to sleep with the prodigal Rayford heir in the hopes of staying safe—not to mention milking the connections that only someone born to Rusted Spur royalty could lay claim to.

Maybe not, she thought, telling herself she'd be drawn to this loving, loyal man under any circumstances. Hadn't she known that almost from the moment she had met him? But did that give her a right to further jeopardize his safety? Could she really risk costing another man his life?

"You're restless," Zach said. "Regretting this already?"

"No," she answered honestly, "but maybe I should be."

"Why's that?"

"Your barn didn't burn by accident. It burned because we were both in there together. Someone meant for me to die."

"You think I didn't know that?" he asked. "It's not like that crowbar jammed into the door was exactly subtle. If I hadn't found a sledgehammer and made myself another exit—"

"I should've told you I was warned," she admitted, before spilling the details about the text she had received only hours before the fire. The text that had threatened that she might soon have another death on her conscience if she didn't leave immediately.

"You were right earlier," she added. "I should've listened. Should've taken the threats a lot more seriously. And now, you could've burned alive in that barn... I'm so sorry, Zach. And I'd understand completely if you don't want to have anything more to do with me."

He pulled her back into his arms, spooning her from behind and speaking low into her ear. "I've served three tours in the war zone. You really think I'm going to let this keep me—let anything stop me—from ever having you again?"

She hadn't known a woman could shiver from heat as well as cold, but his words made her do it. Still, she fought for control, even when his fingers found and tweaked a nipple.

"First, you lost your truck and then your barn and that poor mare," she said. "You aren't sorry you ever met me?"

He stopped caressing her, his voice roughening. "It's

the killer who's going to be sorry. As for me..." He mouthed the pale column of her neck, making her forget her guilt, forget everything but the need to turn around and mold herself to his hard body.

By the time the two of them finally got up and dressed, the sounds of the storm had long since been replaced by the clinks and whirs of Margie working on dinner in the kitchen.

"Let me go down first and talk to her alone," Zach suggested.

"She won't be shocked that you were up here?"

He smiled, shaking his head. "Margie Hunter's not my mother. I'm thinking maybe she'll be more willing to talk if there's not an outsider listening—especially one with a penchant for jumping down folks' throats and demanding answers."

"I would never—" Jessie protested.

"You can take the girl out of the newsroom..." Zach kissed the top of her head. "But the way I figure it, nobody's ever gonna take the newsroom out of this girl."

"Woman," she corrected, but as much as she hated to concede the point, she knew that Zach was right about having a far better chance of extracting information on his own. "How about I come join you in about twenty minutes? I need to call and check on Gretel, anyway, if you don't mind giving me the number to the vet clinic."

He handed her his phone and said, "You'll find it under B for Burton, or maybe V for vet. See you in a bit."

Out of habit, she checked her own phone first, scrolling through missed texts and emails in case one of the news directors or station HR departments she'd reached out to had responded to the résumés she'd sent. Many of the messages in her inbox were spam, but she found one sweet note from an old college friend who'd heard that

Jessie had lost her mother. Once more, however, there was nothing from any of the colleagues she'd spent so many years with—colleagues who treated her as if her recent bad luck was contagious.

Most likely, Jessie decided, they were frightened of running afoul of the vindictive Vivian. It might explain, as well, the lack of response from other Texas news directors, too. The industry was smaller and more incestuous than most people realized, so it was likely that they'd gotten word about Jessie's attempt to "burn" her boss by taking a Metro Update work product—as the story she'd developed for the station was legally considered its intellectual property—to a rival news outlet.

Jessie scowled, furious at how effectively her former boss had shut her down. And even more furious to think how no one would dare comment on, much less question, the impact of the woman's engagement to the billionaire wildcatter she'd been seeing. An alliance that he probably figured would buy him a whole lot of leeway when it came to influencing—or tampering with—elections at virtually every level. But to what end, she couldn't fathom, despite her attempts to sift through his connections.

Apparently, however, not every facet of the media was susceptible to Vivian's and H. Lee Simmons's influence. One of those, the fiercely independent *Lone Star Monthly,* had responded to her query, and several subsequent conversations with an editor as concerned as she was about Simmons's true agenda had resulted in an offer for her to write an extended feature story on the state's biggest power broker.

A thrill of pure excitement ran up her spine. A showcase piece like this would not only draw widespread attention to the issue but might well catapult her career in an entirely new direction, with a book deal and major national media interview requests. Knowing she'd go crazy simply living off her share of her parents' estate, it was gratifying to realize she wouldn't have to settle for a job reading farm reports in Outer Podunk, North Dakota. But what really revved her pulse was the idea of having a platform capable of bringing Henry's murder the attention it deserved—and in doing so, help bringing her sister justice, as well.

After sending a quick email accepting the basic terms of *Lone Star Monthly's* offer, Jessie picked up Zach's phone to check for the vet's number. The moment the dark screen sprang to life, her eyes widened at the long list of missed calls, one after another, many labeled "Home," followed by "Sheriff's Dept."

There were voice mails waiting, too, at least a half dozen, and when she checked, she found that Zach had had the phone on vibrate only, with the sound turned off.

Turned off while the two of them had been making love.

Panic twisting through her, she headed for the door, knowing something had to be wrong. Eden's face filled her vision: an active, curious child being cared for by Zach's mother and an older cook, neither of whom could hope to keep up with her. What if there had been some accident, or she'd wandered off? In her reporting days, Jessie had covered enough drownings, household accidents, even abductions to understand how very vulnerable the young were and how quickly they could disappear.

Just as Haley had vanished.

Terror crowding into Jessie's chest, she tried to tell herself that she was going to feel silly in a few minutes when this turned out to be nothing…or maybe just another minor health scare for his mother.

Even as some bone-deep instinct argued otherwise.

Chapter 16

Try as he might, Zach was having no luck questioning his former teacher.

"You can pour on the charm all you want," Margie Hunter told him as she stirred a simmering pot of her famous bison-and-black-bean chili to go with the pan of jalapeño-and-cheese cornbread she had just pulled from the oven. "There's nothing for me to tell you. Not a blessed thing."

"Who are you protecting, Margie?"

She shook a spoon at him, too annoyed to care about the saucy spatters she was flinging. "You always did have one humdinger of an imagination, all those tall tales you were always comin' up with to explain why you didn't have your homework."

"I'm not imagining that there's something rotten in Rusted Spur, a secret that at least one person's willing to kill for to keep hidden. And since you've always seemed to know most everything that goes on around here, I've gotta figure you know something about Jessie's sister. Something you've been ordered not to share—"

"Is that really you talking, Zach Rayford, or that reporter you've been spending the afternoon upstairs with?" she asked. "Because you oughta know me well enough to figure that anybody *ordering* this cantankerous old woman to keep my mouth shut would guarantee I'd be spreading whatever this big secret was to every corner of this county."

"So tell me, Margie," he said quietly, sensing some shift in her. "When was the last time you saw Haley Layton?"

She jerked her gaze away from his, seeming to notice the mess she'd made of the stove and counter. After dropping the spoon back into the chili pot, she grabbed a sponge and turned her back to him to clean. "It was a while back. I'm not sure when, exactly. She stopped by to see if I had any work for her."

"When?" he asked. "Last summer? Back before she and Frankie took off?"

Behind him, the floor creaked, and a flurry of dachshund tails pattered a greeting from the spot where they were piled by a heating vent. He looked to see Jessie hurrying toward him, his cell phone in her hand and her face ghostly pale. She opened her mouth to tell him something, but convinced that Margie was about to finally talk, he managed to stall Jessie with a raised palm and a quick shake of his head.

"Maybe middle of September?" said Margie. "The local kids were back in school already."

"You're sure?" he asked.

She nodded in answer. "I may be retired, but I'm like an old warhorse that way. Notice the running of the school buses every year. And, of course, the start of football season. Gotta love our Scorpions."

So that was why she'd been so startled to hear Jessie say she feared her sister might have been dead since August.

"So why did Haley come here in September?" he asked.

Jessie froze, lowering the phone in her hand and listening intently to the woman at the stove.

"She'd come and cleaned for me in the past," Margie admitted as she scrubbed another stubborn spot. "Did a good job those days she managed to make it over in that rattletrap old car of hers. This time, though, she showed up all black-and-blue, her poor eye swelled nearly shut, wanting to know if there was any way that she could live here, even if she worked for only food and board. She said she had to get away from him before he ended up killing her."

Jessie flinched, hugging herself.

"What happened?" Zach asked quietly. "Did you let her stay here?"

"I wanted to help her. I truly did," Margie said, "but she and that Frankie, they were always at it, breaking up and making up, the fur flying between them. There was even that one time she went off to some hotel in Marston, and he showed up there with a gun! Can you imagine? Instead of having him arrested, that fool girl decided that it proved he really loved her."

She looked back at Zach, her eyes begging for understanding. Seeing Jessie there behind him, Margie started, then shook her head, regret gleaming in her eyes. "I'm sorry."

"So you sent my sister away?" Jessie asked. "You sent her back to that monster?"

"You have to understand. I couldn't risk my guests' safety, or my own, either, for that matter," Margie told her. "I'd given her money before, helped her research domestic violence shelters. But she always took him back. Every single time."

Her face a mask of misery, Jessie nodded. "Believe me, I do get it. But what about—what about the little girl? Did Jessie have her with her?"

The two women locked gazes, the silence between them loud with mounting tension. All too soon, though, it was interrupted by the muffled thump of the front door closing, followed by the scrabbling of toenails and the raucous barking of the dachshund brigade.

Margie looked away first, turning down the burner. "That'll be the other guest I was waiting for," she said. "I'll need to set the table."

"Please," said Jessie, stepping closer. "Please just tell me, what happened to my sister's daughter?"

Margie's gaze found theirs again, and in hers, Zach saw worry, but before she could respond, she turned her head toward the heavy tread of approaching boots.

"Sheriff!" she said, startling as George Canter filled the doorway, his rain-spotted hat in hand.

At the sight of him, Jessie grimaced, but Canter had no eyes for anyone but Zach.

"Where is she?" the sheriff demanded. "Tell me you have her with you. Your mama's goin' clean out of her mind over there, and you aren't answering your damned phone."

Zach's heart stumbled and his breath caught, so he shook his head, unable to speak.

"Where is who?" Jessie asked for him. "You don't mean Eden?"

Canter's face fell. "So then she's not here with you? I was hoping when we couldn't find her—"

"No," Zach croaked out. "Of course not. I'd never take my niece without telling my mama and Althea. I've gotta get back home now."

He started for the door, panic snapping at his heels. Hard as it was to imagine Eden going outside in this weather, could she have been tempted to explore the sooty ruins of the old barn? Ruins that could easily collapse to trap and injure or even kill a small child?

"I'm coming, too," said Jessie. "Let me grab our jackets."

Zach barely heard her and didn't slow down until Canter blocked his way. "Hold on just a minute—"

"I can't. I have to find her."

"I've got three deputies there looking, and Virgil's got every hand out helping, too. They've been turning the place inside out, both indoors and the property. Found the puppies, locked up safe in the tractor shed, but no girl."

Zach's pulse thumped wildly in his head, so hard he heard it beating in his ears. "Tell me from the start. What happened?"

At the base of the staircase, Jessie froze to listen.

Canter nodded. "During the storm, she was curled up in the family room with a movie. Some kids' thing she was watching with her puppies right beside her. Nodded off after a bit, so your mama left her—I guess she had some sewing project she was keen on getting back to upstairs. A little while later, Althea came through, and she felt a cold draft."

"An open door? A window?"

"That back door closest to the den, wide-open, with the TV in the family room still running. No sign of Eden anywhere."

"Did she have her shoes? Her coat on?" Margie interrupted, her eyes bright with apprehension. She glanced toward a gloomy window, toward the low, cold clouds beyond.

"I'm not sure about that," Canter admitted.

"She could've gotten bored, decided to go outside exploring." He shook his head, thinking of how proud she was of the new clothes she'd gotten, how she liked to keep them nice. "More likely, we'll find her holed up somewhere nice and warm inside, hiding before falling back to sleep. She likes to make herself a mouse sometimes. That's what she calls it, finding hidden nooks and crannies. Lots of good ones in that big house. She could just be—"

"Eden's not in the house. And it turns out she's not all that's missing."

"What else?"

"Your father kept a handgun. You didn't move it, did you? Althea told me it was locked up in a drawer in his desk."

"We've always kept a gun or two around the ranch, for emergencies. But I saw to it myself, put a combination trigger guard on it, just in case," Zach confirmed, the drumbeat of his pulse grown louder. Because a child lost was one thing, even with this weather; a child missing with a handgun was something else entirely.

"Well, that drawer was partly open, the gun nowhere in sight."

Still frozen on the staircase, Jessie asked, "You don't think Eden could've somehow—?"

"Not by herself, she couldn't have," Zach told them. "We keep the key to that drawer way up on the top of the tallest bookcase. No way a four-year-old could've reached it. Even my mama'd have to stand up on a chair to get it.

And I can't imagine that Eden would've known to look for it in the first place."

"Maybe she was playing mouse and saw you hide it one day?" Jessie suggested.

"Definitely not." He was certain of it. "I triple-checked to be sure she was out of sight the day I put on the trigger guard, and I haven't touched it since."

But he had been in that drawer, he realized. Had gone there for another reason. "My father always kept some cash in there, too, in a box underneath the drawer's false bottom. His 'horse-trading stash,' he liked to call it."

Canter shook his head. "We didn't find it. How much was there?"

"Last time I checked, about five thousand."

"Well, it's gone now—and so's this intruder's real chance to score big Rayford money."

Margie's hand flew to her mouth, but it was Jessie who cried, "So you're thinking this was a kidnapping? That there could be a ransom call?"

"Deputy's standing by the phone, waiting with Althea and your mama, just in case."

"But this is Rusted Spur!" Margie burst out. "We get the break-ins and assaults, drunks and bar fights, that's all. We don't have kidnappings. It's just a little town."

"Used to be," said Canter with a glance toward Jessie, "we didn't have any murders, either. Not until your sister—"

"My sister?" Jessie blurted. "Now you're blaming a murdered woman for a murder? A murdered woman I'd bet money that you *knew* about."

Canter glared at her, shook his head and turned back to Zach. But Jessie wasn't finished with him yet.

"I've seen the proof," she said, "or photos of it from before you had it buried. So tell me, are you really most afraid of some random, out-of-the-blue kidnapper who took Zach's—no, *my* niece, from the ranch? Or are you really worried that Haley's killer's come back to finish off the final witness? Because *I* am."

Her accusation slammed down like a thunderbolt, spreading shockwaves across the room. Margie blinked hard, and Canter's hand dropped to the butt of his gun, swift as reflex.

"I saw her bones, too, in that old grill," Zach admitted, gambling that, as much as Canter disliked him, he wouldn't dare to arrest a Rayford. "*Human* bones, it turns out. The same ones you and my mama arranged to have hauled off and buried."

Canter's face flushed, but he looked confused to be tag-teamed by the two of them, and even less pleased to have it done before a witness. *Witnesses,* it turned out, as one of the land men who had come downstairs for supper was standing in the doorway, gaping at the scene.

"I don't know what—" the sheriff stammered. "What the hell are you two jabberin' about, when we've got a child missing? Now that I know that Eden isn't with you, I'm heading to the car to get an Amber Alert going. If we don't find her pretty quick, anything could happen."

"Please, then. Get it done," Zach said. "And think hard about adding the name and description of Frankie McFarland to the BOLO."

Canter shook his head. "You're barking up the wrong tree. McFarland's long gone, I'm telling you."

"Stop trying to cover your own rear, and let's get this child found now," Jessie demanded. "We can straighten all the rest out later. Eden's life is what's important."

Zach shot her a grateful look, though he feared that there'd be hell to pay when that *later* came around.

"I don't have time to stand around here arguing." Canter turned on his heel and said, "Out of my way!" to the bewildered land man, who nearly tripped over his big feet in his hurry to comply.

Moments later, the front door slammed, and Zach watched through the window as the man stalked toward his marked SUV. Then he turned on Jessie, saying, "I'm heading home. Still coming?"

Nodding, she said, "Just try and hold me back."

Jessie turned and headed for the staircase, nearly bowling over another land man who was trudging down for dinner.

Ignoring the gawky older man's startled exclamation, she made quick work of the errand, her pulse careening out of control. By the time she climbed into the running truck with the jackets and her purse, she was breathing hard. Paying her no heed, Zach was talking on his cell phone, trying to calm someone from the sound of it.

"No, definitely don't wake her if the doctor's finally got her resting," he was saying as just ahead of them, Canter sped away, his flashing emergency lights and siren slicing through the twilight gloom. "If I have my way, she'll stay asleep until I can put Eden back in her arms. Just let her know, if she does wake up, that I'm on my way home. And try not to cry, Althea. It's not your fault. I know it isn't."

Jessie's heart twisted, and she thought of every tragedy she'd ever covered. Thought how vastly different it was to watch from the inside, and how crude and intrusive her questions must have seemed to those with lives and loved ones hanging in the balance.

As he ended the call, Margie came running out of the house, a woolen poncho wrapped around her. Jessie lowered the passenger-side window at the older woman's approach.

"I just wanted to say I'm so sorry," she cried. "I only wish I could've made more of a difference for your sister."

"You damned well might've made a difference," Zach ground out, "if you'd told us what you knew before. Told *me* about Eden. You know as well as I do that this secret you and Nate and, for all I know, half the town's been keeping is the reason that she's gone now. Because she's not a Rayford by blood, never has been. You all just figured she'd be better off that way. Isn't that right?"

Pain filled Margie's eyes as she nodded, hugging the fuzzy poncho tight around her. "I—I recognized her, of course, when your mama first started taking her out and introducing her as Ian's daughter, Eden. Haley mostly kept her close to home, but she'd been here with her mama, when she couldn't find someone to watch her."

Though Jessie and Zach had guessed as much, this independent confirmation rocked her to her core. Her sister had really had a child, a beautiful and bright daughter she'd never shared with them or mentioned. A child she'd been too proud or hurt or angry to ask her family to help care for.

Or had it been that Jessie and her father, with their anger and their judgment, had made her feel so unwelcome that she didn't dare?

"You have to understand," Maggie continued. "It was a total transformation. That sad, scared little ragamuffin I'd known, the one who startled at every new voice and tried her best to disappear into the shadows, was gone. This new version was so clean, she squeaked, and absolutely adorable in her new clothes and haircut. Bubbly and outgoing, with smiles to break your heart—the first smiles I'd ever seen on her face. And it was all because she had someone to love her, someone who saw her as a miracle instead of a burden and a nuisance."

Jessie closed her eyes, tears burning as she was stricken by the thought of this child's neglect—terrified she'd never get the chance to make things right. To show Eden all the love her biological mother should have. Because regardless of what Jessie felt for either of the Rayfords, Eden was *her* flesh and blood; a child to love when every other member of her family was gone....

If they could only find her safely.

"What's my niece's real name?" Jessie managed, her voice trembling.

"Go ahead and tell us," Zach called when Margie hesitated. "Maybe it'll help us find her."

"It was Bree," Margie admitted, tears trailing down her pale cheeks. "Short for Brianna, I think. Brianna McFarland."

"So she was really Frankie's child?" Jessie asked.

Margie nodded. "So Haley claimed, not that that sorry devil ever cared a fig about her."

"So how was it my mother came to have her?" Zach asked. "Especially if Haley's really dead?"

"Then you meant what you said earlier?" Margie looked from him to Jessie. "You're sure she's dead?"

"I—I'm sure," Jessie answered, feeling again that icy absence at her center, the spot she'd always hoped her sister would one day return to fill.

Margie shook her head. "I tried so hard to warn her, to tell her how those kind of stories always ended. But she'd just smile and tell me she knew how to give as good as she got. And she loved that Frankie, plain and simple. Or maybe she'd forgotten who she was without him."

Or who she could have been, thought Jessie, if the same life she'd survived hadn't left her twin so damaged. But who could say why lightning forked to strike one tree and not the next?

"I always figured she'd dumped off poor little Bree for free sitting and taken off for a new start with no encumbrances. Or with none but the worst company that poor foolish girl could've picked."

"We have to get moving," Zach said, shaking his head in frustration. "It's getting colder and darker by the minute. If Eden's somewhere out in that…"

A wave of dizziness hit Jessie like the hard dip of a roller coaster at the thought of the child Zach loved so deeply, the child of her own blood, tiny and vulnerable somewhere out there in the freezing darkness. But as dangerous as these endless plains were, with their bitter winds, hidden pitfalls and heaven only knew what desperate predators eager for an easy meal, the animal Jessie feared most was the one who'd killed her sister. The one who'd as callously kill a child, to be certain she would never talk, instead of leaving anything to chance.

But where would Frankie take her? Would any lonely stretch of road do, or would he be drawn to the familiar? To someplace with a special meaning? A place that held some memories for a man who no doubt planned to run off, a man who'd never see his home again?

So before the window rolled up, she cried out, "Wait! Wait, Margie. Was there anywhere that Haley ever mentioned? Any place Frankie liked to hang out? Anywhere that he might go with Eden?"

Zach made an impatient sound, but she stayed him with a raised hand.

"Racing off after Canter might feel good," she told him, "but you heard the sheriff. He has his people at the ranch, and all your guys are all out looking. We need some other place to look, some place they won't think of. And when backs are to the wall, people don't run away—they run to the familiar. Even when it's bound to bring them grief."

She'd seen it a hundred times while covering the night beat. Wanted men and women, even prison escapees, caught in the flypaper of their old attachments. Returning to show off or say goodbye, unable to resist one last glimpse of home or loved ones—where the cops, the U.S. Marshals and the bail bondsman's bounty hunters so often caught up to them.

Margie shook her head and answered Jessie. "I don't know where his kind goes. I don't even want to know. In the summertime, Haley mentioned a cookout or two with Hellfire and his family at the bunkhouse. And sometimes Frankie and his brother'd head over to Elam's garbage pit and shoot off fireworks."

Jessie winced at the mention of what might have become her sister's final resting place. Could Danny be thinking of dumping that poor child there, as well, like trash? Or of killing her in the same forlorn spot where he'd ended Haley's life?

"Either that, or they were off drinkin' up a storm and stirrin' up trouble at the Prairie Rose. Probably left that poor sweet child at home half the time to do it."

"Hard to imagine he'd be stupid enough to show up someplace he'd be known," Zach said.

"But people can be stupid," Jessie argued, "especially people under stress. I'm telling you, he'll be close by, with old contacts. That's how the Frankie McFarlands of this world are always caught."

"All right," Zach allowed as they sped off toward town. "On the way back to the ranch, we'll swing past the bunkhouse site to check for any vehicles, or tire tracks since the ice storm. Then we'll talk to Canter about sending a deputy to Danny's and Clem Elam's, if he already hasn't thought of it himself."

"Maybe we should try the bar first. In case he wants to show off to his old friends, buy 'em one more round on you—"

"It's Monday night. That bar's closed, and we can't run all over the county, chasing shadows." Zach's voice was harsh, the look he sent her even harsher. With a grunt of anguish, he popped the dash with the heel of his hand. "Damn it, I should've been there. Should've been there for them, for Eden and my mama, like I promised. There at home where I belong, keeping that child safe instead of wasting time with—"

"With me," she said, her gaze glancing off his long enough to catch the world of hurt there. The blame, resentment and the anger already poisoning what they felt for one another—or thought they'd felt—in those few foolish hours they had reached out for each other in their weakness.

Even if they found Eden soon, found her utterly undamaged, Jessie knew their situation was impossible, too burdened with conflicting loves and loyalties to do anything but crush them. How would he ever look at her again, without thinking of what that time might have cost him and his mother, how the mess her twin had made of her life had reached out to shatter their peace? And how would Jessie herself ever get past what had been stolen from her family, let alone the quiet conspiracy meant to keep the truth from them forever? Meant to leave her twin interred in a garbage pit?

"I get it," she told him, "I do. But before we rip each other's hearts out—"

"Our hearts aren't what are important. Not now," he said as he mashed down on the accelerator. "All I can think about is what if we're too late already? What if it doesn't matter whose plan we pick, or where we go first, because Eden's gone already? I swear, I'm back in Kabul again, hanging underneath that parachute, watching everything go up in flames below me."

"You can't think like that, can't talk like that," she said, her voice racing to keep up with her mounting desperation. "*We* can't, because we're going to bring her home. I know it. Besides that, I was probably wrong before, about him coming back to silence the only witness to my sister's killing. Maybe it really was about the money all along, like Canter said. Frankie tried to get away from here, and when he ran out of cash, he came back with a plan to get some, even if it meant exploiting his own daughter."

"Yeah, that's gotta be it," Zach said, grasping on to her words like a lifeline. "And whatever Frankie asks, I'll pay it. My money, my land, my life itself—that kid's my family. Maybe she's not blood. I'll admit that, but Eden is my *family,* and that's the only legacy I give a damn about."

Her heart ached for him, for this good man in the most impossible of situations. And the certainty sliced through her, keen and cold as the knife's edge of the winter wind, that though they might part bitter enemies, she would always love him. Love the man for showing her what honor and duty were really all about.

As they sliced through the town's center, honking the horn and flashing headlights at anyone foolhardy enough to get in their way, the bruised glow of the horizon darkened, and the first few stars punched their way through small gaps in the cloud cover.

It served as a cruel reminder of just how early night came in the teeth of the Panhandle winter. And how much colder the bitter darkness would grow before the dawn.

Chapter 17

They were halfway to the ranch, hurtling along thirty miles per hour above the posted limit, when Zach's phone rang. His pulse jumping, he reached for it, so desperate for a report that Eden had been found that he didn't even check the caller ID but assumed it was Canter.

"Tell me you've got Eden," he said. "Tell me she's safe and sound and with my mother—"

"Need to—need to get on over here," a muffled male voice panted.

"Get on over— Wait, who is this?" Zach demanded. *"Hellfire?"*

"Come quick. Not much time."

With a glance toward Jessie, Zach slowed, hearing something ominous. "Come where? Is something wrong, man? Are you hurt?"

As he pulled over, he heard the breathy scrape of some more panting, a groan that finally morphed into intelligible words.

"After the last time I was arrested, I swore on my mama's grave I'd go straight…even if it killed me. That I'd find a way to get the…"

"The Prairie Rose, you mean?" Zach asked, knowing the man's obsession with what he saw as the pathway to respectability. "Is that where you are now? Did Frankie stop by, Danny? Is he there with Eden?"

"What is it?" Jessie asked beside him.

Hellfire said, "Tried my best. Tried to show my brother what Mama would've wanted for us. Warned him to lay off the booze. Warned him to lay offa Haley. But those two couldn't quit their— It was sick, man. The fighting and drinking, the make-up sex and—and that poor, sad little kid of theirs, stuck in the middle of it. She deserved a better life. Deserved to be something better than another McFarland for this town to look down their noses at her whole life."

"Where is she, man? Where's Eden?" Zach demanded, looking over his shoulder before jerking the truck through a three-point turn. "Tell me, and I'll send an ambulance there to you…*Danny?*"

"I tried to stop her, man. Tried to make his life count for some—"

In the background, he heard a desperate outcry, a voice shouting, "Put down that phone! Put it down now!"

There was a loud clatter, but the connection remained live. Live and open long enough to capture the sound of two blasts, the first nearly on top of the second. Zach flinched with the insult to his ears.

"Danny? Danny, are you still there?" he called, his head still ringing.

The only answer, in those last moments before the line went dead, was the terrified weeping of a child in the background, a child crying, "Wanna go back home!"

Gut twisting, Zach roared, "Eden!" But it was too late, too late to do anything but get there, as fast as he could.

"What's happening? Is Eden—is she all right?" Jessie demanded, her eyes rimmed in white as she pulled out her own cell phone.

"She's— I don't know. There were shots. Then she was crying. I think she witnessed—"

"I'm calling 9-1-1. What do I tell them?"

"Tell them to send an ambulance, sheriff's cars—everybody they have to the Prairie Rose on Old Cemetery Ridge."

"So Frankie's back? He shot his brother?" she guessed as she punched out the numbers.

"I'm not sure, but I don't think so," Zach said, making it a desperate prayer to heaven. "And Jessie, it's not Frankie. We've had this thing wrong all along."

Jessie shook her head at Zach, trying to make sense of what he'd told her. Before she could ask him to explain, her call to 9-1-1 connected, leaving her to tell the operator that a man had been shot at the Prairie Rose Saloon. "We think that Eden Rayford's there, too," she added, "along with the shooter. Please, send everyone you have and hurry! We can't let him get away!"

As they roared down the road, she answered those few questions she could. Eventually, however, she lost patience with the dispatcher's request for her to stay on the line and disconnected.

She had questions of her own, questions she couldn't put off another second. Before she could get the first out, Zach said, "It's a small department, spread over a damn big county. Depending on how many deputies are out at the ranch looking for Eden, we're likely to beat them to the Prairie Rose."

She shook her head, not caring who made it there first. Not caring about anything except getting there before the shooter disappeared with her niece.

"What did you mean before," she asked, "when you said it wasn't Frankie? How could it not be him, going back to see his brother? Maybe Hellfire got it wrong, thinking he was there to steal from him again."

"It wasn't Frankie's voice. I'm sure of it," Zach insisted. "I've known that guy, both brothers, since we were all in grade school."

"Voices change. Kids grow up."

"I'm telling you," Zach insisted, "it wasn't him. Not unless he had a sex change I didn't hear about."

She blinked hard. "You're saying it was a *woman?* The person who shot Hellfire?"

Zach accelerated into a curve, forcing Jessie to brace herself to avoid being thrown into the passenger-side window.

"Slow down, Zach, please," she cried, feeling her insides flung to the road's shoulder. "This isn't your old fighter jet! Eden needs us in one piece, not splattered on the pavement."

"She needs us *now,*" he said, "before your sister takes off with her."

"My—my *sister?*" Jessie asked, her head spinning as she shook it. "No, that can't be. Haley's dead. You saw the burned bones near the bunkhouse."

"I saw bones," he said, "charred and human. But not necessarily female. And definitely not Haley's. I'm telling you, it was a woman yelling at Hellfire before I heard the gunshots. A woman with a voice a lot like yours."

Jessie shuddered, her stomach threatening upheaval. "But that would mean…" she said, her mind struggling for purchase. "It's impossible, what you're saying. My sister wouldn't shoot somebody. She's a victim of abuse. Of murder, not a—"

A killer. It wasn't possible. Yet Margie's words rang through her memory, something about Haley telling her she could give as good as she got.

"When we get there," Zach said, "I need you to let me handle this. You just stay out in the truck and wait for the deputies."

"The heck I will," Jessie argued. "Frankie has my niece in there."

"Listen to me. Someone's got to tell the deputies not to just go charging in there, where people might get hurt. People like Eden or your sister."

Shuddering, Jessie rubbed her arms, still unable to accept what he was saying. "Do you really think they're still inside? I mean, surely Frankie won't just hang around, waiting to be caught."

He shook his head. "It's hard to say what someone that unbalanced might be thinking. But whatever the case, I'm not taking any chances with your safety. Yours or Eden's, either."

In shock, Jessie didn't argue. The idea of her sister, not as victim but as perpetrator, kept buzzing wasplike through her brain, its sting somehow more painful than the thought of her buried in a landfill. Could Zach really be right? Could Haley have killed her longtime lover before fleeing? But why come back, then, to take Eden and shoot Hellfire? It made no sense at all.

"Where on earth *is* this place?" she finally asked, as they turned down a road with a hand-lettered sign reading Cemetery Ridge.

"Right up the hill, on the horizon." He pointed out the silhouette of a long, low building, squatting a hundred yards ahead. "Only place in town the neighbors wouldn't complain about the noise."

"You were right before," she said as he pulled into the unlit lot, slowing for the deep ruts. "We did beat the emergency responders. But someone's here. See?"

She pointed out a dark bulk in the lot ahead just as the truck's headlights raked across a rusted old sedan. A wrecked sedan, with its sprung hood crushed against the driver's-side door of a large white SUV—

"Wait," she cried, shocked to see her mother's Escalade. "How on earth would my car get here?"

"Your sister must've taken it when she snatched Eden. The keys were down in the den. But it looks like she cut off this other driver. Or maybe it was the other way around."

"Hellfire, maybe?" she guessed. "Maybe that's how he ended up shot. But isn't that his motorcycle?" She pointed out the dark shape of a parked chopper.

"I think so. I'm heading inside." Zach put the truck in Park. "Get behind the wheel when I bail out. And be ready to get out of here if anything goes wrong."

"Wait," she warned, grabbing his arm to stop him. "Whoever's in there—this person's armed and dangerous. Maybe you should leave this to the sheriff's department."

Their gazes met in the charged space between them, fear reminding her how quickly everything could change. As tough and capable as he was, he was no match for a bullet. Fear froze the breath in her lungs at the thought.

"I've come back from the war zone," he said. "Come back from hell in Kabul. I'll come back from this, too, with Eden in my arms. I'll come back for you."

Shaking her head rapidly, Jessie felt fresh apprehension knotting inside her, crowding out her breath with a dark warning. "Please, don't, Zach. Everything could go wrong."

"Things can go just as wrong when we do nothing," he said, his head shaking. "And I won't take that chance again."

When he leaned to press his lips to hers, her heart stuttered and her breath hitched. Then he left her, a dark figure leaving the cab an instant before disappearing into the shadows. A dark figure risking his life to reclaim the child who owned his heart.

It was Ian's voice that Nancy Rayford heard in her head. Ian, urging her to save his daughter. Guiding her to slip out of the mansion, as the caller had instructed, telling her to do whatever needed to be done.

She imagined her son's strong hands over hers, gripping the wheel of a vehicle no one had imagined she would dare take. But Ian had guided her there, too, in her darkest hour, warning her that she'd be caught if she tried to drive her familiar Mercedes out of the car shed, where too many eyes were watching.

But then Ian, she remembered, had always been so clever about escaping the ranch for his adventures. So it didn't surprise her how she wasn't seen, leaving with the money and the gun he had helped her take from the den.

Because one way or another, she was coming back with his little girl, raising his precious child in the home he'd missed so much. Just as he had missed her. Or at least that's what he'd told her in the dark days after his death.

The wheels bumped, jostling the SUV over rocks and grassy tufts, jerking her fully awake. With a gasp, she hauled on the wheel, getting herself back on the narrow road—and warning herself that she couldn't risk drifting off again.

"Wake up, wake up!" She pinched the tender flesh inside her arm, wishing that she hadn't taken both her anxiety and migraine pills along with those new medications the specialist in Amarillo had put her on for her arthritis. She was going to have to find a way to stop, she knew, stop and become a better grandparent than she had been a mother: a more present and more active influence than the timid little shadow she'd been.

She would see to it, she told herself, as soon as things settled down a little. As soon as the pain became more bearable, and she had Eden on the ranch where she belonged.

Chapter 18

Though he was keeping it switched off to avoid being spotted, Zach gripped the metal flashlight like a police baton, prepared to use it as a weapon. To knock Haley out, if he could, before a stray bullet forever silenced her innocent four-year-old daughter.

But first he had to find Haley, to somehow catch her inside the darkened saloon unawares. As he slipped around to the back, where he thought he remembered a loading entrance, he prayed she wouldn't fill him full of lead the moment he poked his head through the door.

Finding the outer door unlocked, he slipped into the pitch-black and carefully eased the door closed just behind him. Hard as it was, he resisted the impulse to blunder forward, instead taking several deep breaths and allowing his eyes to adjust.

He heard the noises first, a metallic clinking punctuated by the sound of breaking glass. Soft crying, too—

Eden's—in the distance, and farther along this hallway, a hallway leading to... Was that light?

Yes, a dim light, he was certain, ahead and to his right. A light from—he struggled to remember the bar's layout from his brief meeting with Hellfire before he'd banished Zach from the bar. Wasn't there a little kitchen back here, and an office, here in the back?

Still uncertain, he crept along the hallway, following the muffled sounds of conversation: male and female. An argument, he realized, hurrying as the voices swelled into bitter accusations.

"You can't just take her," cried the woman, weeping out the words. "You can't. I have the right to see my child."

"You got no more right to that kid than you did to my money."

Coldness crept up Zach's spine. Let these two argue all they wanted, but where was Eden right now? And how could he get past this door without drawing fire?

"I just—just needed a little more travelin' cash, Danny," Haley said. "Just a little loan. You didn't have to—"

"When you tripped that alarm, I thought you were some damned lowlife, breaking in to rob the place. Guess I—I was right. You are and you were. I warned you what would happen if you came back!"

"You're just covering yourself, like always," she accused, "considering how you freaking sold my daughter to get this place."

Sold her daughter to get this place. The knowledge hit the pit of Zach's stomach, making sense of Hellfire's purchase of the bar, of the undocumented expenditures from the ranch's accounts: gaps he'd blamed on the mess his mother had made of the record keeping.

"It was—" Harsh panting. "It was never about sellin' anybody." Danny McFarland's voice had grown weaker, but a vein of pure stubbornness ran through it. "It was about a real life for my niece. A life better than what she'd have, as a foster kid with a mama in prison for shootin' down her daddy. Or worse yet, growin' up the way that me and Frankie both did, so damned poor and dirty, kids made our lives a livin' hell till we got tough enough to—"

"Rich isn't always better," the woman insisted, her voice a warped, weak version of her sister's. "It doesn't buy wh-what matters. Doesn't buy a mother's love."

Was she hurt, too? Hearing the pain in her voice, Zach edged farther down the hallway.

Danny coughed. "If you really loved that kid, you'd let her go. Let her grow up a high-and-mighty Rayford, with ribbons in her hair and gold-plated ponies."

"I only meant to leave her for a little while, until I could get back on my feet. If I hadn't been so freaked out, I never would've—"

"I told you, told you to stay well clear. Warned you what would happen if you showed your face in this town again."

"How'd you swing it, Danny? How'd you make it pay off? You get your old jailhouse buddy Elam to forge the paperwork? Or'd you have some shyster lawyer connection who would do it for a price?"

Zach flinched, his heart pounding. Was his mother really callous enough to buy herself a granddaughter? Or had it not been about callousness, but desperation? A need to give her meaningless life purpose, a desire to save a child who was obviously in need?

"It was for Bree's own good. I didn't want her growin' up like me an' Frankie. Growin' up the town's trash—"

"Or did you blackmail the old lady to get your money?

Told her you'd let Bree go into the system if she didn't pay up?"

"What the hell's it matter? Everybody made out."

"*I* never got a dime," she said, her voice so hard, Zach started at its callousness, unable to believe this grasping, desperate woman could be related to his Jessie.

"You freaking got away with murder," said Hellfire, "thanks to me 'n' Clem."

"Not murder, self-defense. We both know your brother would've killed me. And now I want my daughter, Danny. I want…to take…her home."

"Home? That dump's been bulldozed."

"That bunkhouse was never home. Home's where I can say my sorries, where I can leave my kid to get raised right. And disappear again, if that's what they want. Disappear where I won't hurt anybody else."

"You ain't taking her. No one is. When I make a deal, it stays made."

Finally close enough, Zach crouched down to peer into a room lit by the dim glow of a desk lamp that had been knocked onto its side. As he searched desperately for Eden, he saw Hellfire sprawled beside an old desk, a dark puddle beneath him and a revolver in his hand.

Across the room, a woman sat slumped beside a wall, a wet streak smearing the paneling behind her. *They've gone and shot each other,* Zach understood, mentally replaying the two blasts he had heard on the phone. Yet even now, the two of them weren't finished, prepared to argue to the bitter end.

But all he really cared about was Eden. Was she hurt, or hiding? Zach risked another few inches, peering underneath the desk and praying that the child had been spared.

A small head cocked as it caught his eye, and before

he could warn her to stay quiet, Eden cried out, "Uncle Zach! You came for me!" and scrambled out from beneath the desk.

"Noooo!" howled Haley as Zach reached in to grab the girl...

Just before another gunshot broke the silence.

Waiting had never been Jessie Layton's strong suit, and Vivian Carlisle was only the most recent in a long line of bosses who could attest to her bullheaded failure to heed orders. And the longer she sat inside the truck's cab, the deeper her foreboding grew—and the more horrified she became at the thought that she'd become the kind of woman who would cower while Zach went inside to save *her* family.

And while he went inside to face what Jessie finally admitted to herself might be her own twin. A twin who'd long ago passed beyond the point of no return, who might be capable of anything.

She took off for the building at a dead run, telling herself she wasn't going to let it happen. Was going to at least try to talk her sister out of whatever brand of lunacy had swallowed her alive.

Maybe seeing her own face in Jessie's would shock Haley out of this insanity. Maybe hearing that their mother had still loved her to her last breath would remind her of better days.

Jessie went first to the saloon's front door, thinking that it might be wise to try a different route than she'd seen Zach take. But when she found it locked, she changed tacks, hurrying around the corner toward the back.

Her heart spasmed at a muffled boom—a gunshot from inside the saloon. "No, Haley. No, please!"

More afraid for Zach and Eden than worried about her own safety, Jessie peered into the shadows, looking for a back door. And shrieking when one narrow slice of darkness separated itself from the rest with a metallic clicking that instinct warned her was a gun.

"Don't move." The thin voice was cold as dry ice. "Don't breathe, or I *will* use this, Haley. I swear, that's what I'll do."

"Not moving," Jessie said, her hands rising slowly. "Not breathing. And also, just for the record, I'm not Haley."

"I—I knew I'd find you here. Knew you were all in this together," the woman slurred, her words sending a shock of recognition straight up Jessie's spine. "Playing me for some old fool, and using that poor child to—"

"Didn't you hear that bang, Mrs. Rayford? It was a gun, inside the building." Jessie's teeth were chattering so hard that she could barely speak. Because it was clear to her that Zach's mother must have somehow driven herself here, in Jessie's own vehicle, mostly likely. As addled as Zach's mother sounded, it was a miracle she'd made it this far. But that didn't mean she wouldn't pull the trigger if anyone startled or provoked her. "Let me go, please, so I can check on Zach and— *Uhhh!*"

Something slammed against the left side of her head hard enough to send her crashing to her knees. *The gun,* she realized, her jaw throbbing madly. That crazy old woman had actually hit her.

"Where is she? Where's Eden?" Zach's mother demanded. "Tell me, and I'll give you the five thousand I brought—but only if I never have to see your face again."

"Eden's inside," Jessie insisted, raising her hand to cup her aching face. "Let me—let me get her for you."

"We'll go in together. You first, Haley, with your hands up."

"All right. Whatever you say." Jessie's mind was whirling, her every instinct warning against taking Zach's mother, in her current state, into an already volatile situation.

Thinking quickly, Jessie exaggerated her discomfort, hobbling forward with her head bowed, then moaning and leaning over as she reached for the door pull.

"Here, let me," said the older woman, reflexively reverting to the genteel manners that ruled her saner hours. But as she moved to help, Jessie exploded into action, shoving the older woman backward toward the step before turning and racing into the dark hallway—and slamming into a wall of what felt like solid muscle.

A wall that instantly engulfed her in a grip as strong as steel.

Chapter 19

Zach took Jessie to her sister first, insisting that there wasn't much time. Considering where Danny's second shot—possibly meant to offer Zach and Eden cover—had struck her, Zach couldn't imagine she'd make it to the hospital alive.

"B-but your mother," Jessie said. "She's outside."

"My mother?" he asked. "What's she doing here? How'd she—?"

"Haley!" Jessie cried, spotting her sister's crumpled form inside the office. Pulling away, she bolted through the office doorway, nearly tripping over Hellfire's groaning bulk. Dropping to her knees amid a scattering of bullets that Zach had emptied from both handguns, Jessie threw her arms around her twin, both of them weeping, overcome by the reunion.

"You can't go," Jessie pleaded, kneeling in a bloody puddle at her sister's chest. "You can't die, too, not now that I've finally found you."

Outside the room, Eden's small hand found Zach's again, shaking so hard that her small jaw chattered. "Want to go find Grandma. Want to go back home."

Lifting her into his arms, he said, "I'll take you out to Grandma. It's going to be all right."

But to his marrow, he knew that he was lying. That neither his loving mother's brand of magic—nor every penny of the Rayford millions—could ever make this situation right again.

Five Months Later...

Standing amid stacks of boxes in her mother's kitchen, Jessie pulled at the end of the packing tape, then said a choice word when it came off the empty roll. Wincing, she looked around, waiting for Eden, as her niece still insisted on being called, to put her little hands on her hips and demand an offering for the Naughty Jar, where the two of them were saving for a trip to see Shamu in San Antonio.

Since it was a five-dollar word—one that Jessie didn't want her innocent niece repeating—she sighed in relief, remembering Eden was on a playdate at the neighbor's, with the world's best babysitter—the now-recovered Gretel—helping to supervise.

With no more tape and at least a dozen more boxes to pack before the movers arrived first thing tomorrow morning, she did a hair and face check and winced at the sight of her bare face, broken nails and messy pony-tail, wondering how she'd ever get herself camera-ready for her interview with the nationally broadcast *Sunday Morning News Hour,* which was scheduled to coincide with the release of her article in the *Lone Star Monthly.* For the moving supply store, however, a few swipes of a hairbrush and a dab of lip gloss would do. Along with her big sunglasses, her casual look would also serve to keep her from being recognized by any of her former viewers, wanting to know when they would see her back on the air.

When Hell freezes over, she thought, now that the book was being rushed into production. The deadlines for both the article and the more in-depth manuscript had been grueling, but her work had also kept her sane as she grappled with her losses, along with the new challenges of single parenthood.

Along the way, she'd found she liked writing better, anyway, liked having the freedom to dig beneath the surface, informing and encouraging people to think beyond sound bites meant to shock or titillate. She didn't at all miss the viewer emails, either, from the disgusting propositions to the even stranger marriage proposals to the constant commentary on her clothes, her hair, even her breast size: everything but the substance of her work. Though there would probably still be a little of that when she did appear on the national news program, she hoped those viewers would be far less interested in her personal appearance than in the secrets she was due to expose, including her discovery of H. Lee Simmons's close ties to hate groups advocating for a shockingly extreme national agenda.

Though she feared there might be blowback when the news broke, she was committed to get the word out before any of these groups—and the billionaire wildcatter funding them—moved forward in an all-out assault on the Bill of Rights. It was important enough to her that she planned to use a large chunk of her inheritance to move herself and Eden to a secure gated community in another part of the country—and buy a Hansel for her Gretel for added insurance.

Grabbing her purse, she headed out to the car and immediately wished she had checked the windows before leaving. Or had her dog with her—not that the Rottweiler could be trusted to ward off this particular evil, since he'd been plying her with steak bits every time he "happened" by.

Zach Rayford waved a greeting from the driveway, where he'd leaned against the bumper of her pickup, his long legs stretched out ahead of him and crossed at the ankles. He looked perfectly at ease there, content to wait forever, and so striking in the warm spring sunlight that he took her breath away.

"I thought we agreed that next time, you would call first," she said coolly.

Taking off his white straw hat, he tipped it toward her, his eyes as blue and clear as the sky above him. "I was just in the neighborhood," he said as if it was nothing for him to jump into his pickup and drive six hours to get to Dallas, "so I thought I'd come by and see if I could say hello."

"Every time you *happen* by, Eden cries herself to sleep nights, wanting to see you and 'Grandma,'" Jessie said, sketching air quotes with her fingers, "and visit Mr. Butters and the puppies. Thank goodness she's not here now, so she won't have to go through all—"

"You know she's always more than welcome to come up and see us for a visit. We really miss her up there."

Jessie marked the longing in his handsome face, the yearning to reconnect with the little girl who still drew pictures of him, pictures of the ranch and her animals and Miss Althea and Mr. Virgil nearly every day. An entire glitter-bedazzled family that adored her, stacked up against her relationship with an aunt it had taken her

months to warm up to. An aunt who all too closely resembled the mother she had never been able to depend on.

Concerned about her niece's well-being, Jessie had
dragged the traumatized girl to session after session with
a child psychologist to help her cope with the horrors she
had witnessed. Jessie, too, had squeezed in a few coun-
seling sessions, wanting to be certain that her own sadness, guilt and even anger wouldn't end up hurting the
child she'd so quickly grown to love.

But that didn't keep fury from flaring every time she
thought about what had taken place in Rusted Spur.

"I know Haley gave Eden to your mother after she
shot Frankie, but your mother *killed* my sister as sure
as if she'd pulled the trigger. And my cameraman, too,
even if Danny McFarland won't admit to shooting Henry
that day at the bunkhouse." She flexed her scarred right
hand, the fingers that still ached when she spent too long
at the keyboard, though she'd recovered more function
than the surgeon had initially predicted.

He looked into her eyes, his own wells of regret.
"Whatever he's admitted to, Danny's being prosecuted
for Haley's and Henry's murders. And he's already lost
the Prairie Rose. He's lost everything."

"While Sheriff Canter gets off scot-free for knowingly
covering up a faked adoption and your mama's still living like a queen inside her palace."

"I can't do anything about Canter, since there's no
proof he intentionally razed that bunkhouse or knew any
of the particulars about how Eden came to be with my
mama."

"Of course he knew," Jessie murmured, though much
as she hated to admit it, it was possible Canter had believed he was acting in Eden's best interest.

"And as for my mother," Zach continued, "I wouldn't

go so far as saying she's living like a queen, but she's certainly living a more comfortable life than Hellfire, thanks to your not pressing charges. I can't tell you how much I appreciate that, Jessie."

"It's not like any Trencher County jury was going to convict her," she said bitterly. *Or that I'd ever do a thing like that to you.* "But that doesn't mean that I'm ready to reward her for what she's done—or risk letting her screw up Eden's head with any more of her brainwashing."

"I won't defend what she did, but I will tell you, that's all over. My mother's changed, Jessie. Changed drastically since she came home from the rehabilitation center. She's not only better than she was before, she's better than I can ever remember—no pills and no sick headaches, since the doctors finally helped her get those migraines under control. And she talks about her mistakes, not only with Eden but with my brother and me, when we were younger. When she couldn't find the strength to keep us safe from our father."

Jessie crossed her arms in front of her. As sorry as she felt for Zach's impossible situation, she still wasn't certain if she bought his mother's whole "drug psychosis" defense, though she'd been assured by a pharmacist she'd checked with that drug interactions combined with extreme stress had indeed been known to alter patients' perceptions of reality. "Of course you would defend her."

"Not to you, I wouldn't," he swore, "not after what you've suffered. But if it makes you feel any better, I can assure you, my mother's suffered, too."

"I know she has. I know it," said Jessie, pressing her knuckles to her forehead as she allowed herself to imagine what it must have cost the woman to lose a child she had loved beyond the point of reason. Jessie allowed herself to see, too, the price that Zach was paying, that both of them were paying, stuck on opposite sides of a line that she couldn't imagine a way across.

Pushing back the sunglasses, she wiped her burning eyes. "I just can't get past— Haley was my twin. My sister. You've lost a brother recently, so tell me. Could you forgive the people who had a hand in his death?"

"I don't know. Maybe not. But let me ask you something. How did not forgiving Haley work out for either of you in the long run?"

Fresh grief stabbed through her center, pain she would carry with her all her life. How dare he use it against her? Use it to try to gain her sympathy for a woman who didn't deserve it? A woman who'd marched her at gunpoint to the building where her sister lay already dying? "I think you'd better leave."

"C'mon, Jessie. Don't be like that. Let me take you to lunch."

"I don't have time for lunch, Zach, even if I had the inclination. I was on my way to run an errand. Then I need to finish getting this house packed up for the movers."

"You haven't told me yet. Where is it you're going?"

"Why, so you can 'just happen by' there, too, after I've asked you not to show up without calling?" Colorado wasn't far enough to keep a man as determined as Zach from driving there, too. "Or maybe your mama will send someone to snatch Eden the first time I take my eyes off—"

"That's not going to happen, Jessie. I swear to you, it won't. Well, the last thing, anyway. The part about me coming by—I'm afraid that I can't guarantee it. Because Eden's not the only one I've been coming here to see."

"Which reminds me, Gretel sends her regards," Jessie said, feeling one corner of her mouth quirk upward.

"I wasn't talking about your dog, and you know it."

"Well, *I'm* not talking about you and me, regardless of how well it would fit into your mother's schemes—"

"I'm not doing this for my mama," he said, "and I'm not doing it for Eden, either, as much as I care about them both. I'm doing it for myself, because you're what I need in this life to make me happy. Because I love you, Jessie Layton. Love the way you're clawing your way through circumstances that would've killed a weaker woman. Love the way you're fighting like a hellcat to do what's best for a little girl who was a total stranger to you. When I get up every morning, it's all I can do not to jump into my truck and drive three-hundred-plus miles for the chance of getting a single glimpse of you. For a chance for a single word, I'd drive to hell itself— and back."

"Here's a word for you—*restraining order.* Because you're sounding more like a stalker than a rancher right now."

He tipped his hat back, pointing out, "That's two words, Jessie, and I'm no stalker. I'm just obsessed with you."

She rolled her eyes, trying to pretend he hadn't become a fixture in her own dreams, coaxing and caressing until he took her to the very edge, where she was invariably left hanging. "Tell it to the judge, cowboy. Now, I need to get to the store. Want to move your truck, or do I have to—"

"Please, Jessie," he said. "Just lunch. That's all I ask."

She looked up into his face, wanting so badly to invite him inside, wanting to press her lips to his again, to pull him closer—so close. But the wave of need that struck churned her feelings over, leaving her so guilty and conflicted she couldn't allow herself to give in.

Instead, she shook her head, not trusting herself to speak for the painful lump in her throat.

He set his jaw and nodded, regret etching deep lines in his forehead. "I see it in your eyes. I'm hurting you, too, coming here. Hurting all of us. So I'll tell you what. I won't be back again. I won't try to follow you to your new place, either, or even call or email. Just know that I'll be waiting for you, waiting for the family of my heart to join me back in Rusted Spur."

Don't waste your life waiting, she wanted desperately to tell him, but the best that she could do was nod.

Pulling his keys from his pocket, he started to turn toward the truck's door, and froze a moment, staring past her shoulder. Staring at something farther down the quiet residential street.

She heard the approaching engine and got a single glimpse a split second before he shouted, "Jessie!" Reaching out to grab her, he slung her down to the hard concrete.

She heard the shots an instant later, a feeling of déjà vu rising in her throat like bile as she rolled over. Rolled over to see Zach lying just behind her, streams of blood pouring down the driveway, running toward the gutter. Blood from the body he had used to shield her own.

Chapter 20

Every time he opened his eyes, Zach saw Jessie, waiting. Standing by the window of the hospital room or sitting by his bedside, her face a mask of anxiety. As much pain as he was in, he wanted to tell her not to worry. Wanted to assure her he was too tough to let a couple of bullets keep him from her.

Speaking, however, was an issue, partly because it sent pain shooting from his injured neck and shoulder and partly because of the morphine he'd been given to float him past the worst hours. Or days, most likely, maybe even longer, he thought as he remembered the glimpses he'd had of his mother. Eden, too, once, shoving a picture his way that had dusted his bandages with sparkles. But Jessie was the one constant, his touchstone with a world he was struggling to fight his way back into.

Cool and shaky, her fingers slid along the stubble of his cheek and she repeated the words he'd seen her mouth form at least a dozen times before. Only this time, he understood her.

"I'm so sorry, Zach. So sorry. This is all my fault."

He tried to shake his head, then gritted his teeth at the pain. But he fought past the blackness threatening to overwhelm him, fought to form words. "Not. Not your fault."

"You—you're speaking." She sighed, relief easing the strain on her face. "Thank God. Thank God. Would you like— Could you drink some water? Your throat might still be sore, but—"

He nodded, abruptly aware that his mouth was dry as sand. When she brought the straw to his lips, he had never tasted anything sweeter or more refreshing. But *sore* was a long way from how he'd describe the tearing agony of swallowing that first mouthful.

He choked, which made things worse, but Jessie adjusted the bed's elevation, and he did better after that. After only a few more sips, she took the cup away. When he reached for it again, she grasped his hand and shook her head.

"Not too much, too fast. Okay?" she said. "If you keep it down, the nurse told me I could let you have more in a few minutes."

"Thanks," he told her, his voice sounding less like a stranger's than when he'd first spoke. "How—how long? What day is it?"

"It's Friday, Zach. You've lost a whole week." Her thumb glided over the rough bumps of his knuckles, a simple, soothing touch that seemed as necessary to sustain life as the water. "After your surgery, the doctors thought it best to keep you sedated. But you've turned the corner, finally. You're going to make it home."

As his eyes focused, he noticed the scrapes along the side of her arm. "Hurt?" he asked. "You weren't sh-shot?"

"Thanks to you, I wasn't. But you were, instead. The same way Eden might have been if she'd been standing out there with me."

He squinted, trying to make sense of it.

"Canter may be a big jerk, worried enough about that big donation your mother promised his department to arrest me, but he was right about this," Jessie told him. "A witness saw the car speed off. Saw the bald man with the neck tattoos behind the wheel with the trigger man beside him."

"Same guy from R-Rusted Spur?"

She nodded in answer. "The very same. Or at least that's what he confessed when the police caught up to both of them, not ten minutes after you were shot. They've been trying to kill me, trying ever since my old boss Vivian Carlisle found out I knew her fiancé, H. Lee Simmons, was bribing politicians. They killed Henry, and they almost killed you, twice."

"The barn, too?" he guessed, remembering the locked door and accelerants, both of which Hellfire had stubbornly refused to admit to.

"I'm so sorry, Zach," she said again. "I had no idea they were after me the whole time. Trying to shut me up before I let the public know what I'd found out."

Worried for her safety, he asked, "They in jail now?"

"They are," she said, "and Vivian Carlisle, too, since she was the one who hired those men from one of the hate groups Simmons was affiliated with."

"What about Simmons?"

"He's probably boiling mad, since the *Lone Star Monthly*'s article ran, and there's a book version coming out next week. He may or may not end up in prison for some of the stuff he's done—he can afford enough attorneys to put that decision off for years—but I'm pretty sure his political influence has come to an abrupt end. And there's no doubt that Vivian will be spending a lot of years in prison."

"Thanks to you," he said. "But what about you? Are you safe now?"

"I'd like to think so," she said, "but the truth is, I don't know that, now that I'm the face of the woman who trashed Simmons's ambition and shined a light on some very ugly groups of haters. These are not the kind of people who are known to give up grudges. And in spite of the precautions that I've taken, there have been a number of threats."

"Credible threats?" he asked her.

She shrugged. "I really can't say. The security people I contracted don't believe so, for the most part. But even with the security people and Gretel watching out for me, I'm going to spend the next few years, at least, looking over my shoulder. Only this time, I'm not risking anybody else's life."

"What do you mean? You can't blame yourself for all—"

"I absolutely can and should. If I'm going to go around tilting at windmills, I have to consider the fact that someone is very likely to get hurt, or even killed." She squeezed his hand again, moisture gleaming on her lower eyes. "Someone else I lo— Care about. Which is why I'm signing over custody of my sister's daughter."

"Wh-what?" Forgetting his neck wound, he shook his head in confusion. "But she's your flesh and blood, and I know you love her like a daughter."

"I love her too much to risk putting her in danger," she said, tears spilling from her eyes. "Too much to keep her any longer from the only real family that she's known. The only family she wants."

If he'd ever wondered for a single moment whether she could really love Eden the way he did, he dismissed the doubt now. For he knew all too well what it would take to give up her claim to her last surviving member of her family. The pain the wound would inflict, far deeper and more damaging than any bullet. "So you've made peace with my mother?"

"I kept thinking about what you said, the day you asked me how not forgiving Haley had worked out for either of us. And she really is so much better and so committed to doing the right thing for Eden. She's looking after her right now. And Eden's so happy to be going home at last, home to the ranch and her animals…." A sob bubbled up, but Jessie kept pushing forward. "And to you, too, Zach, as soon as you're well enough. The doctors are saying you'll make a full recovery."

"But what about you? Where will you go?"

She shook her head. "Far enough to keep me from getting anyone else that I love shot."

Now fully awake, he caught the words, their import. *That I love,* she'd said. "You can't leave. Come to Rusted Spur. Come where I can keep you safe with me forever."

"I was shot in Rusted Spur, remember? And I got Henry killed there, too. You, too, in that burning barn— or nearly."

"But you weren't mine then. I'll keep you safe. I'll watch you every minute of the day and night, if only—"

"I'm sorry, Zach," she told him, for the third and final time. "But I'm not yours now. I never can be. I—I've just been waiting here to tell you one last goodbye."

He tried to argue, but she wouldn't listen, tried to follow her to the door, but there was no way he could get up.

And so, she went to the door, giving him one last look over her shoulder before leaving.

Leaving, because she loved him as she loved Eden: too much to sacrifice.

Three months later...

On a small South Carolina barrier island known for wealthy vacationers, wild behavior and scantily clad beachgoers, a slender woman with wind-tossed, honey-blond hair and a wide-brimmed sunhat didn't much stand out. Not even when that woman, dressed only in a bikini top, denim cut offs and a deep tan, walked an unleashed black-and-tan dog among the dunes at sunset.

From time to time, the former Jessie Layton, now known to her few acquaintances as part-time house sitter/full-time beach bum Jaime Cavanaugh, pitched a squeaky bunny toy to her companion. Each time the dog returned it, her wagging rear and canine grin made Jessie smile, too, absurdly glad she'd ignored her security consultant's advice and refused to give up her last link to her family....

A family whose only living member was as lost to her as the dead.

A different family walked past Jessie toting folding chairs, an ice chest and the inevitable plastic pails and shovels, apparently intent on enjoying the gentler evening temperatures and the painted twilight sky. The smallest of three children stopped to look at Gretel and then asked Jessie, "I pet doggie?"

With waves caressing the nearby shoreline and the tang of salt air in her nostrils, Jessie nodded. "Sure you can, sweetie."

"She's safe?" the father asked her as he studied the powerfully built dog with obvious concern.

"It's okay," Jessie told him. "She absolutely loves kids. I promise you, your little ones couldn't be safer than with her."

After signaling the dog to sit, she watched, slivers of longing driven through her at the sight of the tiny child wrapping chubby arms around the Rottweiler's thick neck. Clearly delighted, Gretel gave the girl's face a lick, prompting both of her older brothers to come and join the petting, each of them collecting a few kisses in the process.

"Thank you," the children's mother told her before taking her youngest by the hand, "but it's time to go now, you three. Don't you want to play in the water before it gets too dark?"

"Bye-bye, doggie!" said the little girl, her piping voice reminding Jessie so painfully of Eden that it sucked the air from her lungs.

As the family disappeared over the dune, Gretel stared after them as Jessie's shaking knees gave way. Sinking down to sit in the sand, she leaned forward, her heart gone hollow, her stomach leaden, as waves of grief and longing crashed over her like a storm-driven surf.

She fought not to give in to it, telling herself she was lucky to be here, hidden like a pearl in this secluded paradise. Lucky her career was flourishing, as well, with another book for her to work on, another project to pass the time and fill the emptiness inside her, even if that work had driven her to dye and grow out her hair, wear blue contacts and hide away in the unoccupied beach house of her parents' wealthy friends, who had decided to spend this summer in their Paris apartment.

But the sight of the little girl, the protective father,

the whole happy family, served to remind Jessie that all the book deals, award nominations and TV interviews meant nothing if she had no one to share them with. Over the past months she'd drifted far off course, her life losing its meaning. Losing everything but sporadic email contact with her editors and agent, along with the occasional offer from the smarmy hair-product millionaire next door—a Jacuzzi shark of a man with flowing, pure-white locks—to provide her with what he'd promised would be some "quality, no-strings sex" anytime she found herself wanting.

The thought was so repugnant she was nearly ill the day he'd offered, yet sometimes, late at night, as she ached for all that she had lost, she wondered, would she ever be touched again the way that Zach Rayford had touched her? Would the tight fist of her scarred heart ever open up again? Or would loneliness break her spirit, eventually reducing her to accepting sleazy, meaningless offers from guys like Captain Good Hair, since she'd grown too frightened of forming real attachments to risk anyone she truly cared for.

Gretel whined in the direction of the family one last time before trotting over and dropping the slobbery toy in front of Jessie. Rather than throwing it again, she hugged the dog, harder than the little girl who'd reminded her so painfully of Eden. Apparently, too hard for comfort, for the Rottweiler whined, backed out of her mistress's embrace and snatched up her beloved bunny. An instant later, she pricked up her ears, then loped away, cresting the hill and racing out of sight before Jessie could stop her.

"No, Gretel!" she cried, rising to keep her dog from abandoning her in favor of the loving family she craved. When the Rottweiler didn't listen—a rare event in itself—Jessie broke into a run, cresting the hill in time to see Gretel drop the toy and bare her teeth, her hackles rising as she glared daggers at her mistress.

Heart pounding, a bewildered Jessie was about to stammer out the *platz* command before the Rottweiler charged past her, growling at a figure rushing toward her. A large, well-built male figure, silhouetted by the bloodred August sky.

Without waiting for a command, Gretel launched herself at the tall man, knocking him to the ground with a shout of pain and surprise before she caught him by the arm.

"Get her off him! Don't let her bite down!" shouted a second man behind her, the man Gretel had been rushing toward with her toy.

The man who had bribed her dog with steak tidbits all too often.

"Zach!" she cried. "What're you doing here?"

"It's Nate your dog has pinned down," he said. "And annoying as he can be, don't let the fanged menace chew him up."

She gave Gretel the release command, freeing her to run back to greet Zach while Nate picked himself up off the ground.

"Are you all right?" She looked over her shoulder to ask the bull rider.

"That animal could give the bucking bulls one heck of a run for their money," Nate complained as he brushed the sanding off his arm. "But yeah, I'll be fine—annoying or not," he added, shooting his friend an aggrieved look.

"And so will I," Zach told her, "now that we've finally found you."

"Why would you do this?" she demanded, pulling off her hat so she could better see him. "Why would you track me down, when you know it could jeopardize my safety?" *To say nothing of my heart.* The very sight of him, so deeply tanned and drop-dead gorgeous in his half-buttoned linen shirt and loose, beachcomber's pants, was enough to crack through her hard-won composure, threatening to shatter it completely.

"I came to bring you back to Texas," he said, "to beg you if I have to."

She shook her head and pushed a few bleached strands from her eyes. "You know I can't risk that, won't risk you and Eden and your mother."

Nate cleared his throat, looking uncomfortable to be here. "How 'bout if I take a walk now?" he asked. "Go check out the surf."

"Only if you take him with you," Jessie told him, gesturing toward Zach.

But Zach was speaking over her, saying, "Sure, man. Go ahead. And why don't you take Gretel?" He looked at Jessie and asked, "That's okay, isn't it? You want to lend him that leash?"

"I—I don't— Gretel watches. She watches out for— for trouble," she said, still too afraid to speak the name of H. Lee Simmons or mention the hate groups he was affiliated with in public.

"That's what I've come to tell you." An expression of relief and joy lit his face. "You don't have to fear them anymore."

"I don't have to—" She shook her head. *"What?"*

"Here," he said, gently taking the leash from her and passing it to his friend to clip on Gretel's collar. "Let the man go walk the dog, or, knowing him, use her to try to pick up one of those bikini babes we spotted packing all their stuff up."

Her head spinning, she gave Gretel leave to go with

Nate. Once the two were out of sight, she simply stood, staring up into Zach's blue eyes, questions buzzing like a thousand insects inside her brain.

"I've come to take you home," he repeated, taking her into his arms first. Pulling her into the strength of his embrace. "Home to Rusted Spur, to Eden, to the legacy that will never mean one damn thing without you."

She felt herself split down the middle, cracked wide-open by her need to recapture the fleeting dream she'd once had. A dream she would give her very soul for another shot at.

But images flickered through her brain, flashes like heat lightning stabbing the horizon. Flashes of Zach's blood, running swiftly toward the gutter. Of Henry's body, lying near the open doorway of that rundown bunkhouse.

"But I can't," she said. "I just can't. They'll never stop. I know—"

"No, *I* know," he corrected her, pausing long enough to press a soft kiss to her temple. "I know that I can keep you safe now, safe where you belong."

Pulling back, she looked up at him. "How? What's changed, Zach? Please don't put me through this, not unless there's some chance."

"For one thing, H. Lee Simmons was arrested. He's in custody, without bail, for bribery of public officials. And from what Canter's been able to find out through his sources, that's the least serious of the charges against him. *Federal* charges, which means no possibility of parole until his sentence has been served."

"You mean, *if* he's convicted."

"To tell you the truth, he may not even live to be convicted. Apparently, there was a big falling out of some sort between him and his favorite hate groups. They found out he was feeding the Feds information about them, so they turned over a bunch of incriminating videos—including one that showed Simmons talking about taking out some federal judges."

"Ordering a hit, you mean?"

"And not only on the judges."

"On me?" she guessed, her skin crawling at the thought.

He nodded, his expression sober. "Yeah, on you. But like I said, at this point, the only person really in danger of getting knocked off is old H. Lee himself."

She shook her head. "But what if— Surely those guys won't forgive me for exposing all this in the first place."

"With the Feds crawling all over their activities like ants and Simmons still firing away at them, believe me, you're the least of their worries. And the greatest of mine, Jessie, because I made a promise to my daughter, a promise that I'd bring you back, safe and sound."

"To—to your—?"

"The adoption's not official yet, but I swear to you I'm going to make it legal. I'm going to be that child's father, to give her all the love and the stability she's lacked. Before the paperwork goes to the judge, though, I want to give her one last gift. A mother—a real mother—the one woman we both love with all our hearts."

"But I— There's still a risk, Zach. Don't try to deny it."

"Everything's a risk. Everything in this life," he said, his gaze tunneling into hers. "But you'll be safe with us on the ranch. You'll have to trust me on this, darling. And finally learn to trust yourself again."

Still, she hesitated, months of hiding warring with the trauma she'd endured. With the memory of her sister, gasping out her final breaths and going still in her arms. Still and cold, her body heat beginning to dissipate within seconds. Her spirit leaving with it, along with her last chance of redemption.

Was she going to die like her twin, wasting her last chance, too? Or would she grasp at life before it was too late?

Zach reached up, tilting her chin gently and stroking her tight jaw with his work-roughened fingertips. "And I have it on good authority that if you do come, there's going to be a *lot* of glitter for you. Glitter, Althea's cookies and a bunch of puppy kisses, too."

"Puppy kisses?" she asked, remembering Sweetheart and Lionheart and wondering how they'd grown. Wondering, too, how much bigger Eden had gotten since she'd signed away her claim on the child of her heart.

But it wasn't the dogs, or even Jessie's niece on her mind when she raised one slender brow to ask Zach, "So that's really the best you have to offer, cowboy?"

Their gazes locked, a frisson of pure desire leaping from one to the other, along with the promise of a lifetime spent deepening the bond.

And as a light breeze rippled through the dune's sparse grasses and the waves murmured the grace notes of a love song, the two of them came together, sharing a kiss that finally answered the last of Jessie's doubts...

A kiss that forged a family where only two lonely and unhappy people had stood moments before.

* * * * *

COMING NEXT MONTH FROM

H HARLEQUIN®

ROMANTIC suspense

Available July 1, 2014

#1807 LONE WOLF STANDING
Men of Wolf Creek • by Carla Cassidy

Sheri Marcoli is searching for two things: her missing aunt and her fairy-tale prince. The damaged and fierce detective Jimmy Carmani is nothing like the man she envisions, but when the kidnapper sets his sights on her, it's Jimmy who rides to Sheri's rescue.

#1808 SECRET SERVICE RESCUE
The Adair Legacy • by Elle James

Secret service agent Daniel Henderson saves the rebellious secret heiress Shelby O'Hara from a cartel looking to pressure her grandmother to drop out of the political race. But when they're forced into hiding, sparks fly and Daniel realizes the biggest threat is to his heart.

#1809 HOT ON THE HUNT
ICE: Black Ops Defenders • by Melissa Cutler

Former black ops agents and ex-lovers Alicia and John are both on the hunt for the team member who betrayed them, but when the tables are turned, they must team up, trust each other and trust in the love they once shared.

#1810 THE MANHATTAN ENCOUNTER
House of Steele • by Addison Fox

When the commitment-phobic Liam Steele agrees to protect the shy research scientist Dr. Isabella Magnini, neither expects the explosive danger they find themselves in or the equally explosive attraction they feel for each other.

YOU CAN FIND MORE INFORMATION ON UPCOMING HARLEQUIN® TITLES, FREE EXCERPTS AND MORE AT WWW.HARLEQUIN.COM.

HRSCNM0614

REQUEST YOUR FREE BOOKS!
2 FREE NOVELS PLUS 2 FREE GIFTS!

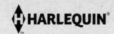

ROMANTIC suspense

Sparked by danger, fueled by passion

YES! Please send me 2 FREE Harlequin® Romantic Suspense novels and my 2 FREE gifts (gifts are worth about $10). After receiving them, if I don't wish to receive any more books, I can return the shipping statement marked "cancel." If I don't cancel, I will receive 4 brand-new novels every month and be billed just $4.74 per book in the U.S. or $5.24 per book in Canada. That's a savings of at least 14% off the cover price! It's quite a bargain! Shipping and handling is just 50¢ per book in the U.S. and 75¢ per book in Canada.* I understand that accepting the 2 free books and gifts places me under no obligation to buy anything. I can always return a shipment and cancel at any time. Even if I never buy another book, the two free books and gifts are mine to keep forever.

240/340 HDN F45N

Name _____ (PLEASE PRINT) _____

Address _____ Apt. # _____

City _____ State/Prov. _____ Zip/Postal Code _____

Signature (if under 18, a parent or guardian must sign) _____

Mail to the **Harlequin® Reader Service:**

IN U.S.A.: P.O. Box 1867, Buffalo, NY 14240-1867
IN CANADA: P.O. Box 609, Fort Erie, Ontario L2A 5X3

Want to try two free books from another line?
Call 1-800-873-8635 or visit www.ReaderService.com.

* Terms and prices subject to change without notice. Prices do not include applicable taxes. Sales tax applicable in N.Y. Canadian residents will be charged applicable taxes. Offer not valid in Quebec. This offer is limited to one order per household. Not valid for current subscribers to Harlequin Romantic Suspense books. All orders subject to credit approval. Credit or debit balances in a customer's account(s) may be offset by any other outstanding balance owed by or to the customer. Please allow 4 to 6 weeks for delivery. Offer available while quantities last.

Your Privacy—The Harlequin® Reader Service is committed to protecting your privacy. Our Privacy Policy is available online at www.ReaderService.com or upon request from the Harlequin Reader Service.

We make a portion of our mailing list available to reputable third parties that offer products we believe may interest you. If you prefer that we not exchange your name with third parties, or if you wish to clarify or modify your communication preferences, please visit us at www.ReaderService.com/consumerschoice or write to us at Harlequin Reader Service Preference Service, P.O. Box 9062, Buffalo, NY 14269. Include your complete name and address.

"That's better than being poisoned, right?"

He was aware of the weight of her intense gaze on him as he pulled out of the animal clinic parking lot. "I'm no veterinarian, but I would think that definitely it's better to be tranquilized than poisoned." He shot a glance in her direction.

She frowned. "That man in the woods broke Highway's leg. I don't know how he managed to do it, but I know in my gut he probably broke the leg and then somehow injected him with something. Highway would never take anything to eat from anyone but me, no matter how tasty the food might look or smell. Jed and I trained him too well."

They drove for a few minutes in silence. "Sorry about the pizza plans," she finally said.

He flashed her a quick smile. "Nothing to apologize for.

I'm guessing you didn't plan for a man to attack your dog and then chase you in the woods tonight. I think I can forgive you for not meeting up with me for a slice of pizza."

"Thank God you came to find me." She wrapped her slender arms around her shoulders, as if chilled despite the warmth of the night. "If you hadn't shown up when you did, I think he would have caught me. I will tell you this, he seemed to know the woods as well as I did, so it has to be somebody local."

"We'll figure it out." He seemed to be saying that a lot lately. "Maybe in the daylight tomorrow we'll find a piece of his clothing snagged on a tree branch, or something he dropped while he was chasing you."

"I hope you all find something." Her voice was slightly husky with undisguised fear. "I felt his malevolence, Jimmy. I smelled his sweat."

"You're safe now, Sheri, and we're going to keep it that way. Highway is going to be fine and we're going to get to the bottom of this."

"So…so, what happens now?" she asked.

"Since we didn't get our friendly meeting for pizza, we're going to do something else I've heard that other friends do," he replied.

"And what's that?" she asked.

He flashed her a bright smile as he pulled in front of her cottage. "We're going to have a slumber party."

**Don't miss
LONE WOLF STANDING
by Carla Cassidy, available July 2014 from
Harlequin® Romantic Suspense.**

HARLEQUIN®

ROMANTIC suspense

SECRET SERVICE RESCUE
by Elle James

The Adair Legacy

Heartstopping danger, breathtaking passion, conspiracy and intrigue. The Adair legacy grows...

Secret Service agent Daniel Henderson saves the rebellious secret heiress Shelby O'Hara from a cartel looking to pressure her grandmother to drop out of the race. But when they're forced into hiding, sparks fly and Daniel realizes the biggest threat is to his heart.

Look for the final installment of *The Adair Legacy*—*SECRET SERVICE RESCUE* by Elle James in July 2014.

Don't miss other titles from *The Adair Legacy* miniseries:

SPECIAL OPS RENDEZVOUS by Karen Anders
HIS SECRET, HER DUTY by Carla Cassidy
EXECUTIVE PROTECTION by Jennifer Morey

Available wherever books and ebooks are sold.

Heart-racing romance, high-stakes suspense!

www.Harlequin.com

HRS27878

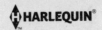

ROMANTIC suspense

HOT ON THE HUNT
by Melissa Cutler

ICE: Black Ops Defenders

**Lust and danger collide in the Caribbean in this
ICE: Black Ops Defenders title!**

Burned black-op ICE agent Alicia Troy spent years
plotting the perfect revenge on the man who left her for
dead...until her plan is foiled by her ex-teammate and
lover, who taught her the meaning of betrayal. She can't
trust John Witter...so why can't she stop wanting him?

Look for *HOT ON THE HUNT* from the
ICE: Black Ops Defenders miniseries by Melissa Cutler
in July 2014. Available wherever books and
ebooks are sold.

**Also from the *ICE: Black Ops Defenders* miniseries
by Melissa Cutler**

SECRET AGENT SECRETARY
TEMPTED INTO DANGER

Available wherever ebooks are sold.

Heart-racing romance, high-stakes suspense!

www.Harlequin.com

HRS27879